EXcapades

DEBRA KAY

ISBN 978-0-9894286-0-6

This book is a work of fiction. References to real people, events, establishments, organizations, or locales are intended only to provide a sense of authenticity, and are used fictitiously. All other characters, and all incidents and dialogue, are drawn from the author's imagination and are not to be construed as real.

DEDICATION

This book is dedicated to the special people who comprise my rainbow. You are a burst of color, even on a dark day. And most of all to my sunshine; I would wither without you. Thank you for your encouragement, especially when I stopped believing in myself. I am forever grateful.

CHAPTER 1

If love is a game, I am a loser.

At least my golden retriever loved me, but if I left the door wide open, she would leave. My dog might come back; sadly, my husband didn't.

Really, I didn't always wallow in self-pity, but I had been crushed by his departure, and I just could not shake the sorrow of being alone. The handsome, swarthy handyman I hired to help restore my house was the closest a man had been to my bedroom in over a year. And I admired his strong, dexterous hands as he fiddled with the broken faucet.

While he manipulated the stainless steel nozzle, I leaned against the marble counter, stared at his thick, callused fingers, and fantasized. Almost every man I looked at now had me wondering what his caress might feel like: rough and rugged with a cowboy, skilled to perfection from a masseur, or right on key by a musician. I bet the repair man's skillful, experienced touch would leave me breathless for more. And when he turned to ask me a question, he jolted me back to reality, exactly where I didn't want to be.

He looked at me steadily with intense brown eyes. He pointed to the stained glass that filled the entire window over my Jacuzzi tub. "Is that the artwork you want me to remove before you sell the house?" he asked. I nodded, staring at his full, succulent lips, wondering—if I kissed him would he stop me? Or return my advances? Would his kiss be soft and inviting or hard and passionate? After a minute, I realized I was gaping at his perfectly sculpted mouth and muscular chest.

Embarrassed, I looked down so he wouldn't see the yearning in my blue-green eyes.

Meanwhile, he seemed oblivious to my desire and shook his head. "Sorry to tell you this, Ms. Baxter, but if I try to detach that colored glass from the window frame it's adhered to, it will break. And the art is stunning. I know you want to take it with you when you move, but not shattered."

I just sighed, defeated. No, I did not want it broken like everything else in my world. "Thank you anyway. And please call me Lila."

He smiled thoughtfully and apologized for his bad news while gathering his tools. He told me he would let himself out and be back tomorrow to finish the projects. A few minutes later, I stepped into my bedroom and listened to the sound of the front door closing. The sky was growing brighter with sunlight flooding the room between the open silk curtains. I stared at the king-size bed with one monogrammed pillow propped against the mahogany headboard. I plopped down on the disheveled, purple satin sheets and sighed.

Realizing I was alone, I wondered whether it was better to have "loved and lost" than to have never loved at all. I kept asking myself that question this past year because I'd had my heart pulverized and stomped on by the very person around whom my world had orbited. I didn't just love my husband; he was a part of me. He was my universe, my family, my compass. It's not that my identity completely hinged on him, but I thought we were a team until he dropped a bomb on my world, crushing my hopes and dreams.

Exactly one year ago, my husband, Peter, and I went to Parents' Day at the University of North Carolina at Chapel Hill to visit our only child, Jenny. I wanted to make sure she was settled in for her freshman year in college. After a hectic day, we began the thirty-minute drive home to Raleigh. I looked at Peter, smiled, and asked softly, "Can you believe our baby is grown?" Before saying another word, I reached over and gently caressed his arm, only to be met with a slight jerk as he yanked his arm from beneath my touch.

He snarled in a voice I had learned to accept, focusing ahead on the road. "I'm just glad she earned an academic scholarship." His once-friendly tone had become a distant memory, replaced with a gruffness that had intensified over the years.

I sighed and wished time had not passed so quickly. "She makes me proud. I feel so lucky that I was able to work from home, for our business. I loved being an art teacher before she was born. But I don't regret quitting that job to help with our family's needs."

"Thanks to my hard work, my company grew and prospered," Peter said brusquely.

"Yes . . . your hard work," I said, forcing a smile.

"What? You don't appreciate what I've done for you?"

I nodded. "I do." I sat confused. I managed part of the business, too. I thought we had a partnership, but what did I know?

"Without me, you'd be just another middle-class gal. I gave you the finest. Don't forget that."

I shook my head. "My family had everything. We didn't need material things. We had love. Lots of it. I tried to make sure Jenny had that same feeling growing up."

Peter mumbled. "Right. . . ."

Once our discussion about Jenny ended, we sat in silence except for the whistling air. Peter insisted we keep the top to his new Porsche convertible down to enjoy the warm, sunny afternoon. Strands of brown hair slapped at my face. Out of the corner of my eye, I could see the long piece of jet-black hair that Peter usually combed across the top of his head flapping in the wind. I saw him struggle to tame the flyaway hair with his left hand; however, it wanted to sail free in the breeze.

At that instant, I noticed something missing: his wedding ring. I gasped. When did he stop wearing it? Instead of asking, I sat quietly, shifting in my seat, staring at my dainty, manicured finger. I twisted the sparkling band, around and around, and then concentrated on the puffy white clouds floating freely in the royal blue sky.

When high-rise buildings appeared in the distance, I knew we were almost home. A few minutes later, Peter pressed the remote, opening the iron gate. Gritting his teeth, he drove without braking along the meandering tree-lined drive leading to our house. And suddenly, it looked more like a haunted hotel in the distance rather than a comfortable home.

Instead of parking in the four-car garage, he pulled into the circular drive in front of the house. Without even turning off the engine, Peter hopped out of the car, yanked open the front door, and raced across the foyer, almost slipping on the shiny, polished marble floors. Once inside, he disappeared upstairs.

I took a crystal glass from the cabinets and poured myself a glass of iced tea. A few minutes later, he waddled into the kitchen. I looked up, bracing myself for a cutting remark.

I smiled. "Wow, you look handsome. Are you going somewhere?"

He stared at me with his vacant, dark eyes. But he didn't say a word. His stone-cold gaze made me shiver. Finally, he broke the silence by asking, "Do you like this new silk shirt on me?" I looked at his black shirt and noticed that the buttons didn't pull tightly across his belly. Maybe he finally broke down and bought an XXX-large.

"You look great." I paused. "Why don't we go to the club for dinner and let me show you off?"

He stared at me without blinking, and for a second it looked as if his face had become molded in wax. His labored breaths reminded me of our neighbor's bulldog. After clearing his throat, he said, "I'm going to buy new clothes. You can just keep the old ones. In fact, you can keep everything we've accumulated. I don't want it anymore, and I don't want you either."

In a shaking voice, I asked, "What are you saying to me?"

"Isn't it obvious? I want a divorce. I just feel like I need new stuff and a new life, too.

And since you'll hear about it soon enough anyway, you might as well hear it from me. I'm moving in with Sabrina, and she's pregnant with my child."

I gasped. His words nearly punched the life out of me. I searched my brain. *How do I know that name?* Finally, it occurred to me: Sabrina was our babysitter a few years ago. For crying out loud, she couldn't be more than twenty-five years old. And to add to the drama, she looked like a younger version of me.

"Sabrina doesn't argue with me like you do," he said.

"You just don't want to hear my opinions."

"Why should I? You know I'm usually right. Didn't I make a fortune with *my* car dealership? You could never have done that yourself," he said. He didn't stop there with his hurtful words. They just kept firing at me like a machine gun. "You know, in North Carolina we have to be separated for one year before the divorce is official. I'll tell you what, you keep the house. It needs a lot of work anyway, and I don't want to be bothered with it. You know, I have a new baby to concentrate on. So do what you want with the house. In fact, do what you want with all of the stuff. I'm leaving."

He rushed out the door without looking back. I didn't even have a chance to fight with him. In a flash, our life together ended. He was gone. I never dreamed my empty nest would include my husband.

If he had died suddenly, I could have grieved his memory. But instead, he left abruptly and I had to go on living, knowing he was playing house with another family right around the corner.

Even a year after his hasty departure, I struggled to deal with my memories of him. *I just want to forget, but how is that possible?* We can't just take an eraser and wipe the past away. Can we? It's an imprint that's forever etched into our brains— whether we like it or not.

After twenty years of marriage and what I thought had been a partnership, I was alone in the stately home we once shared. The only sound was my rapid breathing and the faint hum from the air conditioner. I picked up a crinkled photograph and a tiny matchbox off of the nightstand. My trembling hand nearly knocked over a crystal vase filled with sprigs of lavender.

With the tip of the match, I struck the flint. In the next instant, I lowered my eyes and fixated on the translucent flame while it danced along the wooden matchstick and brought the piercing heat dangerously close to my manicured fingertip. *Ouch!* I rotated my wrist slowly to stall the movement of the rapidly approaching flame. To avoid torching my long tawny hair, I tucked the loose strand behind my ear, away from the fire that waved uncontrollably from the blast of cold air.

In my other shaking hand, I lifted the creased photo and stared one last time at his attractive face. *Quit taunting me with your perfect smile,* I wanted to shout. But my words would have echoed in the silence of our abandoned home. Why did you want to leave me? How many times had I studied that timeless image of him looking so dashing in his black tuxedo? That special day now only a distant memory, captured always and frozen forever in this photograph.

I squinted my red, swollen eyes so that I could see the outline of his face more clearly. My tears dripped on the photograph, and the drops of moisture distorted and blurred his image. I hesitated for an instant but continued to merge the flame and photo. Meanwhile, I watched with a bitter smile while the burning photograph dissolved into ash. If only it were that easy to delete the painful memories from my traumatized mind.

Burning his picture might seem like an unusual way to celebrate becoming divorced. Today it was official. I was free, no more paper handcuffs.

Oh, the irony that I almost caught my French-manicured fingernails on fire. He always insisted that I keep my nails groomed. Just like he insisted that I keep everything about me and the house perfect. It was all a facade that only fooled me. *It is time finally to peel off these fake nails, remove my mask of thick makeup, and be free.*

I played the role of the compliant, devoted wife, and sometimes when one assumes a part, one gets lost in the character. *I need to find myself.* What good did my efforts of perfection do for me? Nothing. Try as I did, he left anyway. And after all those years of dutiful marriage, he discarded me without a thought; like loose strands of hair tossed out a car window, he hurled me into the wind.

And now I wondered, should I stop burning his photographs? Maybe. But that wouldn't be much fun or provide enough cathartic release. Perhaps burning a few more would be therapeutic. I stumbled while stretching to reach the top shelf of my closet. Although still somewhat nimble, I was not limber like I had been years ago as a competitive gymnast.

The muscles of my former athletic self were pliant, but soft, although I would like to think in all the right places.

I reached up to grab the box labeled *Memories* on the shelf above my tidy row of dresses. As I grasped the box, a sharp pain ripped across my body, tearing into me like an invisible blade. I winced and just as abruptly as the piercing pain started, it stopped, leaving me gasping for air in its wake. The pain in my abdomen had become familiar, but seemed to be getting worse.

Wild thoughts ran rampant through my brain as I tried to imagine what just happened. Maybe I pulled a muscle this time. Or could it be more? Could heartbreak radiate through the body in the form of true physical pain? Somewhere deep inside me, warning bells were ringing.

An instant later, the box tipped over and fell toward the marble floor. I gasped as a lifetime of mementoes crashed and tumbled to the ground and then sighed in relief after seeing the box intact. My curiosity drew me toward it, and I felt like those past events were calling out to me. But today, of all days, could I really handle seeing the contents? I should lock the box and spare myself the pain of reliving the past. *Hidden secrets . . . secrets hidden.*

What was the harm? Come on, one quick peek. With hesitation, I raised the top of the box and peered inside. Sifting through it was like stepping back in time. "No way, I forgot about you," I mumbled, lifting a tiny black bikini from the box. Peter bought this for me on our honeymoon. He thought it was a good idea for me to parade around in two minuscule pieces of fabric. I shoved the bikini back in the box. *At least it doesn't take up much space.*

But the item next to the bikini really caught my attention. I sighed and held a picture for closer inspection. I wiped the smattering of dust that had accumulated on the glass and stared at the image of my youthful face. In the photograph, a young man draped his arm across my shoulders. We squinted in the bright sunlight, with playful grins as if we shared a secret. At that moment, we were both blissfully unaware of obstacles that lay ahead.

I smiled, recalling the image of my college boyfriend and my first true love. "Blake," I whispered. *I am not about to burn this photograph.* Just bringing up Blake's name brought a feeling of longing to the surface. That picture reminded me of warm summer days without a care in the world and made me feel an unfamiliar stirring deep inside. But what was that yearning for: to see Blake again or have those halcyon days of my youth once more? Maybe it was both or something else. Was it possible to reclaim the excitement of those years of discovery?

Blake had a power over me and could talk me into just about anything. My parents thought he was a negative influence and didn't want me to be with him. Maybe they were right?

I looked at a faded round scar on my forearm. In fact, I never told anyone how I got the scar. But Blake knew. And if I brought the scar close enough to my face, I could still see the faint outline of, well . . . some things are better left unsaid. Some memories should remain in the box—hidden secrets, secrets hidden.

A deluge of memories shot through me at lightning speed. My favorite had always been our first intimate encounter—the night we both lost our virginity during our freshman year of college. But the memory that zoomed to the forefront was the *last* time we made love.

I looked at the image of Blake's face. This photograph became a portal, a time machine. All I had to do was stare at this picture and back I went to college. We attended a prestigious private university. We were both awarded athletic scholarships—his for football and mine for gymnastics. Without our scholarships, neither of us could afford the steep private school tuition.

What started out as a dare became a tradition. The Friday before Blake's home football games, he slipped notes under my dorm room door, inviting me to meet for a tryst. The first time he challenged me, I agreed.

Much to his surprise and delight, I showed up and quickly loved the excitement the new locations offered. He tried to convince me our afternoon sex helped him relax before the big games, but we both shared in the thrill. After his practice, we met in the school gardens, behind the football stadium, and the list of our escapades grew over the months. Each rendezvous became more adventurous as Blake tried to outdo himself. My competitive nature led me to stand up to each challenge. *Or should I say lie down, bend over, kneel . . . the list kept growing.*

Today, I was fascinated by his request to meet in the small study room. As I walked sprightly through the library with my backpack bouncing on my shoulders, I glanced around, but it felt deserted. Everyone seemed to be outside enjoying the warm fall sunshine. The halls were silent, and only the faint smell of decaying paper wafted through the air. I ran up the stairs, anticipating what was to come.

We had been to parties at Blake's fraternity. We had enjoyed numerous romantic dinners and beach trips. But it was our adventures that excited me the most.

Eagerly, I bounded into the study cubicle on the second floor. The small room consisted of a table, chairs, and nothing else except a window with an angled view of the campus, slightly obstructed by a thicket of trees. As always, the first sight of Blake made me gasp. Today was no exception. He stared at me when I walked into the room. He ran his fingers through his thick chestnut hair while leaning his back against the window frame, fixing his eyes on me. He spread his fingers across what looked like the start of a dark beard.

"Hi, pretty girl," he said, giving me a boyish grin. "Close the door and turn off the light. I've been thinking about kissing you all afternoon. I could barely get through practice."

"I know what you mean. I almost jogged over here from class. Are you ready for your last home game this season?" I asked, flipping the switch.

"Yes, if you'll help me relax. And I'm sorry I couldn't meet you for lunch today. My schedule will ease back up next week. But I promise I'll make it up to you."

"You will. How?"

"I'll show you. First, let's start with your dress. Take it off slowly for me."

Sunlight cut across a corner of the space, leaving the remainder of the room shadowed. We were alone. I stood in the darkened section, lifting my dress. Blake's eyes were fixated on me in a penetrating stare. His fervor turned me on, and suddenly I felt adrenaline surging through my body. I tossed my dress onto a chair.

He smiled. "Now come here."

I wanted to run into his arms; instead, I walked slowly, teasing him with the sway of my hips. He watched me without blinking. He rubbed his lips together. Stepping into the warm sunbeams and next to Blake, I could smell his freshly showered scent. Without pause, he pulled me close and hugged me as if we hadn't seen each other in months.

He stroked my hair and lifted my chin to look into his eyes. No one had eyes like Blake. They were more golden than brown and at the moment seemed to be predatory like a tiger's stare. And the intense look he gave me was filled with hunger, like he starved for my touch.

I thought he was going to kiss me, but he startled me by saying, "I have loved you since the first moment I saw you. I'm glad I waited until college to make love, because you made the first time unforgettable, like everything about you." He ran his hand down my arm and squeezed my hand. "These past couple years have been the best of my life."

"I love you. Happy anniversary," I said.

His face lit up. "You're something else. I know what I want to do to you."

"Kiss me?"

In the next instant, he leaned his face down and brushed his lips against my cheek. I felt a surge of warmth, anticipating his exploring touch. He slid his hand behind my head, tangling his fingers in my ponytail, tugging on my hair. He pressed his mouth flush against mine. His tongue parted my lips, searching for its playmate.

At the same time, he rubbed his other hand down my side and behind my back, unhooking my bra. He leaned over, placing tiny kisses on my throat, and cupped my breasts, squeezing them tenderly. He sucked one sensitive nipple while he fondled the other. I could feel wetness spread between my legs.

Using his other hand, Blake traced the outside of my panties in a circular motion. "You're so wet. You want me, don't you?" he asked.

I could barely speak, but managed to say, "Yes . . . please."

He rubbed back and forth across my panties. "Oh, I'm going to give it to you."

I stared at his wide grin. "Promises. Promises."

"I deliver. You know I always do."

Blake rotated my shoulders until I faced the open window. In the next instant, he rubbed his hands down my sides and along the curve of my hips. He flared his fingers across my bottom, squeezing my burning flesh, and skimmed his tongue along the base of my spine. He surprised me when he began sucking and biting at the soft skin on my round bottom.

"You like it when I touch you like this?" he asked.

"I want more."

I leaned forward with my arms sprawled across the windowsill and stared outside. With my chest angled toward the sunlight, I watched the students walking across campus. Anyone looking up would have been treated to the sight of my bare breasts.

Blake dropped to his knees. I let out a gasp as Blake knelt beneath my spread legs, holding my thighs. With his face pushed up against my panties, he began blowing hot breaths onto the silk. My moist skin underneath the fabric tingled in anticipation. He curved his finger around my panties and pulled them to the side. My exposed, well-shaven flesh throbbed with desire.

He wrapped his lips around my satiny skin. He pulled my slick folds inside his mouth and sucked. My clit sprang to life, becoming fully engorged and throbbing with sensitivity. Working in rhythm, he pushed two fingers inside me and rubbed his tongue back and forth. My moans resonated through the room, filling the silence as my body clenched. He licked. And sucked. I could hear the faint sound of him moaning. My body tightened. My thighs wrapped around his head until finally a wave of warmth swept across me.

After I shuddered in ecstasy, Blake stopped and hopped to his feet. "Let's really live. I dare you to go out onto the ledge with me and make love," he said, his eyes pleading.

I looked over the ledge, clamped my teeth together, and saw the ground far below. I told myself to go for it, but to not look down. Swallowing hard, I reluctantly complied.

"I'll climb out first, and then you follow. Once you're safely out there, climb onto me, straddle my hips, and ride me." His naughty laugh filled the room. "Don't worry, the ledge is wide enough to hold us."

Before I could answer, he removed his shirt, revealing his flat stomach and defined abs. A few seconds later, he slid his shorts off and was standing next to me in only his boxer briefs. He hoisted his leg over the windowsill, climbing slowly onto the ledge. He crawled forward a couple feet and then rolled onto his back. With one foot dangling over the side and swinging in the breeze, he motioned me forward. "The sunshine and the warm air feel incredible out here. Come straddle those cute legs over mine."

"Why should I?"

"Because you want it."

He knows I can't resist.

Carefully, I scaled the windowsill and clambered across the ledge on all fours and slowly climbed on top of his feet. With my legs draped across his toned calves, I began scooting up toward his hips. Slowly. Slowly. I maneuvered my way along his body until I was sitting astride him. I felt his stare. When I glanced at his face, he showed no signs of fear; only amusement flickered in his eyes as he pushed his boxer briefs low enough for his erection to aim toward the sunlight. *Oh . . . wow.*

Although I could do flips on a balance beam, my nerves were getting the best of me. I tried not to look down. I sucked in my breath. My heart pounded. *Focus. Focus. Don't think about the huge drop to the ground or that anyone looking up might see us. Don't look down again.* I tilted my body, trying to steady myself as my legs dangled over his hips. In a calming motion, he stroked his fingertips down my back to my hips, his touch leaving a path of warmth. I looked into his eyes and saw desire staring back at me.

With my legs straddled across his hips, I pushed my crotch against him. He took my hand and placed it on his penis. My mouth curved upward in a smile of amazement. Although I had seen his cock many times before, the size continued to astonish me. One hand was not enough to accommodate his manliness.

Reluctantly, I let go of my grasp on the ledge. I reached over with my other hand and continued to stroke him. The more I rubbed my hand up and down, the larger and harder he grew. *Lucky me*, but I didn't say it out loud.

Blake, however, was more vocal. "Oh no, don't stop. Don't ever stop," he murmured. His lips puckered in a playful smile. He slid my red panties over to the side and expertly slipped his finger inside my warm, wet center. I could feel the gentle breeze brush against my wetness. My breathing quickened to match his.

After he eased one finger inside me, he slid in a second. I opened my legs wider. I pushed my hips closer to allow him full access. At that moment, I would have done anything he wanted me to do. But he knew that already.

"I can't get enough of you. Ever," I said.

"Tell me what you want, Lila."

"I need you," I said breathlessly.

In one quick motion, he gripped my hips, lifted me, and pushed my warm flesh on top of his penis. Secretly, I loved how he took charge. I leaned forward and dug my nails into his biceps, watching his face smile with pleasure. I tilted my hips side to side, easing myself onto his long, hard shaft. I sucked in my breath as I could feel his thick cock stretching me, every inch of him pushing inside my tightness.

"You feel so good," he said. He moaned from my warmth as my inner muscles clenched and released, pulling him in deeper. In the next instant, he traced his fingers around the tenderness of my throbbing clit.

I smiled. "I want you deep inside me."

After fully mounting him, my hips took over the rhythm, pushing my pelvis against him, increasing our friction. He felt like a wild bull I was trying to tame undulating beneath me. He was totally uninhibited and wild.

The motion of my hips took over, and I began to rock against him, grinding myself into him. I pinned his hands above his head, holding them down, kissing him. At the same time, he lifted his pelvis to thrust against me like he was dancing inside. I tried to remain in control but couldn't.

"No one will ever love you as much as I do," he whispered breathlessly in my ear. My moans penetrated the gusty air. I was at the point of no return. My tingling flesh clung to him, sucking him into my depths. Two orgasms gripped me in quick succession. As I climaxed, the muscles deep inside me squeezed him, pulling him closer. I felt him tense under me. Someone groaned—me, him, or both in unison.

My greenish gaze looked down into his twinkling golden eyes. "I love you . . . always," I said.

Now it was time to make him have a multiple orgasm of his own. After he came, I didn't let him go. I held him inside me. I squeezed and pumped his penis for round two. A scream ripped out of him. And another scream. He continued to yell as his body tightened.

Finally coming to my senses, I pushed my forearm into his mouth to restrain and silence him. Blake clamped hard, tearing into my soft skin. I looked down and saw a couple of students pointing up at us. Frantically, I tried to hop off of Blake and scurry back to the window.

But in my haste, I slipped. I lost my footing and began to slide down the roof. I shrieked. I clawed at the roof. My fingertips tore. I slid. And slid. I couldn't get traction.

Blake grabbed for my hands, trying to stop my fall. His fingertips touched mine; however, his attempt failed. I skidded out of control, bouncing off of the roof line and tumbling into the tree below. Acting instinctively, I managed to grab a limb to slow my fall, but my swinging body was more weight than the branch could hold.

A moment later, the limb tore away. I fell the remaining ten feet to the ground. The foot that first made contact took the greatest impact from the fall. My bone snapped. I lay on the ground, naked except for torn panties, writhing in pain. I tried not to look at the bone protruding from the top of my foot. What happened next was a blur in my memory.

Ultimately, there was disciplinary action. And with a shattered foot, I lost my gymnastic scholarship. Not to mention the whispers that followed, as the word of my naked disaster spread across campus. Of course, Blake slipped his clothes on before he raced outside. His reputation remained unscathed because no one knew for sure that he was involved. I kept our secret. Unlike me, he retained his scholarship.

As a result of losing my scholarship, I could no longer afford to stay at the expensive private school and transferred to the state school close to my home. Blake felt horrible that I had to suffer and that he walked away without tarnish to his reputation. But his sorrow did not change our fate. And our relationship unraveled after that day.

So many years ago, so many things left unsaid.

CHAPTER 2

Just looking at the scar made me tremble, remembering the most intense day of ecstasy I had ever experienced. And pain. . . . I needed to push those memories back, deep within the recesses of my mind. But now, I just couldn't. My mental time travels were interrupted by the distant sound of my barking dog. The noise swiftly shook me back to the present.

That's right, my neighbor and best buddy Jane said she was going to stop by with a celebration gift. What in the world do you give as a divorce celebration gift? Leave it to Jane to find just the right thing.

I should wear this tiny bikini to greet her when she gets here, and make her laugh. She would fall over at the sight of me spilling out of it. But should I really put on Peter's torture device? Oh, why not! I slid off my loose-fitting sundress. I yanked the bikini bottoms up and over my padded hips.

As I struggled to fasten the top, I had to blow the air out of my lungs. Finally, the clasp hooked. *I don't remember this bikini fitting so tightly.* Almost breathless with laughter, I slid on my stilettos and sashayed into the bathroom in search of the full-length mirror.

But what I saw in the mirror surprised me. The face staring back at me had to be my mother, right? Not me. *Is this actually me? When did my face start to look so much like hers?*

I almost could hear my mother's trilling voice: "Dixie Elizabeth Baxter, is that any way for a proper lady to conduct herself, wearing that tiny bikini?" Even though she was chastising me, it rolled off her tongue like she was singing in church. Although I preferred to be called Lila, she would never call me that.

And somehow, she always knew when I misbehaved. To this day, she was the only person to call me Dixie—Dixie Elizabeth to be exact—unless she was really upset and then I got all three, the full arsenal of names blasted at me.

About two years ago she and my father moved to Florida, to judge my sister on a regular basis instead of me. I had lived my entire life in Raleigh, North Carolina, and don't have any plans to move. Thanks to the telephone, I don't feel her absence. Although occasionally, I wished I didn't have any method of communication.

I loved my mother dearly, but sometimes her voice resonated in my head. She was one of those people who kept telling me it was better to have "loved and lost" than to have never loved at all. I knew she meant well, but her opinion of love felt like total nonsense after what I had been through this past year.

Further study in the mirror made me inhale sharply and gasp. Were those muffin tops hanging over my bikini bottom? Reluctantly, I turned to get a better view, and what I saw startled me. I let out a moan of anguish. Was that back fat rolling across my rib cage? When did that appear? I glanced at my reflection in disbelief. *What were you thinking, putting on this old bikini? It didn't work to keep your husband; it is not going to entice a man now. Anyway, what man? Go change.*

I tried to contain my laughter but couldn't. When the sound wheezed out of me, my tummy roll released and fell over my bikini bottom. I gave up trying to pull my stomach in and simply looked down in disgust at the pudgy roll hanging over the fabric.

Quickly, I brushed my wavy hair that hung in strands down my back. Although a natural brunette, I enjoyed having a few highlights, blond or red, depending on my mood. This year, I wanted that summer blond look that reminded me of my towheaded youth.

I flipped my chemically-enhanced hair away from my face, rotated from side to side, and stared one more time in the mirror. *Maybe I can learn to color my own hair.* As I leaned in closer to inspect myself, I feared that the glow of my youth was beginning to fade. New lines by my eyes? Good grief, maybe I could Botox my entire face like a statue.

I was only forty-one years old, but today I felt creaky and ancient. *Enough . . . Step away from the mirror*.

As I left the bathroom, my stained glass caught my eye. A bright burst of sunlight lit the colors of the glass, fully illuminating the bathroom. I tried to figure out how many hours I worked to create this masterpiece. I painstakingly merged broken bits of glass, piece after piece, with lead, slowly transforming them into spectacular art. And now, sadly, it was time to leave it behind. All of it. The legal documents were signed; it was official, and today I was divorced. I couldn't afford this house and didn't need the space anymore.

Some might argue that I was now free, but I had not yet come to terms with this newfound freedom. Although, reality was slowly sinking in, and I was not completely sure how I felt about it yet. My feelings were a weave of fear, sorrow, exhilaration, and uncertainty. What I did know, for sure, was as a newly single woman, I needed to downsize. I didn't expect to feel this jolt of sadness about selling this house. But the tears welling in my eyes had made the decision for me, and when they spilled over my eyelids, they revealed my sorrow.

At that exact moment, my perky golden retriever, Elky, danced in excitement at the front door, from the mere sound of a truck pulling into the driveway. Her barks echoed across the marble floor, and the commotion brought me out of my trance-like state. Was the handyman here to finish his work? In the distance, I could hear someone slam the backyard gate. In addition to the interior work, I hired a handyman to repair the broken tiles and restore the pool. There was no way I could handle all of this work alone.

A few minutes later, my thoughts were interrupted again, this time by the sound of the doorbell. *Jane*. The bell echoed while I raced across the house in my tiny bikini and stilettos. My outfit was going to make her laugh so hard she might have to cross her legs or pee on herself. I giggled at the thought. An instant later, I opened the front door and shouted, "Janeeeeeee," but to my surprise it was a fresh-faced handsome stranger.

I gasped and stepped backward, stumbling to find my balance. My face froze in a surprised expression, with my eyes round and wide like a startled owl. I laughed as I realized I stood nearly naked in front of him.

"Do I look like a Jane?" asked the male version of perfection staring at me. A wide smile flexed across his flawless face, and he chuckled as he stepped forward and introduced himself. "My name is Chase," he said in a deep, husky voice while I assessed the brawny body that filled my entire doorframe. Instantly, I perked up from my dour reflections.

I would guess he was about twenty-one years old. *Don't look at him that way*. He sure was gorgeous, but he was much too young for me. I wished some of his youthful shine could rub off on me. He stepped toward me, narrowing the distance between us until I could feel his breath. His gaze traveled down my body, and to my surprise, slowed at my breasts. Another smile lit his face, and then he continued scanning my body.

So here I stood, in front of a beautiful man, wearing nothing but a scant piece of fabric that barely contained my soft, marshmallowy flesh. Finally, Chase's ogling ended and his glance returned to my eyes. I had wishful thinking, at least, that his look was in appreciation of my female form and not in disgust. He was smiling, after all. And not once did I see him fall down laughing.

"Hello, I'm Lila."

He extended his hand toward me. His brawny hand encompassed mine, and rather than shaking it, he stroked it softly. "It's my pleasure, my great pleasure, to meet you." The trail he touched along my flesh prickled from his heat.

I started beaming and then, once again, remembered my outfit. I had to look down to avoid his eyes. "Oh, the pool boy," I found myself whispering softly as my head dipped down toward my chest. *Oops. Did I say that out loud?* I felt the blood rush to my cheeks.

Acting as if he didn't hear me, Chase continued. "My father was here earlier repairing your bathroom and pool. He finished the tile work and now I'm here to clean the pool." As he spoke, the muscles across his chest tightened. "Will you show me where the equipment is stored?"

The young man had the same friendly smile as his father. They were both attractive. "Sure, come on in." I smiled widely, proudly revealing my perfectly whitened teeth. I think my teeth might be blinding. *Did he just cover his eyes with his hand? Too white, too artificial. Okay, glow stick, close your mouth.*

As Chase stepped into my house, I studied him. He had bronzed dark skin, soulful brown eyes, and rippling muscles. His tight tank top with the "Pool Professionals" logo barely covered his muscular chest.

"How are you doing today, ma'am?" he asked, bursting my bubble. *Go ahead, burst my bubble.*

My expression hardened slightly, and I was not sure how to respond. He addressed me like his mother. Actually, I was probably older than his mother.

"I've been busy working on this house. In fact, I'll be listing it for sale this week. Chase, you came at the perfect time," I said in a soft drawl. But the moment the remark slipped out of my mouth, I regretted it.

Chase met my gaze and did not hesitate. "Yes, ma'am," he said with his charming smile. "I always do know when to come. I think it's a skill I've perfected." He winked. "Would you like me to show you some of my . . . tricks?"

My lower jaw dropped. Good thing it was attached or it might have hit the floor. I stood there, with my mouth still ajar, making some kind of mumbling sound. I finally regained my composure. "Oh my, let me show you the pool."

While he walked across the house, I thought even his wink was sexy. I couldn't help notice that he had the swagger of a man who knows how to satisfy a woman. He peered into the dining room and stared at the low-hanging crystal chandelier that twinkled in the sunlight. "Wow, this house is even more beautiful on the inside than the outside. Ev-er-y-thing is beautiful here," he emphasized as he looked around admiringly.

In order to prepare the property to sell, I spent the past year painting, landscaping, cleaning, and organizing every inch. I was proud of the fact that I did most of the work myself, except for the large projects. But Chase was here to help put some of the finishing touches on my efforts.

He glanced down at my dog. She was wagging her tail excitedly and running in circles. "And, of course, hello to you, too, pretty puppy." He knelt down and offered his face for her licks. Elky kissed him from cheek to cheek and wiggled in delight. He stood and brushed the dog kisses off his cheeks. "Both of you ladies look stunning."

"Her name is Elky." I tried to hide my exhilaration, but I was certain my eyes betrayed my delight. *I want to do a happy dance, too.* I looked away to hide my face, which had become ablaze with excitement.

Chase leaned close. "For the record, I'm a pool professional." Chase pointed to the logo on his shirt. "It says it right here on my shirt, 'Pool Professionals.'" He let out a delicious laugh and, at that point, I was close enough to smell his manly essence.

I stood dumbfounded in horror. *Did he hear me say pool boy?* It had been too long since a man had stood this close to me. Wow, I lost my composure entirely. I just opened my mouth, and the words tumbled out.

I really wanted to look down to hide my embarrassment, but I struggled to take my eyes off of his broad shoulders and strong arms.

Oh yes, I regretted calling him a pool boy, which sounded so demeaning. I tried to hide my humiliation by smiling demurely. And whether the pool boy comment was a cliché or not, there was a woman's secret fantasy, standing intimately close to me.

He was tall, dark, and oh, so handsome, in nothing but a tank top and tight shorts, staring at me intently. But I barely noticed because I was fixated on his skin; I was thinking his skin looked like creamy caramel. *Yummy enough to lick.* I'd had this daydream before. This entire scenario was almost too good to be true.

Chase's lips parted in a seductive smile while he brushed his shaggy, unkempt hair from his eyes and looked intently at me. He stood close. Feeling his warm breath on me left me struggling to find my next words, and to my surprise, I realized

I wanted him even closer. With my brain reeling from this newfound excitement, I felt conflicted.

A part of me wanted Chase to touch me, to push me up against the wall and devour me with kisses. But the other part of me wondered what I was thinking. I had not been touched by a man, other than my husband, in twenty years. And I had not been touched *at all* in over a year. What were these feelings stirring inside me? My body's eagerness took control of my mind. A strange sensation of warm tingles traveled to my loins.

This excitement was foreign to me, but I could learn to like it. Finally, I regained my composure and shook myself back to my senses.

I jumped away from Chase and cleared my throat. "The storage shed has the equipment you probably need." Actually, I couldn't remember the last time anyone had cleaned the pool. For that matter, I couldn't remember the last time anyone had used the pool. What a waste.

And today was the perfect cloudless day for his arrival. It was a sweltering September day, even by North Carolina standards, with the sun shining bright and the air thick with steamy humidity. A dip in the pool, for the first time in a very long time, seemed refreshing.

I had been so tired lately, and I continued to be haunted by an unsettling sensation that I felt to my core. No matter what I did, or how much rest I got, I just couldn't shake the feeling that something was wrong. This disturbance occasionally felt like an alarm going off in my head, but I could handle only one apocalypse at a time. I had enough going on with the divorce.

Anyway, sunshine would be my medication for today. Living in the South gave me an abundant supply of radiant heat. But I probably didn't need the extra brightness today; just looking at Chase warmed me.

I wondered if he could feel my thoughts while I led him through the expansive house to the back veranda. We walked down the stone steps to the lap pool, which was surrounded by fuchsia crape myrtles still in bloom.

After we stepped into the sunlight, he said, "Your long hair looks so pretty in the light. It is so shiny and smooth that I want to run my fingers through it."

Stunned by his words, I turned toward him, shielding my eyes from the intense afternoon light, and saw him still staring at me. Our eyes held a lingering gaze for an extended moment. Or was that just my wishful imagination?

I handed him a key to the shed, and his hand slowly brushed against mine, stroking his fingers across the tender skin inside my palm. His fingers felt rugged and strong. What would more of his touch feel like?

I felt startled as Chase's voice brought me back to reality. "Can Elky play in the yard with me while I work?" And to my astonishment, I watched Elky leap, paws first, onto him, licking his face. *She really likes him.* After Chase pushed her down, I watched Elky wag her tail so hard she almost toppled over onto her side.

"Of course, she would love to play," I said. *Can I play with you, too?*

Chase reached down and picked up a tennis ball and tossed it to an excited, panting Elky, who scrambled to return it. He scratched her neck.

Although I did not think flirting with Chase was the right path to take on my journey of life, it was fun for today. Watching his muscular arms while he cleaned the pool would help divert my focus. I needed to take his picture to show Jane. Maybe when he was working I could sneak a quick photo, but what if he caught me?

Perhaps he was the distraction I needed to get my ex-husband's image out of my head. Nothing Peter told me was true, it seemed. Are trustworthy men an endangered species? I thought our life was fine. Well, maybe not a perfect marriage, but we fit together comfortably enough. But Peter had been busy creating a new life and family; meanwhile, I did not have a clue.

And when I finally heard about his lies, my entire world was ripped away from me in an instant. It made me sick as if my life had become a scandal. At that moment, I vowed never to trust a man again. Maybe learn to have fun again, but never completely believe the words that I heard.

Behind us was a loud crash. We turned. Elky stood still, wagging her tail and holding the tennis ball in her mouth. Next to her was a terra cotta planter broken on the ground.

I laughed. "Well, I never really liked that planter anyway."

Chase shook his head. "I'm sorry I got her so excited."

I smiled at that comment. "I'll just sweep up the broken pieces while you transform the pool."

"When I'm done netting these leaves, you'll be able to enjoy it again." He wiped his brow. "Today is a scorcher."

I nodded. "We might have a few more weeks of hot weather."

I went inside the storage shed to get the broom. The light was broken. I searched in darkness. A moment later, Chase stepped up behind me.

"Oh, my." I gasped, turning to meet his gaze. My heart began to beat faster.

He grinned at me. "I walk softly, but that's all I do with a light touch." He inched closer. I could feel his breath. "I guess you want me to get started cleaning the pool?"

I took a small step backward, bumping into the wall. When I spoke, my voice was shaky. "That . . . might be a good idea."

He moved closer to me. "Are you sure you don't need help with other projects first?"

I forced myself to keep my voice steady. "I'm . . . fine." I hesitated for an instant while I looked down at his tight shorts. And then I pointed to the net and pool supplies. A few seconds later, I grabbed the broom and raced out of the shed.

After refilling Elky's water dish, I began sweeping the broken planter pieces. At the same time, I quietly watched him. With escalating delight, I stared at Chase's thickly muscular arms scooping leaves with the net. He was in perfect shape. I used to keep fit until the separation. Then I stopped exercising. I used to work out every day; it once made me feel invigorated.

Before the divorce, I would swim laps in the pool to stay in shape. But depression took over my life; it consumed me, and then I consumed everything in reach. And the scale numbers climbed. And climbed. Looking back on it all, I realized it was not a coincidence that *stressed* written backwards spelled *desserts*. If stress could burn calories, I would be skinny now.

I wasn't totally oblivious of my increased weight; I just didn't care. Sure, I could tell my pants didn't fit the same, so I bought some new ones. Maybe I realized the full extent of my weight gain the day I started doing jumping jacks and heard applause, but when I looked around, I was the only one in the room. *That mental image of my fat chunks slapping together still makes me gag.*

And now a year later, I struggled with a different problem. I lost my appetite. Suddenly, I started losing weight. In fact, I had layers of excess skin to battle.

The truth was, it would be nice to be proud of my naked body again, but not that it mattered at my current pace. It had been such a long time since I was intimate with a man. Not being asked out on a date for the past year didn't help my bruised ego. But I had enjoyed those long romantic walks to the refrigerator.

The sound of the doorbell startled me in the midst of my mental assessment, or more accurately, dissection. Suddenly, I remembered I was standing in a tight bikini a few feet away from a gorgeous man. I quickly excused myself. Then, without another word, I raced inside.

CHAPTER 3

Before going to the front door, I slipped on a bathing suit cover-up. *Finally, I came to my senses.* I stopped to compose myself. This time, I would look out *before* opening the door. As I peeked through the glass panels, I saw a familiar face.

Seeing my friend and neighbor, Jane, usually cheered me up instantly. She always had a way of just being there when I needed her. I was usually glad when Jane stopped by for a visit, but today I hesitated. I was not sure if I wanted to share Chase with her. Maybe I wanted to enjoy watching him all by myself.

I stood there floundering in indecision as to whether I should open the door, but too late now; Jane caught me looking through the glass sidelights. She waved her arms crisscross in the air at me. *Darn.* I opened the door and Jane greeted me, giving me an embracing hug.

Jane was pretty with a magnificent mane of long black hair, creamy dark skin, and expressive brown eyes. Her demeanor was animated when she talked, and she had an infectious laugh and an effervescent energy.

Jane's personality was so big and bright that she could light up a room. I felt like a shy wallflower in comparison. Although in truth, I might be only a few shades less vivacious than Jane. I was definitely not quiet. And together we were just silly. The simplest things made us laugh uproariously.

"Hi, Lila, did I miss the show?" Jane bellowed as she walked into the house. She flung her hands in the air in an exaggerated gesture of exhilaration. "I saw a very handsome man driving a truck in your driveway. I can't believe you didn't call me right away." Jane had an excited smile. "I raced over here as fast as I could."

I sighed in defeat; I would not keep this experience to myself after all. "His name is Chase, and he's still here. But you better hurry if you want to see him." Even though we were two middle-aged women, we giggled like teenagers as we raced across the house to the window with the best view.

When we entered the kitchen, I flipped the switch. Prisms of light illuminated the granite countertops. Jane flung her oversized handbag onto the table. A moment later, we stood next to the picture window and pulled the curtains back that obscured our view. We now had a clear angle of the lap pool. Jane gasped and leaned forward to savor the sight.

Chase stood next to the pool, holding a large net and wearing nothing but tight shorts. "Oh, look at him," Jane said, practically panting. "He's male perfection like Michelangelo's *David*. No. He's more like a male stripper," she cooed.

She whipped her hands to her chest with dramatic flair. "I really need a pool," she said with a breathy sigh. She looked at me and gasped. "What are you wearing?"

I pulled the gaping opening of my cover-up apart to reveal my outfit. "What, you don't like my string bikini and stilettos? They don't scream sexy?"

Jane raised her eyebrows and looked at me. "It screams something, but sexy isn't it, girlfriend. Sure, wear that outfit to the club if you want everyone to know you're having a mid-life crisis."

I burst out laughing. "Are you telling me my high horse is really a mini pony?"

"If normal is how you see yourself, and if that helps you sleep better at night, by all means, think what you want."

I teased. "Look at you in your sexy momma miniskirt you chose to wear over here. If it was any smaller, we could call it a bathing suit."

Jane gave me a twisted smile. "Are you trying to say the expiration date has lapsed on this look? I know what you mean, though. You should have seen me climbing out of my minivan in this tight skirt. My kids had to tug my arm to help me get out of the driver's seat."

"Really?"

"Just kidding. Actually, I squeezed into it just to come see this cutie. And didn't I see a different handsome man drive up earlier? Are you hiding him somewhere?"

This time I let out a full belly laugh, and Jane joined in. "You don't miss much, do you? That was Chase's father. He has a separate repair business and will be back tomorrow."

"Two of them?"

"Yes. I don't see a sight like that every day. Can I offer you something? Coffee? Tea?" I said, motioning toward the coffee maker.

"You're having a good-looking man parade. I should've brought a flag to wave. No caffeine for me, thanks. But I'll snatch one of those chocolate éclairs I see in plastic wrap, if you're offering," she said.

I pushed the tray toward her. She stuffed a piece of éclair into her mouth and chewed as if in rapture. She wiped the crumbs from her mouth.

"Would you like champagne to wash it down and to help me celebrate the start of my new life?" I asked.

"Tempting, but I better not," she said.

"You know, as of today, I'm officially divorced," I sighed in resignation.

"I know. Today is a difficult day."

"Yes, I have so many mixed feelings. But I need to get over Peter. He has a new baby now. You know, we could have spent thousands of dollars in marriage counseling, and it would not change the course of that sinking ship. Peter was the captain, and he had been in our marriage, too."

She crinkled her face sympathetically. "You're better off to chart your own course than follow his," she said.

I nodded. "He stopped being a team player, for our team at least. And then without pause, he moved from one woman to the next, like he was the baton in a track race." My voice cracked. "Sadly, I was the last to learn that I was part of the event. It stunned me how quickly he could jump from one life to another."

"I'm angry with you, and for you," she said.

"In a blink of an eye, it was like I didn't know him at all. How's that even possible?"

Why didn't he just leave me and then go look for a new life? The coward, he couldn't be on his own for a day.

"Marriage can give us a false sense of security," she said. "Chris and I aren't exactly on a perfect path either. I'm here for you, but I'm no expert." She shoved another bite of chocolate éclair into her mouth.

I sighed. "I should have seen the warning flag when he insisted on getting married on February 29th, Leap Year. I thought it was his odd sense of humor, but really he only wanted to keep up with our anniversary every four years. And when he filed for divorce, he tried to claim that we were married only five years instead of twenty!"

Jane looked at me curiously. "It took me a moment to realize you were joking. I know today's a challenging emotional day. Are you okay?" she asked.

My voice choked up. "I know we've been over this, but . . ."

"It's okay, honey. You're still going through it."

"Yes," I said with a tight smile. "It doesn't seem fair to be left alone after all those years of devotion to him, his business, and our family. I got caught up in his world. And I forgot to live up to my own potential. But I'm ready to rebuild my life into something that'll make me happy, and not just a life that revolves around his needs."

"I know what you mean. My two boys and my husband keep me busy from morning to night. It's easy to get lost in other people's demands."

I shrugged. "He always used to tell me to quit arguing with him. But after he left, it occurred to me that he considered my *opinions* arguing. He was telling me to quit giving my opinion and essentially to do everything his way. No thanks, this is my life, too, and I shouldn't just live it the way he wanted. I guess it's time to step out of his shadow and let the light shine on me," I said.

"It is time for you to live for yourself," she said.

"When he left me for another woman, I begged him, 'Don't go, Peter. I need you in my life.'"

Jane looked down. "Okay."

I laughed. "After I begged him to stay, I said, 'I'm just joking, Peter. Close the door on your way out.'"

Jane tried to hold back her laughter but couldn't. "You're just figuring out what a selfish jerk Peter can be? He needed his ass kicked long ago," she said, pretending to kick him in the backside using an exaggerated swinging motion with her foot.

I would not want to be on the receiving end of her kick. Jane's legs had power. She and her husband owned a fitness center. And when her elementary school-age boys were in school, she taught cardio classes part-time. Her husband looked like he could flip small cars with his fingertips. Chris looked like a mirror version of Dwayne "The Rock" Johnson. Watching them together reminded me what a marriage should be like. They respected each other and worked together.

"At least I got something good from my marriage. Because of Peter, I have Jenny. She will always be my gift."

"That makes you a lucky lady." In the next instant, she picked up another éclair, bit into it, squirting the crème across her mouth. She leered at Chase through the window. Jane turned to me, licking the crème off her lips, in a somewhat obscene manner, and asked, "Do you think Chase would like a more mature woman?"

"I'm not sure what his first impression will be like if you don't wipe that éclair crème off your face." I grinned. "You and your lascivious nature."

Jane smiled and spun around with her arms crossed over her chest as if dancing with Chase. "I don't think he scares that easily." She continued in an upbeat playful manner. "Don't even go there with a bad cougar joke. Who came up with that title anyway? So, if we're called cougars, what does that make Peter?"

I shrugged. "You don't want to hear me start cussing, do you? Plus, as soon as I start swearing, my phone rings. I'm not sure how she does it, but my mother must have a tuning device that picks up on my misconduct." We both snickered.

"Your mother is something. Remind me whose idea was it for her to move to Florida?" Jane asked.

"We shouldn't go there, or the phone will start ringing." I glanced back out the window at Chase. "He sure stays in amazing shape," I said admiringly.

"That's what sexy looks like," Jane said.

"Your husband is in perfect shape."

She nodded. "Okay, this one is for you."

"He's too young. But maybe one of these days, I'll date again."

Jane pointed toward the window and then looked at me. "He's just a reminder to have fun. You're never too old to enjoy yourself."

I paused and watched Chase as he tipped a red soda can to his lips and appeared to guzzle the entire drink. He wiped the sweat from his brow and stared at the kitchen window.

I turned back to Jane, hoping he couldn't see us. "I still feel too wounded to want to try to enjoy myself. The good thing is that anger has a way of making any unresolved feelings of love go away. Or at least masking them." I did not meet Jane's gaze; instead, I looked down at the tea I just poured, using it as an excuse to turn away.

"Yes, it's true; we can be hurt the worst by the people we love the most," Jane said.

"Peter should have come with a warning label." *He needed more than a warning label. He needed a warning tattoo.* I could tell by my wavering voice that I was deeply hurt by him. It was out of character for me even to discuss our relationship. But I was simply relieved to vent.

Jane reassured me that it was fine by saying, "We've been friends for more than ten years, and never once had I heard you say anything negative about your marriage until he dropped this bomb on you. I know it still hurts. You need to talk about it."

I smiled. "Thank you, dear friend. I just feel overwhelmed and confused by my feelings today, since it's finally over. I can't let go, but I want to. I have to."

"You'll feel better when you do."

"Really, this divorce is for the best."

"Yes, the best is yet to come."

My nod in agreement was interrupted by a sharp pain in my side. The agonizing pain forced me to gasp for air and bend over to find relief. I labored to catch my breath and lifted up slowly as the pain subsided.

Jane, watching it all, was caught off guard by my behavior. "Are you all right?" she asked, startled.

Forcing a smile, I looked Jane straight in the eye. "Oh, yes, sure, it must've been something I ate today. Or maybe I'm letting the anger out, like steam." I tried to joke. But deep down I had an unsettling feeling that something was wrong . . . terribly wrong.

My intuition knew that behind my tired eyes, something else lurked. The sad reality was I had not been feeling like myself lately.

Wanting to change the subject quickly, I asked Jane jokingly, "Ever just want to empty your head of all your memories and start over? Lately, I want to untangle the web of memories in my mind and tear them out. Except for my sweet daughter and my dear friends like you, who I love, I think it would be a good idea to start over with a clean slate."

Jane turned to me. "Are you serious?"

I smiled warmly. "Am I ever really serious?"

"You have a point there, my friend. You and your quirky personality."

We both laughed. Just talking about the finalization of the divorce was helping me. I felt slow relief from my frustration, and at last, peace.

My close friends had become my family, but for the first time in many years I did not have a special man in my life. Maybe that was good at this point. "Thank you for always being there when I desperately need a friend."

"I'm always here for you," Jane said.

Glancing out the window, she sighed, "Chase is beautiful to look at, and I bet he would be fun to touch."

"Oh no, I would never do that," I gushed.

"What's stopping you, girlfriend? You're single now. And even though that no-good ex-husband of yours probably never told you, you're very pretty, too. If nothing else, flirt with Chase a little. Do it for me and all the married women out there who are stuck in a sexual rut. Speaking of all of that, I brought you a gift to celebrate your divorce." She rummaged through her handbag and handed me a pink box tied with a large white ribbon.

I pulled the ribbon, opened the box, and blinked, trying to focus on the contents in stunned silence. "Is that what I think it is?"

"I bought you something that every newly divorced woman needs. Okay, *every* woman needs." She giggled.

I lowered my voice. "You bought me a vibrator?" I asked, looking at her in disbelief. "I never had one before."

Jane's mouth dropped open, and her eyes grew wide. "Are you serious? Well, it's about time you did."

I lifted the pink vibrator, squeezed the thick rubber shaft, and tossed it on the counter. "I could never do that." And I began to blush from the mere idea.

She could not hold back her look of surprise. "What, touch yourself? You need to let loose a little bit and experience life. I'm starting to think you forgot how. Touching Chase might be a good first step. If nothing else, touch him with your mind," she said.

I looked at her curiously. "What do you mean?"

She looked at me as if she was explaining this to a virgin. "Fantasy . . . let your imagination have an adventure," she said.

"Jane, you're such an amazing friend, and you know what? You just gave me the answer I needed."

She looked puzzled. "I don't recall you asking the question. But yes, you need to start living again," Jane said. She had a warm smile that met mine knowingly. "You're aware of what you need to do, right?"

I nodded. "Have fun with a hot guy. But you know I'm joking. I wouldn't do that."

"Enough joking about it—do it. Live it." Jane grinned. She loved instigating wicked fun.

In the next instant, she blurted out something about picking up her boys from tennis practice. She grabbed her purse from the table and walked to the door. Thinking about that vibrator, I was still giggling when I followed her.

Jane stepped outside and turned back to me. "You're stronger than you think you are," she said.

At that precise moment, it occurred to me: life is not a destination, but a journey to be enjoyed.

"Thank you. You're a dear friend," I said.

She reached over and hugged me. "Oh, say good-bye to Chase for me." We both giggled again like schoolgirls.

I went back inside, paused while looking at the pink box open on the table, and wondered if I should do what my instincts were shouting for me to do. *Do it!*

And without giving it a second thought, I tucked Jane's gift back into the box like I didn't want anyone to know my secret, and then I carried the box to my bedroom and closed the door.

All those jokes I had with Jane. My mother would be horrified. She certainly would tell me that a proper lady would never repeat them aloud. I almost could hear the telephone ringing.

Jane was a unique friend, but many people probably would find me mentally unstable from those comments, not funny. And what would my friends think if they knew what I was about to do? They probably would gasp in horror. *My dirty secret.* I washed the vibrator and tried to figure out how to work it. Let me see—slow speed, medium speed, and high or probably mind-shattering speed.

I yanked the long silk curtains shut except for a tiny crack that let in a slice of sunlight and enough space to watch *him.* I pulled the cool leather chaise lounge chair up to the window as close as I could get it. I sat down with my knees tucked under me. Through the tiny slit in the curtains, I had a clear view of Chase, who was netting the pool.

I let out a sigh while I admired his hard, tanned-to-perfection body that was ripped with muscles. I had become captivated by his every movement as he pulled the long metal pole back and forth.

And oh, I was thinking about moving with him. I shook my head because I couldn't believe I was having these erotic thoughts.

A shiver went down my spine, and a rush of warmth spread between my legs. I had never pleasured myself before, but today I wanted to touch myself *there.* I was divorced and alone now; however, I was still a woman with needs and desires.

Once my lewd fantasy began, I spread my legs and slid one hand down my body into my bathing suit bottom. Instantly, I could feel my body growing warm with excitement.

A glint of daylight poured through the tiny gap in the curtains. Continuing to peer out through the small opening, I thrust one finger inside my warm folds, fantasizing about having Chase's hard manliness inside me.

With my free hand, I untied the string on my bikini so I could touch myself easily. I kept the finger inside me. With my other hand, I rubbed small circles on my most sensitive area. I caressed myself slowly at first but liked it so much that I quickly built up speed.

My heart began to pound. I watched Chase, thinking about what it would be like to have him on top of me—moving as one, rubbing his toned body, and feeling his warm kisses. My breathing became rapid as I touched myself with increased intensity. Should I, could I, take it a step further? Why not?

I looked at the pink vibrator hesitantly, and then gave myself the mental go-ahead. I held it nervously. I examined it for an instant. I squeezed the thick rubber shaft and wondered if it would be an appropriate substitute for the real thing.

And then I pushed the vibrator inside myself slowly, as if one of us might break. Once fully inserted, I flipped it on . . . *HIGH, WOW! Meant to put it on slow, but oooooohhhhhhhhhh that feels amazing.*

In my delirium of excitement, I lost all of my common sense. I wanted to get a better view of the tantalizing male in my backyard, so I lifted my feet and pushed them against the window. And then I spread my feet in an attempt to pull the curtains farther apart.

Before I knew what had happened, I yanked too hard on the silk material and ripped the entire curtain rod and fabric to the floor. Fully exposed! My nearly naked body immersed in sunlight. There I lay, spread eagle on the chair, looking down at Chase. Much to my surprise, he was staring up at me! He parted his lips, and his white teeth glistened in the sunlight. He winked and beamed a knowing smile. Or was it?

Did he know that this entire time I had been watching him? Could he hear the hum of my vibrator? Was he really able to see me touching myself now? Probably not since I'm on the second floor, but maybe? My cheeks turned as red as the surface of Mars. Somewhere within, I found bravery and leaned closer toward the window, focusing my eyes on his firm body. *Don't stop now.*

Much to my surprise, I could see the outline of his hard erection straining against his shorts. He reached his hands into his shorts and started stroking his rock-hard pride and joy.

I stooped closer to the window, wanting him to lift it out of his shorts, but he didn't. *Let me see it. Show me. Pleeeease.* He teased me with his touch and his grin.

And he did not flinch from his smoldering gaze, nor did he take his hands from his shorts, as he stared up at me with his chocolate brown eyes from across the yard. At this point, I could *feel* his undaunted stare. His erection seemed to have a life of its own, and he had reason to be proud. I smiled broadly. No wonder he had that cockiness; with a cock like that he had every right.

I just stared at his smug smile, like he had a secret on the tip of his tongue about to bust out of his mouth. His good looks combined with the confidence of someone not yet jaded by life's setbacks, a deadly combination. He still had that youthful self-assurance. And really, how much stress could this gorgeous young man face each day?

I thought about all of his attributes, while I stared at him through my window, spellbound. To my amazement, he continued to fasten his seductive stare on me, at the same time stroking his manliness. His muscles tightened, and his breathing rate accelerated.

I became entranced as I watched him increase his rhythm and intensity. He never for a second looked away. Without hesitation, I pressed my face closer to the window. I could feel my hot breath on the glass—breathing faster and faster— steaming a small circle.

For a few moments, our eyes locked in a concentrated stare. Excitement twinkled in his gaze. And mine, too. My arousal built while I continued to manipulate the vibrator, never taking my enthusiastic eyes off of him. He continued to stare wide-eyed as his body stiffened, his gaze never leaving mine.

With my legs spread, I guided the vibrator deep inside me. In and out it surged. The vibrations pulsated through my body. I imagined his hot breath against my neck. My body trembled.

Every nerve ending ignited, and then a sudden surge of warmth exploded, sending a shock wave of contractions across my body. I stunned myself with a shallow moan as my muscles tightened and brought with it a surge of bliss.

Still never breaking eye contact, I watched his entire body tense as he rubbed his cock harder and faster. I saw him shudder as if volts of energy shot through him. And then he relaxed. He smiled ear to ear as he slowly lifted his hand out of his shorts.

I leaned my head back on the chair and sighed. I couldn't remember the last time I had an orgasm. "That was exciting." I laughed out loud, but I needed the actual touch of a man. I didn't want to become a voyeur; instead, I needed romantic evenings and someone to share some exciting adventures.

What I wanted most of all was a life filled with laughter. I did not like the negative and cynical person I had become this past year. I needed to find more joy in my life. The corners of my lips lifted. I took a deep breath. I almost could feel the cheerful energy fill my lungs.

It was time to make my own choices. My life's story was unfolding in front of me. The start of a new chapter, but what direction would it take? I always loved the stories with happy endings. Would I be so lucky? I continued to smile, but I wasn't sure what provoked me. *Did I hear the faint cry of my hidden diva self, screaming to be released?*

I stripped out of my bikini and dressed while thinking Chase was beautiful, although much too young for me. I needed an experienced man who had lived a full life. Someone I could relate to on a more mature level, not just a hot body. Maybe I was not giving his maturity or intellect enough credit, but who was I trying to kid here . . . myself? I was old enough to be his mother.

And was wearing this bikini and then masturbating in front of my visitor cutting my last thread of self-respect? Was I a lost balloon now flying rogue—cut from the cluster only to disappear into oblivion? Had I lost it all completely?

I inspected my reflection one more time, turning my face from side to side . . . *Ready or not, here I come.* I laughed and then proceeded downstairs.

A few minutes later, I heard Chase's footsteps behind me. "Would you like me to do anything else?" he asked, stepping next to me.

I turned abruptly. "Oh, you startled me."

I looked up into those dark, mischievous eyes, and they flashed back at me. "Yes, I guess I'm full of surprises," he said and smiled seductively. He glistened with sweat and smelled of sun-warmed skin. He looked at me with those intense brown eyes. "Am I finished with my services here today, ma'am, or is there anything else you would like from me?"

The naughty voice inside my head shouted—yes—kiss him!

But in reality, I could barely look up to meet his stare. Suddenly I felt my age and embarrassment that he witnessed my voyeurism.

I avoided his eyes, and with my voice just a whisper, all I could manage to say was the word, "no." And thank goodness I had come to my senses and put on my normal clothes.

He stood next to me, and my mind screamed, *let's keep this our dirty secret.*

Much to my surprise, I saw Chase just about devour me with his eyes. He stepped closer. "Can I help you with something else? Anything. You just tell me what you want," he said. There was no trace of reluctance in his voice or on his face.

Eyeing him questioningly, I met his gaze, which was insistent. Finally, I gave him a demure smile. "Thank you for everything today," I said.

He opened the door to leave but paused. "When can I come back?" he asked.

I stood at the door, trying to mask my discomfort. "Ummm, let me think about that one."

"It was a pleasure to see you, Ms. Lila." He winked and let himself out the front door. I sighed in relief when I watched him walk toward his truck.

My eyes followed his every move. "Good-bye and thank you, Chase. You made my day," I said, wondering if it was out of earshot. Then, without another word, he waved and opened the door to his truck. *My new house will definitely need a pool.*

While I stood on the front porch, watching him climb into his vehicle, I breathed in the humid air. I looked at the cloudless sky, and the blue vastness of it made me think about the endless opportunities that lay ahead for me. Life, I knew, was going to be different now . . . better. I was going to live for today and for the future. *Dear past . . . thank you for the lessons. Dear future . . . I am ready.*

No, I would not allow the shadows of my past to haunt me. I would look to the future, a better future. At that moment, I removed the handwritten note I had shoved into my pocket earlier and read it: *Urgent! Call doctor about scheduling follow-up appointment for test results.*

I squeezed the note in my hand, crushing it until my fist turned red. *I really didn't want to know the results from my biopsy or imaging scan.* I tossed the crumpled paper into the bushes.

As I watched his truck drive away, I wanted to shout after him, "Thank you, Chase, for chasing away the last hint of darkness in me."

CHAPTER 4

And when I sat up in bed the next morning I didn't realize my entire life as I had known it was about to change.

My morning started out like every other day. Even though I was emotionally drained, I felt determined to overcome any negative thoughts. I jumped out of bed eager to start a new art project. Stained glass would make a perfect gift for Jenny to brighten her stodgy dorm room. *Day one of starting a new life.*

No, I was not going to sit around waiting for someone to rescue me. Another idea shot through me. I needed to make a list of what I wanted out of life. I should figure out what I would like to do. It was time to start living!

But creating this list of desires was not a simple task. I had so many ideas about the future. What were my dreams? What did I fantasize about? *Let's see, where to begin? Hmm . . .*

Just as I was thinking about what adventures I wanted to put on my list, I felt that sharp pain in my abdomen again. The throbbing pain was followed by that sudden surge of uneasiness. Maybe a warm shower would help? It didn't; something felt terribly wrong.

While getting dressed, I glanced at the window with my decorative glass artwork glistening in the sunlight. I used broken glass to create my craft. Discarded glass . . . considered trash and useless. And that was how I felt for the past year of my marriage separation, like my ex-husband's trash—used and dumped.

In that same instant, I decided that I valued myself too much to be discarded goods. Enough feeling sorry for myself; I would look at my stained glass as inspiration. Much like fusing broken glass, I could pick up the fragmented pieces of my life and turn them into something beautiful—transform the shattered into something spectacular!

I had given up my career as an art teacher to help manage my husband's company and raise Jenny. All the while, I dreamed of opening an art gallery to display my creations. Perhaps I could partner with another artist.

Suddenly, I felt inspired and ready for action. I slipped on my comfortable jeans, red T-shirt, and flip-flop sandals. I applied my makeup basics, mascara and lip gloss. And then I brushed the tangles from my hair and left it to dry naturally. I hopped in my Ford Explorer and headed downtown to my favorite art supply store.

While walking along the crowded sidewalk, I thought I saw a familiar face. Could it be? Was that Blake, my first love, strolling by on the other side of the road, walking in the opposite direction? I huffed in frustration because there were four lanes of cars zooming between the two sides of the street, obstructing my vision. Plus, it was beginning to drizzle.

Should I turn around, cross the lanes of traffic, and chase after him? *Too impulsive.*

Could it be true? Was it possible that was Blake? *No, that must be my wishful imagination playing tricks on me.*

Despite my burning desire to run after him, I decided not to be that impetuous. *Maybe it wasn't Blake, anyway.* After all, I had not seen him in years, nor heard any news about him. I had stayed in our hometown, but the last thing I heard years ago was that he had moved away.

I wanted a fresh start with my life. But wouldn't that be a step backward if I pursued him? Besides, I broke up with him years ago and I had my reasons that made sense at the time. Right now, I felt a twinge of regret for ending the relationship. But it was best to push those thoughts of a reunion out of my head.

My destination, the craft store, was located in a busy section of town lined with trendy brick-front restaurants, fashionable boutiques, and coffee shops. My favorite shop was a relic from the past, its wooden door covered in thick layers of chipped paint. A bell chimed as I stepped inside.

Walking into the historic shop was like stepping through a time portal. The store had remained the same through the decades. It was built before central air conditioning and had fans running in every corner. The air movement only stirred the lingering smell of cigarette smoke and dust. I always wondered how it stayed in business, since the store was usually empty. Today was no exception. I must buy enough glass supplies to keep them afloat.

A familiar voice greeted me. "Hello, Lila." The store owner shot me a crooked smile as he approached. Steve had a weathered face. The gap between his yellowed teeth looked as if he'd had a cigarette dangling between them for years. His wispy silver hair was combed back with gel. He didn't seem to put much thought into his appearance with his rumpled clothes, but his art was perfection. He put his efforts into his paintings and glass work; he was a master craftsman.

"Hi, Steve."

"Are you okay? You look like you just saw a ghost."

I felt the last bit of warmth drain from my face. "I . . . just caught a glimpse of a face from the past, my college boyfriend. It may have been an apparition. Really, I'm not sure."

"What, you think your imagination is playing tricks on you?" Steve had dark circles under his eyes. He probably hadn't had a good night's sleep since the big box store opened up around the corner.

My stomach made a tickling flutter from nerves or excited energy. "I had a rough week. And I don't know what to think anymore. I thought about chasing him down, but I got a grip on myself."

We were standing near the plate-glass window that took up most of the storefront. When I looked out toward the street, I saw a shadowy figure glance into the store. By the time my eyes focused enough to zoom in on the face, it disappeared.

Steve sighed wearily. "A sight of my ex-wife would have me running in the opposite direction." He let out a sarcastic laugh. I would have joined in, but I felt a little choked from the musty smell.

"I just got divorced. I know far too well what you mean."

"You look like you might pass out. You better step away from the glass section. Can I get you some water?"

"I'll be fine. But you're right. Maybe I'll check out the fabrics you have in stock first."

"That might be a good idea." Steve led me to the back of the store and pointed to the yarn and fabrics on display. As we walked, Steve looked at me. "You know when one door closes, another door opens."

"I keep hearing that, but it's the hallway I find scary."

"You got that right." He sounded a little out of breath. "Let me know if I can help you find anything."

"Thank you, Steve."

I watched him limp to the cash register wishing I could afford to buy all of his sheets of glass. The store had definitely seen better days. After making my selections, I paid and promised to return soon.

As I walked to my car parked at the curb, my eyes scanned the crowd. No sight of Blake. I drove home in the drizzle consumed in thought. With a smile lighting my face, I raced along my walkway, thinking about Blake. It began to pour. Even though I parked by the front door to unload the car, I decided to wait until later. For several minutes, I stood on the porch, watching the rain, and then turned to enter the house. I hesitated in the doorway, stepped inside, and closed the door. I leaned against the doorframe, glancing around. I was greeted with silence. Even my dog was silent.

I stepped over Elky, sprawled across a foyer rug, thinking she wasn't much of a watchdog. She opened one eye to glance my way, curled up her lips in a doggy smile or maybe just a twitch, and then continued sleeping.

Standing alone in the stillness, I heard the sound of a ticking clock resonating through the house. *But I don't own a ticking clock!* Was that my heart pounding in my ears? I plugged my fingers in my ears and still heard the ticking noise, but this time faster—and faster.

Tick . . . tick . . . tick . . . tick . . . tick . . . tick—BOOM!

I grabbed the fluffy pillow from the foyer bench, covered my mouth, and let out a muffled scream. *The ticking stopped.* A moment later, I tossed the pillow onto the bench, shook myself back to reality, and slowly walked through the house. My flopping sandals echoed like blasting gunshots across the floor and walls, breaking the painful silence. From room to room I walked, alone. *When will this empty feeling finally stop?*

As I peered into each silent room, I saw only shadows from my past. Hard as I tried to quell the memories that whispered here, they were all around me, impossible to subdue. I felt a pang of loneliness and wondered what I should do about the gaping holes in my life.

I snapped my finger as the answer seemed to appear magically. My first stop would be the gateway to the world— my computer. And there I sat, swiveling in my chair, in front of the computer, reflecting on my life. I leaned back and pondered about what was missing.

Maybe for distraction, just a quick trip down memory lane would be fun. I could look up some old friends and try to reconnect. My first priority, I decided, was searching for Blake.

Since discovering that photo from my memory box, I couldn't get him out of my mind. Was that him today? We did have amazing chemistry, back in the good old days. It seemed like such a distant time, so long ago. And if that was Blake, he was as handsome as ever.

What if I just sent him a quick hello on the computer? He must be easy to look up. What was the harm, right? If he's not interested, then he won't reply—easy enough. My heart beat faster.

Luckily, Facebook made the search easy. I typed his name and much to my surprise, I found him. He does use Facebook. And looking at his tiny, blurred picture created even more memories. Why did I wait so long to do this?

Oh, why not? I started to type him a message: *Remember me? It has been a long time, but I wanted to say hello. Love your Facebook picture. You look the same after all these years. It would be wonderful to talk to you about old times.*

I sat lost in thought. Should I send that message? We did have great times together. The first time we made love left such an indelible impression, I could remember every detail. Maybe he remembered that day, too? We were each other's first. Who could forget losing their virginity? I once told Jenny to choose wisely because that person will stay in your mind forever.

I placed my finger on the enter button to send the message and hesitated. Was it even fair to try to reconnect with him? After all, I was the one who ended our relationship.

And what if he doesn't respond to me? What if he doesn't remember me? That would feel devastating. I shuddered, and my mind began to race with negative scenarios. *Why do I want to subject myself to this agony?*

I distracted myself by glancing up to the enormous cork board hanging above the computer, cluttered with photos of Jenny at various ages. Although several were recent photos, most of them dated back years ago and had faded and curled edges.

My eyes gravitated to the oldest pictures. I stared at two photos of Jenny as a baby. I sighed briefly, thinking about how quickly my little girl had grown into a mature young lady. Finally, my gaze skipped over to a note scribbled in Jenny's handwriting taped to the wall next to the cork board. I stood, walked over to the board, and traced my finger around the edges of the note that was a reminder to call the doctor.

I removed the note from the wall, stared at it without blinking, memorizing the words, and shoved it into my pocket. How many of these notes were scattered around the house? How many times had they called with the same message? They called too many times to think about now. *And they can't make me go for that follow-up appointment. Sometimes ignorance is bliss.*

At that exact second, my telephone rang. Grateful for the distraction, I answered it. There was a calm steady voice that I didn't recognize coming through the phone, asking for me.

"Yes, this is Ms. Baxter," I said.

The soft voice said politely, "Doctor Young would like for you to come into the office to review your test results. We have been leaving messages for the past few weeks, but we still don't have you on the schedule."

"I need to do that," I stammered. "But I'm busy this week . . . and the last few weeks were extremely hectic," I said. I scanned the room, searching for a distraction.

Unrelenting, she continued. "The doctor wanted me to tell you it's essential for you to come in for your follow-up appointment. He wants to speak with you and has tried to call you numerous times. He said he left messages, but never heard from you. Lucky for you, he has a cancellation tomorrow at nine a.m., and we would like for you to fill that vacant slot." *Yes, lucky for me.*

I should have at least listened to his messages. I guess I was not ready. *But am I now?*

I listened to her with my eyelids squeezed together and my lips pressed tightly. I wished this scenario would end. "I hear you." I paused. "Okay, okay, I get it. This appointment is important. I appreciate that you worked me into his busy schedule. I'll be there tomorrow morning, I promise." I released a deep sigh and hung up the telephone. I stared at the phone as if it was the source of my problems, instead of the messenger.

A sense of impending doom began to build within me. I quickly shut off Facebook, relieved I never actually sent that message to Blake.

Reconnecting with him was a special thought, but I would not interfere in his life. I would treasure the times we shared, but that was then and those days were history.

Maybe I just wanted someone to fill that current void in my life. Right now, I felt empty inside. I should make myself feel complete, on my own. I needed to find my internal strength. I enjoyed sharing my life with a man, but this past year of marital separation had taught me that I don't need anyone. Although I would appreciate a companion and it would be fun to find romance again, I would be fine on my own.

At last, that doctor's office finally caught up with me. Did I have the strength to face the truth from my doctor? I was not sure what those test results were going to indicate, but I was pretty certain I did not want to hear the news.

The next morning came quickly. A few minutes before nine a.m., I stepped out of my car, jiggling my keys in my unsteady hand. I meandered toward the office building as the dread built inside me. My mind wandered all morning; I was completely absorbed in thought. I felt so engrossed with consuming anxiety that I barely knew what I was doing.

Walking toward the building, I tried to remember if I even brushed my teeth or my hair this morning. *Did I apply makeup? Does it even matter?* And I chose to wear a comfortable loose-fitting pink sundress and flat black sandals that I slipped on, not giving my appearance much thought.

The thumping in my chest intensified as I approached the building. I breathed in slowly and exhaled, but nothing worked to steady my nerves. *Breathe.* I kept walking forward, resisting the urge to turn, flee, and pretend none of this was happening. No, I needed to face my problems and not evade them.

I thought about how life could change in an instant, in just a flash.

And then it happened. In the distance, I heard a distinct male voice shout my name. "Lila." That voice. My mind was in a frenzy. How did I know that voice?

My head whipped around, searching for the source. My eyes opened wide while I scanned the landscape. But the glare from the morning sunbeams impeded my vision. I could see—no one. Out of the bright light stepped a figure, his face only a shadow, obstructed by the intensity of the beaming rays.

This mystery man hidden in his own shadow had a towering, broad-shouldered frame—six feet tall or more. I looked up when he stepped next to me. And suddenly his face took shape.

I saw the most stunningly handsome man I had ever seen in my entire life. The face, now visible, beamed a smile that radiated ear to ear while he looked down at me.

I knew that face and those mysterious golden-brown eyes from my past. And then what played out next seemed to happen in slow motion. I felt like time stood still when I realized it was Blake again, after all these years.

In front of me stood my past, my future, and a smile that could restart the fire within me for an eternity. Momentarily, I became paralyzed by shock. And then a rush of adrenaline shot through me, flooding my body.

Neither of us said a word; we just stared into each other's eyes in disbelief, until finally Blake broke the silence. "Lila, is that really you?"

I tried to swallow, but I couldn't. There was a lump in my throat and a knot in my stomach—and both twisted at once. I opened my mouth, but no words came out. And there I stood, wide-eyed with an enormous smile until finally I came to my senses enough to nod.

Blake reached over, took me in his strong arms, and gave me a gripping hug. He caught me off guard. His embrace had me swooning. And I felt as if my next actions were automatic. Without thinking, I hugged him in return, but my mind spun in a stunned haze.

After a few moments, he released his grip on me, and I started to stumble, fighting for my balance. In the next instant, he caught me, stabilized my body, and stood me up straight. *How embarrassing is that? I am a bumbling clown. I haven't seen him in all these years and I fall over looking at him!*

With his hands still on my shoulders, he looked down into my eyes. "You remember me, right? Blake, from college?" he asked, chuckling softly.

Finally, I gave him an ecstatic smile and found my words. "Of course I remember you." *No one forgets their first love. And no one forgets the first passionate touch . . . or especially, the man who takes your virginity. Your first love—that person will stay in your heart forever.*

He shot back a mischievous grin, very similar to the one that made my heart flutter years ago. Could this gorgeous man really be Blake? Serendipity!

I nervously studied him. The years had been good to Blake. His chestnut brown hair was sun-streaked with slight hints of yellow. The highlights interlaced various strands that framed his face. I wanted to reach out and run my fingers through his bangs that brushed to the side in a slight wave. *Oh, such are the thoughts of a woman. A man simply would think his hair is brown.*

His face appeared more sharply defined, without the baby fat, and his cheekbones were more pronounced than when I knew him. His face looked freshly shaven. He smelled like aftershave. But what stood out the most were his eyes; I remained captivated by those eyes that looked the same—all these years later. His eyes were an unusual shade of brown; they were more golden than dark with a unique brightness and intensity. The only difference from years ago was that the corners now wrinkled when he smiled. *We both have had many smiles over the years, it appears. Mine crinkle, too, Blake.*

At one time, I thought they were the most beautiful eyes I had ever seen. And today I was still entranced by his striking appearance.

He startled me. "Do you still live in Raleigh?" he asked. His voice seemed deeper, sexier than I remembered, with no trace of boyishness in it.

Before I uttered a word, I continued for a brief instant, admiring his form. He was impeccably dressed. Blake seemed taller than I remembered. I didn't recall his thick neck and shoulders being so broad, like an athletic superstar. Oh my, that powerful body he still had! And from the look of his physique, he spent a lot of time engaging in physical activity. Whatever he did, it worked for him.

Eventually, I came to my senses enough to answer him. I kept my gaze steady on his face. "My parents moved to Florida a couple years ago, but I never left town. I live a few miles from where we grew up," I said.

"Then you live close to my parents because they still live in the house I grew up in." He sighed as if longing for those days from his youth. "I moved away years ago when I joined the Marines."

"Wow . . . Blake."

"You seem surprised. Don't you see me as a career military officer?" he asked.

My look must have intrigued him. I wondered if my mouth had fallen open. "I admire your dedication to our country, immensely. I'm just stunned to reconnect with you after so many years."

"I'm shocked to see you, too."

"And there's so much I don't know about you. I guess I'm sad that we lost touch," I said.

He was wearing the same mesmerized expression as the day I first met him. "Is it too forward to tell you I'm captivated and startled by your timeless beauty? You really haven't changed much over the years." Without turning his gaze away from me, he continued. "Honestly, in my mind, I can still see you wearing your gymnastics leotard."

I giggled. "Well, that won't happen again. You better use your imagination on that one."

"Not that I'm surprised, but you still look athletic and carry yourself with the grace of a dancer, although now you have those beautiful curves," he said.

I never was a thin woman, but loved being athletic and strong. I was sure my face had filled out, too. And thank goodness he was calling my extra weight curves.

Sure, curves . . . love it.

His gaze lingered as he continued. "But most of all, I'm still mesmerized by your striking teal eyes. They're almost iridescent, like a peacock feather."

His kind words thrilled me, but I couldn't help wondering if he noticed how the corners of my eyes crinkled when I smiled, especially standing in the bright sunlight.

I tried not to be self-conscious, but I could tell he continued assessing me. I just hoped I received a passing grade. From the look of his upward curved lips, I believed the review was favorable. Or so I hoped.

More than anything, I felt overwhelmed by nervous energy, enough to make me bite down on my lower lip. It took a few seconds to register the pain, but then I thought that at least the pressure from my teeth would give my pouty lips a tinged red hue.

Since I skipped makeup this morning in my haste, maybe this action gave me a much-needed burst of color. *Leave it to a woman to think like this, to turn a case of nerves into a fashion and makeup opportunity.*

My nervous lip-biting response did not go unnoticed. His eyes followed my tongue when I brushed it across my mouth as if maybe my lips enticed him, making him want to kiss me again. Or possibly I was confused by my own desires because I wanted to kiss his perfectly sculpted lips. They were irresistibly sexy. I had an urge to lean over and press my mouth to his. And here we were standing—at arm's length away.

From the awkward pauses in our speech, I think we both, for an instant, felt like gawky teenagers again. After staring for what seemed like an excessive amount of time, Blake finally blurted out, "I just dropped my dad off for his medical appointment. My mother is picking him up as soon as she runs her errands, so my morning is free. It would be great if you're available to get a cup of coffee. Would that—"

I nervously interrupted him. "How are your parents?" I asked with keen interest.

He looked down and clenched his jaws. "I'm sad to report that my father has early stages of Alzheimer's, but we're all making the best of a bad situation. My mother is an amazing caregiver for him. And I have been doing my best to help them."

"I'm sorry they're going through all of this. You know, I always admired your parents."

He sighed. "I often feel guilty because I can't help as much as I would like. And my younger brother, Brady, moved to Hollywood, seeking fame and fortune, and never looked back. I'm sure you remember him."

I nodded. Of course, I remembered his brother. They looked like twins. And I could tell all of this news about his parents was a difficult admission for him, and I appreciated that he shared it with me. I could imagine that caring for ailing parents could create a strain. His parents were good to me years ago, and I suddenly found myself wishing I could help them.

Before I could discuss the topic further, he asked about my family. I stammered as I reluctantly gave him sketchy details from my life. Blake took this as his opportunity to ask, "Can we go somewhere more comfortable to get reacquainted? How about we go somewhere quiet and talk?" He looked at me with pleading eyes.

"Well . . ."

He persisted. "Let's get coffee and catch up on our lives and share some old memories. There's no harm in sharing a drink or two and getting reacquainted." Although he posed it as a statement, we both knew it was a question.

I nodded. "No harm in that, right?" I acted cool as if I needed the idea to percolate through my mind. In reality, I found myself so excited that I wanted to jump for joy. I could hardly think of anything else.

"Remember that bakery and coffee shop we loved on Main Street? How about we meet there in an hour?" he asked.

"Yes, perfect."

"Here's my phone number if a conflict occurs," he said, handing me a card and let his fingers linger on mine.

We exchanged good-byes. I rushed inside the office building and took a huge, gulping breath. Blake again after all these years!

One last glimpse of him; I need one more look-see.

And with that thought, I pressed my body flat against the interior wall and slowly turned my head and peeped out the window. A stolen moment, or so I hoped.

But to my surprise, he turned and looked, too. *He sees me. I know he sees me.*

He winked in my direction and turned forward. I watched his figure get smaller and smaller until he disappeared behind a row of cars. *Was that a wink or was that a lopsided narrowing of his eyes from the sunlight? Or am I overthinking things again?*

I slumped forward, hiding behind a tall fern, and peeked out for another glimpse of him. He was gone.

And with a couple of minutes separating us, my thoughts became a little clearer. I quickly realized seeing him again reminded me of a way I used to feel. Unfamiliar thoughts raced through my mind. And a wave of emotions cascaded through me. I recognized for the first time in years what had been missing from my life: passion for a man, but most of all passion for life. I couldn't help but wonder if the universe was sending me a message. *And I am listening!*

It took a little while longer to regain my composure and then I raced from the building. I scurried toward my car with the intent of returning home, freshening up, and regaining my thought clarity before meeting Blake.

From the car, I called the doctor's office and apologized profusely, fibbing that I couldn't make my appointment today.

I explained, rambling in too much detail, how I needed to review my overbooked schedule before I could set a new appointment.

And then I tossed the telephone into my purse and pushed the thought of rescheduling the doctor's visit to the back of my mind. I felt excited all the way home, like the first time he asked me on a date, so many years ago.

CHAPTER 5

The coffee shop, Main Street Bakery, where we agreed to meet was around the corner from my house. The business had changed hands a couple of times since I started coming here as a child. The brick front had been repeatedly painted over in a creamy white, and the black awning looked new. It took only a few minutes to get there, but I spent the entire hour getting ready. I had makeup to put on, hair to brush, and clothes to change.

With my stomach tied in knots at the thought of our reunion, I walked slowly to the entrance. How many years had it been since we dated? *Many.* I hesitated in the doorway, smoothed the wrinkles from my skirt with hands that trembled slightly, wet my lips, and threw the bakery door open.

I was met with the sweet smell of warm cinnamon and fragrant coffee wafting through the air, a heavenly blend of aromas. Before stepping beyond the entryway, I took a deep breath and viewed my surroundings. The coffee shop was nearly empty. There were a couple of cashiers working and one attractive man sitting alone reading the local newspaper, *The News and Observer.* I looked across the empty seats. Even from a distance, it was obvious that was Blake because there's no mistaking his flawless profile.

The moment seemed surreal while I walked to his table. I could see his head tilted down reading, and I wondered if he could feel my presence. My mouth suddenly went dry as I observed him pull the paper closer to his face and shift in his seat.

In the next instant, he tossed the paper onto the table, glanced up, and instead of saying a word, he just smiled broadly. It was an exuberant, maybe relieved, grin. For a minute, our eyes fastened; I felt my heart beat faster, but neither of us said a word. As my eyes stared into his, I was dazzled by their sparkle; they still had their mystical powers. *Quit hypnotizing me with your eyes, Blake.*

His jaw appeared to flex as if rehearsing what he was about to say. When he finally found his words and spoke, he did so slowly, with emphasized pauses and a hint of a drawl. "I'm glad to see you again. Your smile still warms me up inside."

"Well, that's quite a greeting. Thank you."

He motioned to the empty chair across from him for me to sit down. "Seriously, you have grown into such a lovely woman. How is it possible for you to be more beautiful now than in college?"

"I have to compliment you, as well. You left me fumbling for words earlier. You're a handsome man."

"Thank you. Don't take this the wrong way, but that awkward young girl I once knew has blossomed and matured into a sophisticated and poised lady," he said, making me blush. His kind words were music to my ears, and just what I needed to hear. I couldn't help but wonder when the last time was that my ex-husband told me how lovely I looked.

The reality was, I couldn't remember, not that it mattered. Even if Peter had said the right words, he never looked at me the way Blake just did. Blake just looked at me with the same expression of excitement as a child first seeing the toys Santa left under the tree on Christmas morning. I think every woman should be lucky enough to have a man look at her with such excitement at least once in her life. *Lucky me, today!*

But I also enjoyed the view seated in front of me; I was still attracted to him—maybe even more than in college—with his intelligent, inquisitive eyes perfectly balanced by his chiseled chin. He looked almost the same as he did years ago.

I noticed his furtive glance at my left hand at nearly the same time I was checking his finger for a wedding ring. *Oh, relief. Nothing.* Why didn't I think to look for that earlier? I must have been in shock from seeing him again.

"You switched outfits." He smiled and added, "And you look fabulous." He was very observant and had noticed I changed out of my blousy sundress and into a more form-fitting outfit—a slim navy skirt that hugged my curves. I felt thrilled that my efforts were rewarded. I loved every second of his attention.

Not trying to be explicitly sexy, but at the same time, I was meeting my extremely handsome ex-boyfriend, so I left the top three buttons of my white silk blouse open, slightly revealing my ample cleavage. Although I learned how to play up my femininity, I preferred to think I was beautiful on the inside. Either way, Blake made me feel special today. And ignited.

I noticed Blake's eyes slip down to the opening in my blouse. His eyes were drawn to my full breasts, and then moved back up to my face. He gazed at me, almost dreamily. He looked as if he had become absorbed in thought about the first time he explored my body. Our faces mirrored each other with our expression of yearning—pining for those days of lost innocence and the exhilaration of first touches.

Blake's lowered gaze that fixed on my buttons made me wonder what it would feel like if he eased them open and slowly slid my shirt down my arms, exposing the swell of my breasts as he stroked his fingers across my willing flesh.

The waitress interrupted my fervent thoughts when she stepped next to our table for our drink orders. And then she promptly returned with two coffees.

Before I knew what had happened, Blake and I were talking effortlessly about old times. We reconnected quickly, rekindled our long-ago friendship. In just that brief time, Blake lifted my spirits with his hearty, contagious laugh. I remembered his positive energy and happy-go-lucky personality from years ago.

As the robust brew slid down my throat, I contemplated the situation. Something inside me was definitely coming back to life. For the first time in months, I felt energized.

Blake gave me a boyish grin. "I can't believe we ran into each other today. Fate must want us back together, at least as friends."

I lifted my coffee mug. "Cheers to friendship."

He tapped his mug to mine. "You always had a way of making me laugh and I still think you can light up a room with your cheery disposition. You have that same quality you had as a young woman."

His kind words made me question a future with Blake. *Should we give this a second chance? Is he even interested?* But we hurt each other the first time. Maybe he was actually the one worth suffering for. As the saying goes, everyone is going to hurt you at some point. You just have to figure which ones are worth the pain. But this time, if we try again, I would be going in with my eyes wide open, especially fresh from my recent heartbreak.

I watched him intently as if understanding his mannerisms could help me read his thoughts. It appeared that he didn't want to take his eyes off of me. Could he be thinking the same as me—that I wanted to kiss, now?

Once again, he had charmed me; I was falling under his spell.

From across the coffee shop, we heard a female voice. We both turned and looked toward the source. "No way! Great seeing you here, Lila," shrieked an exuberant voice. It was Jane. I waved her closer.

I looked from Jane to Blake and then back again. Blake was cordial to Jane. He stood to greet her and offered his hand. He looked so professional in his introduction.

Jane glanced at me out of the corner of her eye. She tilted toward him as if saying, where have you been hiding this one? Her eyes prodded me.

"Jane," I explained, "Blake and I were friends in college." After I said those words, I lifted my left hand behind Blake's shoulder, out of his sight line, but for Jane to see. I crossed my middle finger over my index finger. Jane looked up at my crossed fingers curiously and gave me a puzzled glance.

"Close friends," Blake chimed in, elbowing me teasingly, totally unaware of the gesture behind him.

"I see," said Jane, with a face distorted as if full of questions.

His eyes moved from me to Jane, from Jane to me. "Ladies, if you'll excuse me. I have a matter to address. I'll be right back."

After he excused himself, Jane pulled me toward her. "I should've worn my sexy miniskirt here. You know I'm joking, right? I know he's your man, but what in the world are you crossing your fingers for?"

I giggled. "You're right, girlfriend, this one's for me. The gesture I made behind his back was an "X." Blake is my ex-boyfriend from years ago. My first love," I said. Her eyes flickered in delight.

Before we could discuss the topic further, Blake returned. "Did I miss anything juicy?" he asked. We turned and smiled innocently and shook our heads.

"I hate to have to dash, but obligation is calling," Jane said, in her usual excitable manner. "My little boy, Thomas, is sick and begged for these muffins." She paused, lifted her pastry bag, and held it up for us to see. "I need to hurry home."

"Give him a hug for me," I said.

"I will. He was probably ready to go back to school yesterday, but I'm one big softie. And I must say, if you haven't tried the raspberry muffins, you need to." And with that comment, she waved the wax paper bag in the air and excused herself. "Nice meeting you, Blake," she exclaimed, gathering her purse.

"You, too, Jane. Any friend of Lila's must be a great gal. Hopefully we can all hang out soon. I'd like to go out with Lila again, if I can get her to agree."

Jane stood next to us, looking into our faces. "I'll leave you two alone to work on that one. I'll call you soon, Lila," she said, smiling at us. She waved good-bye and zipped across the coffee shop.

After I explained that Jane was my dear friend and neighbor, I told him how she had been my savior during this past year.

Ever so briefly, I explained my recent divorce. But I was much more excited to tell him about Jenny. I mentioned the career as an art teacher I sacrificed after giving birth and my indecision about what job steps to take next, now that she had started college. And then I asked Blake about his career.

He told me how he chose a life in the military. Blake's eyes were warm when he looked at me, like we had remained best friends all these years. "I live about two hours from here, near the Marine base, Camp Lejeune, where I work now. I've devoted my life to serving our country."

A forlorn expression took shape on his face and then disappeared. "I tried to finish college, but it just felt like something was missing in my life. After our breakup, I felt troubled. And I had lingering guilt about your scholarship," he said.

"Really?" I asked. "I didn't know it bothered you."

"And besides, I didn't have money to see the world, but felt like it was calling me. I answered that call by enlisting in the military. It was a win-win deal. I was proud to serve my country. I moved up in the ranks, and at the same time, I traveled often."

I looked at Blake curiously. I was not used to seeing him in that light. "Your life sounds so fascinating," I said. His dedication to our country and preserving our freedom impressed me more than I showed. I had traveled on a limited basis, but Blake had taken on the world.

"My military career brought me back to life and became my existence. And I feel like I am serving something beyond myself. And over time, my upsetting memories no longer ruled me."

I cradled my coffee mug and looked at his face through the floating steam. "You must be very proud of your accomplishments," I said.

He shrugged. "Yes. I work hard at all of my assignments. They moved me, quite frequently. Eventually, I was able to work my way back home to North Carolina. I was disciplined with my duties, learned quickly, and soon became invaluable to them. I advanced rapidly through the ranks."

"That's impressive. And you still find time for other activities?" I asked.

"It's a busy, hectic life, but I still try to stay social with friends. And when I'm not working, I write short stories from my experiences, as a creative outlet. My goal is eventually to compile the stories into a book."

I listened intently, captivated by this worldly man. He was full of surprises. Excitedly, I said, "It also looks like you immersed yourself in fitness. You look fabulous." I leaned back, looked at my cup, and took a sip from my coffee that I had been lingering over because I didn't want to say good-bye and part ways.

He pushed a stray hair out of his eyes with his long fingers. "My fitness routine keeps me distracted. Plus, as part of my job I need to remain in shape, and I take pride in staying active and healthy."

A moment later, I looked into his kind eyes and wondered what they had really seen during his years in the service. There was a long silence while I studied Blake, in admiration but also trying to figure out the person he had become. Although he was a man now, something in his face reminded me of our youth.

Looking at his beautiful face again took me back to college when I would sneak him in the dorm at night. "Blake, you always could talk me into anything. Because of you, I caught a few glimpses of the wild side."

He smiled. "We did know how to have fun."

I wondered if he still had the power to ignite my senses. What would it be like to touch him again? After my imagination explored his body, I shook my head, trying to keep my mind in the present. But everything about him took my thoughts back to those carefree days.

While my mind was trying to stay focused, my body was losing control. I was starting to feel a warmth creep across my body. My nipples grew hard. I started to feel a yearning and aching between my legs. It was as if my body screamed at me to touch him again. I wondered if he shared some of those same feelings.

Our eyes locked, and looking deep into his, I thought I saw his answer. Was it mutual attraction? Maybe he, too, grew in excitement just sitting close to me. Perhaps he imagined what it would be like to take me into his arms again.

He was attractive, no doubt, but I had met many handsome men in my life. Yet there was always something about him that went straight to my libido, putting my desire on high alert. I used to think it was just my youthful urges that drove me wild; however, sitting next to Blake now, I knew it was him. He made me hot from head to toe. Other men did not have that same effect.

He glanced down, took my hand, and lifted my arm to his face for closer examination. He focused on the round scar on my forearm. A moment later, he raised my arm to his lips and kissed it.

Using his other hand, he stroked across my nubby scar and looked at me knowingly. When he looked deep into my eyes, his body tensed. It was as if a flash of memories shot through him.

His words confirmed my suspicions that he, too, saw glimpses of that day. He leaned close. His breath was hot on my face. "Seeing this scar is like looking through a window of time. That memory of us making love on the ledge began to seem so distant. It's almost as if it happened to someone else, but seeing you next to me brings that image crashing to the surface. It feels like time is unraveling."

"And what an adventure it was. We really knew how to live," I said.

"I'm sorry I gave you a scar," he said in a breathy whisper.

"Yes, you left me with a party favor."

"That was a loaded comment, Lila. Left you? You mean you left me for good when you broke up with me," he said, with frustration in his voice. "But that was then. This is now."

I shook my head. "I don't know what to say. We can't change what happened when we were younger, but we're sitting together now."

He smiled. And then he lifted my arm and pressed the scar to his lips again. In a husky voice, he asked, "Maybe we can re-create some of our playful times?"

"I like the sound of that."

I tried to look away when Blake repositioned his burgeoning crotch, which I surmised, had begun to awaken and stir. He tried discreetly to shift his bulge; however, my eyes followed his hand with keen interest. *Hello, long-ago friend.*

He leaned forward. "You may not believe this, but I must tell you, on dark nights in the service, alone in my bed, you were there in my mind." He looked into the distance as if watching his memories on a movie screen. "I've lived our escapades over and over in my mind."

I sighed. I wanted to reclaim all those lost years. "You have no idea, Blake, how many times I replayed our adventures, too. Even to this day, our trysts stay in my mind." I lowered my head and softly whispered, "If you look closely at the scar, you can still see faint teeth marks."

He leaned in closer to get a better look. As he eased his hand across my skin and rubbed it gently, my arm quivered beneath his touch.

Maybe this time Blake and I could skip the relationship part and just have fun. Is that really possible? And how could Blake get past the reality that I left him years ago?

And Blake seemed to answer my questions when he said, "You can't believe how excited I am to see you again." His face lit up when he spoke, his youthful energy infectious. *You better be careful with this one.*

"I feel that way, too."

"Lila, it's your turn now that your daughter is grown. What do you want from life?"

I want to live pain-free, both physically and emotionally. I need to make whatever is causing this stabbing pain that comes and goes to disappear magically from my body.

But instead of speaking my inner truth, I bent my head toward Blake as if to confide something important. It was at that exact instant that I knew what I needed to do next.

Suddenly, the words flew out of me. "I'm going to share my secret desires with you. I made a list of goals." Immediately, I could see the question in his golden eyes.

I paused. Should I really be discussing my fantasy life with him? I inhaled a deep breath, taking in the savory coffee aroma, and took a small sip, letting the warm liquid fill me with warmth. Without looking directly at him, I revealed how I had some unfulfilled dreams and a long list of things I wanted to see and do in life.

"I need a traveling companion." My voice suddenly filled with excitement. I paused and met his gaze. And my eyes widened as if an idea struck me. "I would like *you* to be my travel companion. Do you have any interest in sharing this adventure with me?" I shot him a quick smile. And silence followed.

"Ummm . . ."

Questioning my candor with someone I haven't talked to in years, I quickly back-pedaled. "After the first trip, if you don't want to continue, I'll understand. And don't feel like you have to agree to anything," I said.

Blake beamed. "You're making a tempting offer. I'm flattered, but don't you want to take a girlfriend?"

"You might want to see my list." I opened my purse and pulled out a pink sheet of paper. We leaned our heads together to review the list.

The top of my list revealed wish number one: *Romantic Beach Getaway.*

Blake gaped at me in stunned silence. "Oh, I think I get it now." Much to my relief, his face lit up. He grinned from ear to ear. "I'd be honored to be your travel partner, and you never know, maybe it could evolve into something more . . . meaningful. You were always a very exciting woman to me," he said, stroking my arm.

I laughed, again second-guessing my offer; maybe this was a crazy idea. "You know, it doesn't have to be romantic, but let's try for enjoyable."

"Is that open for interpretation?" he asked. His question caused me to give a modest shrug and giggle. "Your laugh," he interjected. "I forgot how much I liked your laugh."

"You're making me happy."

Blake did not hesitate. He did not even pause to think about my offer. "Well, with all of this in mind, I better start planning," he announced. "Perhaps now *you* are the one who can talk *me* into anything." We looked at each other and shared smiles.

In that interval of time, I just started to recognize how much I missed his friendship. I had no comprehension of the impact he would have on my life in the future. I happily pretended to strike the first item off of my list. At that instant, I was beginning to like my new life after all.

"Are you sure?" I asked.

"When can we get started? I'm available next weekend," he blurted out.

I searched his eyes for any hint of hesitation but found none. They looked delighted, full of adventure and twinkled with excitement. It was as if I could see a bolt of energy shoot through Blake—rejuvenation. Maybe he, too, was in desperate need of a new adventure and had not realized it—yet.

Blake offered to take the lead in the planning since he lived closest to the coast. He called the next day to say that his friend, on several occasions, had offered his beach house. And this time he decided to take his pal up on the invitation. Luckily for us, it was available this upcoming weekend. Skip and his wife couldn't join us but offered their house anyway. Nervously, I prepared for our private getaway.

CHAPTER 6

For once in my life, I was ready ahead of schedule. With my bag near my feet, I sat on the front porch, fidgeting and squeezing my phone as if it could speed Blake's arrival. As soon as I saw his car winding along the driveway, I raced down the steps and stood on the walkway. He pulled up next to me, rolled down the window, and shouted, "Are you ready for some fun?"

"I've been ready all week," I said, hopping in the car.

"Fantastic. I just left my parents' house, and they're doing fine. Maybe I'll pop in again after I drop you off on Sunday."

After driving a couple hours, we arrived at the small coastal town that afternoon, garbed in our end-of-the-summer beachwear. He was dressed casually in his khaki shorts, navy button-down short-sleeved shirt, and ball cap. I wore a form-fitting red sleeveless blouse with an eye-catching low-cut neckline, white pants, and flat sandals.

We sauntered down the sidewalks through the peaceful town and spent the afternoon shopping in the quaint beachside gift shops. It was a magnificent day with the sunny, bright blue sky and the warm sea breeze. I breathed in deeply, picking up the scent of the salty ocean air mixed with the aroma of fresh bread wafting from the nearby bakery. A perfect day. I looked up at Blake, and his smile beamed down at me.

An instant later, he slid his protective arm around my waist, pulling me close as I strolled by his side. We couldn't resist the delicious aroma and stepped inside the bakery. My eyes lingered on the glass case filled with pies, cupcakes, and cookies. Blake laughed. "I think your eyes are salivating more than your mouth. What should I get us for this weekend?" he asked.

I smiled and pointed to the homemade milk chocolates molded in the form of miniature seashells. Gesturing to the woman behind the counter, Blake said, "We'll take a pound of those milk chocolates, another pound of dark chocolate truffles, and a loaf of your French bread."

"You really know how to take care of a lady." I teased.

With our arms full of shopping bags, we ambled along until we reached the outskirts of town. I glanced around but saw no one. I felt this sudden burst of energy, dropped my things, and climbed onto the elevated brick wall. Much to Blake's surprise and maybe my own, I did a quick cartwheel, turned, and smiled at Blake.

"You can still do that trick after all these years?"

"Once a gymnast, always a gymnast." I laughed. "Okay, that's not true at all, but I can try."

He chuckled. "I like your unbridled enthusiasm. You're forty-one going on twenty-one."

"And that's how I want to live."

He cracked his knuckles. "Okay, I'll take you on later. You just wait until I get my hands on you." When he looked at me with his ball cap blocking the intense sun from his face, I gasped. Something about that ball cap and the way he looked at me made my mind confused between then and now. It was as if we had lived that exact scene years ago.

We arrived at the house late that afternoon. As we gathered our bags and entered the ocean-front cottage, my thoughts swirled in fear about spending the night with him—alone in the darkness. I heard the sound of the front door shutting and the bolt locking. Blake leaned against the door with that hungry look in his eyes. "I have you all to myself," he said.

"What do you have planned?" I asked. But I already knew the answer. His naughty grin that followed spoke a thousand words, all words I longed to hear again.

Sliding his hand from the latch, he took mine and led me through the open, sun-filled home. The beach house was mostly one large living area with high, vaulted ceilings. The kitchen and family room were connected, and there appeared to be a few bedrooms down a hall. The back wall was made almost entirely of glass, with French doors leading to a deck. Against the side wall, there was an oversized denim sectional and a floor-to-ceiling bookcase. The coffee table displayed back issues of *Southern Living* and *Coastal Living* magazines.

Standing in the sunlit family room, Blake looked exquisite with copper and yellow streaked strands of his hair shimmering in the light. He touched my back softly. "There's something I want to show you," he said.

While opening the doors leading outside, I took in the fresh, warm ocean air. Stepping onto the expansive deck, I saw a chaise lounge, a round metal table, and chairs bursting with colors from the yellow, orange, and red toss pillows that were scattered across the furniture. We admired the four large terra cotta pots that overflowed with pink and white petunias.

When we looked into the distance, we saw a breathtaking panoramic view of the ocean. Sunlight spilled out over the water. A glimmering splay of golden light flared across the rippling waves. The afternoon sun slowly dropped to the horizon, where light blue sky appeared to merge with the royal blue sea.

The glistening beige sand was the only thing that separated us from the backdrop of layers of blue. And up and down the beach, large colorful umbrellas dotted the landscape like an open box of crayons.

We heard the crash of the waves, and it became rhythmic music in the background. "This is a little piece of paradise," Blake said. He turned to me, his golden eyes glistening, making me want to kiss him right there.

"It's just what I needed."

"How about we get some wine to celebrate our brief escape from reality?" he asked.

I followed him into the house, and found it impossible to keep my eyes off his tight bottom. A shiver of excitement poured through me, followed by a tingle of warmth that spread across my pelvis.

Oh, how I longed for a man's touch, Blake's touch. That thought consumed me as I lifted the crystal wine glasses from the cabinet and opened a bottle of Cupcake Chardonnay. I filled our glasses, handed one to Blake, and felt his fingertips brush against mine.

He boomed in a festive voice, lifting his glass, "Cheers, to fun times and reunions. Your assignment, should you accept it, is to relax and enjoy the weekend."

I tipped my glass toward his. "To new beginnings."

He smiled. "Yes. And no pressure from me for anything. But I'm getting hungry. Let's start on that shrimp feast," he said.

While cooking dinner, we caught each other up on gossip about mutual acquaintances. Blake asked me about my marriage and my daughter. Without getting into too many details, I shared how I felt like my married life became all about compromises, especially with a child involved. "The way I see it, if one person ends up making more of the sacrifices then the marriage can become off balance. The person who always has to give in becomes frustrated; in this case, it was me. I eventually realized that I was always forced to make concessions, to keep him content. And when I started to stand up for myself, and express my opinions, he moved on to a younger version of me—probably one who would cave in easily to his demands." *And I don't think I even need to elaborate further on his desire for a younger partner.*

Blake shook his head in disbelief. "You seem to have a good perspective on it, though," he said.

"Really, what choice did I have?" I shrugged.

Blake looked at me with compassion in his eyes. "I'm sorry you had to go through that," he said.

I nodded. "I didn't really realize while I was married how distant Peter and I had grown. Sometimes it takes a while to recognize that the happiness has faded away. You start to wake up each day with a stranger and no longer even have a bond of friendship. That's what happened in our relationship; I became so lonely."

"Married and lonely? That's no good."

"When I wasn't working, I would spend my days while Jenny was in school, shopping and buying stuff that I didn't need, to fill a house that was too big for us to manage and enjoy. When in reality, my life was empty. I was trying to fill that void with stuff. I'm starting to realize that real happiness can't be bought; it comes from within."

To my dismay, Blake actually seemed interested in learning the details of my life, as he leaned forward and asked, "And how are you now?"

I shot him a stunned sideways glance. "After the marriage disintegrated, I had to remind myself of the value of friendships. And now, I realize my trusted friends are my extended family. Sometimes your inner circle changes, whether you like it or not," I said.

Blake smiled warmly. "I hope you'll count me as one of your friends. And I can't understand why your ex-husband didn't see the treasure he had with you."

Blake, who had been chopping vegetables while talking, stopped what he was doing. He looked into my eyes. "Some people just can't seem to appreciate what they have and always feel the need for more. Not only are you witty and clever, but strikingly beautiful, too. I have been enamored all day."

"Thank you. You always know the perfect thing to say. Actually, I'm glad to start my life over and to reevaluate choices that were made along the way." I met his half-smile with my own.

"I'll toast you again to that comment," he said, lifting his glass.

"Cheers to starting over and rekindled friendships," I said. And with that comment, Blake clinked his glass with mine.

I paused. "And you understand that if I talk about Peter, it's my way of saying good-bye to him and to what we shared. It truly is time to move forward and live in the present. Not to forget the past, but to learn from it and grow."

"The way I see it, sometimes the things you want so badly don't work out because there's something better for you around the corner waiting to be discovered. It's not until you look back that you realize this is true," Blake said reflectively.

I wanted to stand up and applaud his words, but instead I said, "You're right on with that one. And sometimes things don't work out because we were too young and inexperienced to realize a good thing when we had it." We stopped to give each other a knowing, thoughtful look.

Blake smiled. "That's true."

"We didn't get to talk much about your travels with the Marines at the coffee shop last week. I'd love to hear more about that."

He looked into the distance as if gathering his thoughts. In the silence that followed, I could hear the faint sound of the waves crashing. Was the tide was rolling in?

"My life became focused on my career. Let me tell you about it after we try some of those chocolate truffles we bought today."

"Chocolate truffles—you're introducing me to trouble. What else do you have planned? I remember how you can be persuasive. I caught occasional glimpses of that dark side when we were young."

Blake handed me the cellophane bag of chocolates. I reached in and pulled out a ball of dark chocolate with white sprinkles. I handed the bag back to him. He selected a dark chocolate ball with brown sprinkles. He bit into a gooey chocolate center and grinned.

"Okay, sometimes I was the bad boy. But I can thank the military for straightening me out. It's a demanding lifestyle. You're given an assignment and then you have to focus on your job. And it took me on adventures around the world."

Blake shared stories of his various assignments that had him stationed in Washington, D.C., Iraq, and Afghanistan, not to mention several locations in North Carolina. And then his voice trailed off, and he appeared lost in thought.

"Right now, I'm involved with training at Camp Lejeune. I like working with the young recruits. Their enthusiasm is infectious. It's a pleasure going to work every day. I didn't feel that way about every assignment I had over the years. I've seen the world from many angles."

"Sadly, my view has been pretty straightforward from the suburbs. My life seems a little narrow compared to yours."

"I wish mine had been a little out of focus. I've seen more than I want to think about right now."

During our discussion, I thought there were hints of the young boy I knew years ago, but overall, he had, without a doubt, transformed into a confident and knowledgeable man.

Listening to him made me feel so proud of his willingness to dedicate his life to the service and the honor he felt in defending our country. I admired everything I knew about him at this point, and I felt intrigued and wanted to know more details.

And knowing that he was capable of handling so many challenges was such a turn-on. I started to look at him dreamily and wondered if he had any idea what a rush it was to be with such a confident and accomplished man. I knew I would lose myself completely if I saw him in uniform.

"After serving in Iraq for a couple years," he explained, "I was sent to Afghanistan."

I looked at him with respect and astonishment. Although I had traveled out of the country, I never spent years away. I leaned in closer. I wanted to know everything, to hear more about his assignments and adventures, but at the same time, I did not want to barrage him with questions.

He hesitated and appeared to be cautious about sharing his past, especially what he said about his career. He gave sketchy details about his assignments. From his reluctance to share, I couldn't help but assume that the military instilled a stoic nature to the demands of the assignments.

He continued slowly. "Both were stressful assignments. I'd rather not weigh down our good time with this discussion tonight. Let's talk about it another time."

"I understand." There was no need to find out too much about his responsibilities tonight.

Leaning in closer, Blake said, "Tell me more about Jenny."

Before I spoke, I wondered if my life seemed small to him in comparison. "Well—"

"Lila," he said, as if reading my mind, "I think being a parent is the most important job a person can have. I admire the effort you've put into Jenny's upbringing. You, no doubt, did a great job raising her." His face had never seemed so endearing. "Tell me about her."

"Where do I start? She's her own person. She's picky about the boys she dates and hasn't really had a serious boyfriend. Over the years she has put academics, her community service, and athletics first. And she excelled at everything she put her energy into. She was on the swim team since middle school and usually placed in the 100-meter freestyle." Even I noticed the uplifting musical lilt in my voice describing being a mother.

"She has a lot going for her, like her mother."

"I'm lucky because Jenny is an incredible, thoughtful person. She was even an easy teenager."

"Is she an artist like you?"

"Yes. She loves to help me with my projects. And boy do we have fun. There are times we laugh so hard we nearly fall over." I had to shake myself a little to stop. "Sorry. Proud mom. You asked. But really, I feel grateful that I got to raise her."

"I love hearing about her and hope I get to meet her one day."

"She's about the same age we were when we first started dating. And she thinks she can take on the world and win. Just like we did."

Blake listened intently with his head leaned in, his chin resting on his fist. "That's an interesting way to put our youthful exuberance, that nothing-can-stop-me attitude," he said, looking at me thoughtfully. "I'm still trying to win. I haven't completely lost that attitude and hope I never do."

"The two of you would get along just fine."

"Great. And I think a parent's influence goes a long way in raising a child, and no doubt you did a terrific job."

"Thank you."

I needed to remind myself this was a vacation—time to have some fun and relax. I glanced around this spectacular house in admiration. The home had quite a setup for any place, especially a beach house. The kitchen was new and spacious. We had plenty of room to maneuver while we prepared the meal.

Blake clapped his hands together. "I'm starving. I hope you'll like my specialty, shrimp wrapped in bacon with a sweet barbeque sauce," he said. And following that declaration, Blake went to the refrigerator and began rummaging through the shelves. He pulled out the shrimp, bacon, onion, and lettuce.

In the cabinets, he found a large skillet and placed it on the stove. Meanwhile, I turned on the radio. Instantly, the sound of "Beautiful Day" by U2 carried through the house and the deck speakers.

Blake cheerfully whistled in tune with the melody while he diced an onion and tossed the small pieces into a saucepan next to the bacon. A few minutes later, the house was filled with the smell of bacon frying and the tangy aroma of onion.

The song faded and a new song began—"Dancing in the Dark" by Bruce Springsteen. Blake surprised me when he started to dance. "I can't believe this song is on now," he said. His voice was almost inaudible with the loud music. He snapped his fingers in tune, walked over to the bar stool I sat on, and began stroking my hair. I was chopping vegetables for the salad but stopped.

"Remember when we used lie in the warm sun, studying and listening to this song?" he asked.

"Like it was yesterday. Funny how a song can transport a person back in time."

Blake grinned. "I know what you mean. Sounds and *smells* are gateways through time. Does that seem odd, or do you know what I mean?" he asked.

"I think I do."

"Let me test out that theory. Stand up and let me take in your scent," he said.

Not wanting to argue with his request, I stood next to him while he draped his arms across my shoulders. Blake leaned his head down next to the nape of my neck and drew in a deep breath.

And I followed suit with his experiment. I inhaled his essence and at once his inimitable scent took me back.

I gave him a startled gaze. "That was exhilarating. Just one sniff of your scent and my mind raced back to the first time we kissed."

"Shouldn't we re-create that scene?" he questioned.

"I thought you would never ask," I teased.

"Honestly, I wanted to kiss you again from the first second I saw you." He reached both hands across my temples, slid his hands down my cheeks, and held my face between his strong hands.

His lips touched mine slowly; his delicious kiss was soft, tender, and loving, with his warm breath against my mouth. He ran the tip of his tongue across my lips. And I whimpered a soft sigh as his tongue began exploring my mouth.

Then, suddenly, we were interrupted by the pungent smell of burning bacon.

"Good grief, I burned it," Blake cried out, pulling away. "I forgot my kitchen responsibilities. You seem to have that effect on me."

Blake began scurrying around, taking the pan off the hot stove. I opened a window to let the smoke clear out. When I turned back around, the crispy bacon was on a plate. Blake was straining the boiling shrimp. And now steam filled the kitchen.

Relieved the crisis was over, I washed the fresh blueberries and placed them in a serving bowl and then followed the same routine with the strawberries.

Next, I helped Blake cut the French bread into sections, and we slid them onto the serving plate. He swirled the olive oil and herbs. He began tearing his bread and sopping it in the mixture. "Yummy. You need to try a bite of this bread. The fresh herbs we mixed in with the oil are scrumptious," he said.

While he spoke, I leaned forward on the bar, propping my chin between my hands. I watched him dice a cucumber. "Imagine this, a gorgeous man who is comfortable in the kitchen and likes to cook. That's sexy."

He paused, looked up at me, and smiled warmly. "Spend Thanksgiving with me and you'll really be turned on."

I laughed. "Now you're talking, a day in paradise. You and me rolling in mashed potatoes and dripping butter."

"Should I start licking at the top or at the bottom?" he asked. He laughed and I joined in, feeling jovial and content. "How about I start with your white meat and then finish with your dark?" He flashed a naughty grin. "But I like my meat a little on the pink side," he continued, chuckling.

"Should we wait until Thanksgiving?"

He stirred the barbeque sauce and licked the spoon. "Better not wait. I'm hungry."

I pushed the shredded lettuce into a bowl. "Yes. Very hung . . . ry, as I recall." My eyes focused on him intensely.

I realized that we just got each other's humor. *No matter how silly.* He had been the first and only man to make me feel so comfortable just being myself—where I felt as if I could let my hair down and say my goofy jokes.

Years ago, he had been the first man to make me feel at ease naked. And just thinking about those hot summer days lying together undressed made a warm tingle spread across my abdomen. I shook myself out of my reverie. And to my delight, my reality was nearly as evocative as my daydream.

My eyes followed Blake as he walked across the kitchen to the sink. I admired how fit he had remained, his bottom tight like I remembered. My focus also fastened on his broad shoulders and toned muscular arms. He must have cast a spell on me. Or better yet, he tossed out a fishing line and I was hooked. *Release me, please.*

My eyes were fixed steadily on him when he handed me a crystal wine glass. "I mixed a drink for you. I hope you like it. It's my summertime favorite, Chardonnay with a twist of lime mixed together with a splash of citrus soda," he said.

I beamed. "Wine mixed with caffeine; I love it."

Using his strong hands, he crushed the lime into the glass to make himself a drink. He cupped his hand around the lime and squeezed. At that moment, I wanted to curve my hands around his firm rear end and squeeze.

After drying his hands on the dishtowel, he turned back around and looked at me. I couldn't take my eyes off his rippling arms, but I tried not to be too obvious. I suddenly realized how long it had been since I'd had sex. And my desire to see him naked continued to stir something deep inside me that had been dormant for much too long. This awakening felt like the roar of a lion. *I wonder if he can hear that roar. I hope not; it might scare him away.*

Blake added a little more wine to our glasses. We carried the drinks and food onto the deck, setting them down on the small metal table. We were just in time to see the last sliver of glowing yellow lowering on the horizon.

I walked to the edge of the deck. And for just a moment, I was a silhouette against the orange-tinged sky. Blake joined me, stretching his arm across my shoulders. His hand brushed against my breast, warming my skin. And when he wrapped his arms around me in a firm embrace, I had a sudden surge of happiness that nearly lit my internal fire. *Are you relighting my fun flame? I hope it still works.*

Being in Blake's arms again while sharing this spectacular sunset might just be a glimpse of paradise. In the fading light, we turned toward each other. Blake leaned his face close, his eyes seeking mine. His piercing gaze held fixed for an extended period. *If only it could always be this perfect.*

As the sun slipped beneath the horizon, a prism of shadowy colors erupted across the twilight. And then slowly, the last trace of red and orange faded into darkness. The sky seemed to blacken in a just a couple of minutes. As the darkness enveloped us, we sat down across from each other at the small table. I turned on a small light.

"I feel so lucky to be here with you," Blake said, his deep voice conveying emotion. "It's amazing to reconnect with you after all of these years."

I moistened my lips. "I feel grateful we found each other again."

"You know I do."

A little while later, I pushed my empty plate aside. I could see the moonlight reflecting in Blake's eyes, making them gleam. And behind those sparkling eyes, I knew there was a clever and sensitive man.

He shot me that radiant smile, took my hand in his, and led me to the chaise. After we stretched out, he squeezed my shoulders and started to rub my back. My body jerked in a slight shaking motion; I was both shivering from the cold and the excitement.

Blake took off his jacket, wrapping it around my shoulders. He used the weight of his arm to cradle me. Nestled in his embrace, I rested my head against him and closed my eyes briefly. I had not been happy for months, but one embrace with Blake and all of that anger and frustration melted away.

We sat wordless, listening to the crashing waves. He stroked my smooth hair over and over, as if in tune with the pulses of the sea.

After a few minutes, we looked at the rising full moon that cast a beam of light across the ocean. The water below glistened, twinkling in the darkness from the reflecting stream of light.

I turned toward Blake. Our eyes met and held a steady gaze. He slid his hand from the back of my head toward my chin, cupped it, and looked at me longingly. I froze in fear. Was he about to go further than the kiss we shared earlier?

My mind whirled with emotions. *I knew your touch years ago. I was terrified when you took my virginity back then, but you were so gentle.* And now it was like being a virgin all over again.

I leaped to my feet and walked in a nonchalant manner across the deck as if looking for something. But in reality, I was searching my mind. I needed an answer. Should I have a romantic night with him? But I did not have romantic encounters with men on the first date. Okay, if I count the coffee shop, this was our second date.

But did that make it any better? Maybe I could look at this evening as a continuation from where we left off years ago. Now that made sense. Besides, look at the man he had become: an honorable, dedicated officer. And although it had been years, I always loved his touch. *Enjoy it again.*

I glanced in Blake's direction and saw him drape his legs over one side of the chaise, rocking it back and forth at a steady pace. The uneven chair legs created a rhythmic noise that mimicked the sound of a heartbeat. He continued rocking. And then he stopped.

Without looking at me, he leaned back in his chair, staring up, with his fingers knit together on top of his head. The chair creaked under the weight of his brawny, sturdy frame. He was quite a man—powerful—physically and in character. I rejoiced in being with him again.

Yes, I missed you. I would like to start over. It was time to put the ghosts of our past to rest.

CHAPTER 7

Blake's voice broke our silence. "The beach looks deserted tonight."

"It's peaceful," I said, fidgeting with my necklace.

"Do you remember the time we lit a bonfire?" While he spoke, I studied his face in the moonlight.

"I remember like it was yesterday."

"Would you like to go for a walk on the beach now?" he asked.

I felt giddy with excitement. "Yes." *Oh, wait, all alone?*

"What's stopping us from lighting a bonfire now?"

My eyes consulted his. "Sounds . . . ummmm . . . wonderful. Let me set the plates in the kitchen and grab my sweater." I carried the dishes into the house and quickly put them in the dishwasher.

Trying to release my nervous tension, I paused and took a deep breath before stepping onto the deck. The glass door slammed shut behind me with a thud.

Blake stood by the railing, looking in the direction of the sparkling water. He turned to me, excused himself, and vanished into the house, only to reemerge a few minutes later carrying two blankets.

With his free hand, he reached for mine. Just holding his warm, strong hand sent radiating heat up my arm and into my body. Together we climbed down the stairs and onto the soft ground. We had the beach to ourselves. There were only a few porch lights from the nearby houses, but most seemed empty this weekend.

The night air felt crisp, and the wind intensified the farther we stepped away from the protective barrier created by our house and the other scattered homes. As we approached the water's edge, the air seemed colder with the gusty breeze lifting strands of my hair, whipping them across my face. Even the sky seemed to hang lower. The stars twinkled bright above our heads—it was like Christmas in the sky. *Time to unwrap some presents.*

The unforgiving night air blew through my light sweater. I let go of his hand. Blake saw me wrap my arms together and shiver. "I prepared for this chill," he said. "I have the matches in my pocket to start that bonfire."

"I like hanging out with a military man, so prepared for action."

He smiled at me, and I watched his expressions, intently memorizing the details of his face. Deep inside me, I felt worried that soon I would have only memories from this night. I just had this strong feeling that this was all too good to be true.

And there was just something about him that made me want more. Not just physically, but emotionally. This one could get into my heart. Could these feelings really be real? Or was this just lust?

"You seem lost in your thoughts," he said.

"Oh, do I? It just seems so relaxing out here."

We strolled across the soft sand inches away from the surf. We were surrounded by darkness except for shining points of light that dotted the sky and the moonlight that sliced through the blackness. The nearby pier was only a shadow. Even though we couldn't see far ahead, I felt protected when Blake wrapped his arm around me. He seemed to have a destination in mind as he led me along the moist sand.

He guided me toward the secluded dunes. We stepped lightly through the tangle of briers and sea grass as we climbed the sandy crest. Our feet slipped in the sand when we descended into the valley of the dunes, a secluded enclave that offered protection from the cool breeze.

After finding the perfect spot to build our fire, Blake began searching for wood. My eyes trailed him while he navigated the dunes, gathering twigs for kindling. Each step he took in the shifting sand made his bottom muscles tighten. I stared, captivated. When he bent over, I admired his broad back and toned shoulders. And when he reached for the wood, goose bumps speckled my skin while I watched, enthralled. His triceps sprang to life with each fluid stretch.

When he knelt and prepared the kindling, I forced myself to look away long enough to spread the blanket out a few feet from his rudimentary fire pit. And to my amazement, he had a crackling fire started in a matter of minutes. I felt hypnotized by the play of light that cast a warm yellow glow, illuminating his raw masculinity. As he stood among the waving shadows and the flickering light, I could see his golden eyes staring intently at me.

"Good-looking and handy. You're a keeper," I said.

"You are, too."

"Blake, your eyes seem majestic in the firelight."

He flashed his disarming smile. "They're just happy because they're looking at you." And he grinned wider when I motioned for him to join me on the blanket. He sat down beside me, so close I could feel his body heat.

We sat in quiet observation of our surroundings. The rhythmic sounds of the waves, crashing into the sand on the other side of the dunes, mixed in with the popping of the dry wood from the crackling fire. Together they created a soothing blend of sounds. Blake and I were being entertained by nature's music.

The flickering flame warmed the air around us, making our secluded nook feel cozy and safe. We could hear the gusts whipping overhead, but we were shielded, wrapped in our blankets, and nestled in the middle of the dunes.

Blake reached his hand across my shoulder, wrapped his other arm around me, and pulled me close. With the warm comfort of Blake's strong arms encircling me, I let out a contented sigh. *What else did I need?* Those arms became my sanctuary, my escape from the world, even if it was temporary.

With our bodies pressed together, we stared into flames that swayed in the breeze. The soft firelight cast shadows across his face and created an aura of mystery. Even through the shadowy light, I could see Blake still smiling. I wanted to spend every night with him.

And as if my thoughts were spoken aloud, Blake turned to me. "I've been enjoying a single life, yet I always knew something was missing. Now I can't help wonder if it was someone. I mean you, Lila. There's just something about you that makes me want more in life—like a partner."

"I was just thinking that sitting with you is about as good as it gets."

He brushed a long strand of hair from my eyes. "Then you forgot how exciting it was for us to touch."

"I would like for you to . . . remind me," I said, surprising myself with my boldness. My hunger for him came with surprising force.

He gazed deep into my eyes. "I want to make you as excited as I am and show you pleasure, just like we did years ago." Clearing his throat, he added, "Trust me when I tell you I am as healthy as the day we lost our virginity together."

"Me, too," I said nervously. "And I know that we can trust each other's word." I wondered if he noticed my shocked expression.

But I also questioned if he could see the yearning in my eyes. Had my face given away my growing desire for him? Ripples of longing flowed through me, making me want to kiss him. And suddenly I felt as if I had been starving for his touch. I had an uncontrollable urge for Blake to caress me with those luscious lips. *Kiss me now,* my mind started to shout, but I had no time to finish that thought. As if reading my conscious yearnings, he cupped my chin and lifted it toward his face. I inhaled sharply and then released a slight moan.

He leaned in closer and closer until our lips met. The kiss was slow, tender, and warm. Our lips pulsed together from the surge of excitement that engorged them. I enthusiastically kissed him back, my mouth welcoming his gentle touch. Then Blake pulled his mouth away and glanced at my fire-lit face.

"Is there something wrong?" I whispered.

His eyebrows shot up. He turned his head and met my eyes. "I just had the strongest feeling of déjà vu. My present and past, for an instant, felt as if they merged when I kissed your lips."

I nodded. My eyes fastened on his mouth while he talked. His lips were soft and full. They fit perfectly to mine. And even after all these years they felt like a match. A moment later, he let out a heartfelt sigh, gently pulled me back onto the blanket, and leaned on top of me. He gave me a deep, sensuous kiss, using his full lips to devour me as if he were starving.

Maybe he was as famished to feel my touch as I was to feel his. He gently slid his tongue between my parted lips, and used his moist mouth to make love to mine. I released soft moans, and my eyes popped open only to find him excitedly watching me.

"I really like your sweet kisses, Blake," I found myself saying. "They make me melt." How wonderful to lie in those familiar arms. *And to have this second chance to get it right.*

He traced my mouth with his fingertip. "Your lips are so soft."

I parted my lips. He pressed his finger gently into my mouth. I sucked, pulling his finger all the way in, and tickled him with my tongue. He eased back out. I sucked him back in. He stared at my lips and gave a tantalizing smile.

We could hear the distant sound of the waves crashing on the other side of the dunes. The full moon glowed as it traveled high across the darkened sky, illuminating its path.

"The moon is spectacular," I said.

"It's one of the most beautiful things I've ever seen," Blake said, when he turned and looked at me. And I quickly realized he might not be talking about the moon.

As he touched my cheek and looked into my eyes, I knew that nothing ever would be quite the same. And I sensed he shared that sentiment.

"Lila," he whispered in my ear in a warm breath. "I fantasized about one day being with you again."

I smiled. It felt so good to be back with him. And it took all my control not to shout, "I want you, Blake."

I was coming alive again, and felt emotions I hadn't experienced in years. I did not realize how much was missing from my life until today. Maybe a wiser woman would have figured it out more quickly, but none of that mattered at this instant—it was perfect. I wanted more from him, needed more, now. The kiss, so delicious, but I wanted his touch.

"Do you have any idea how much I want you again, Lila?"

"Show me."

Glancing down, he slowly unbuttoned my shirt, slipped it off, and exposed my swelling breasts that were covered only by my lacy bra. He brushed his fingertip across each erect nipple that tried to poke through the transparent lace.

In the next instant, he reached around and unhooked my bra. He squeezed my breasts gently. I silently wondered if I might pass out from sensory overload because it had been so long since I enjoyed a man's touch. Meanwhile, he traced around the outside of my hardening areolas and then tweaked my taut nipples with the tip of his thumb and fingers.

"You're stunning," he said.

I sighed. "I missed your touch."

"This is only the beginning," he said, cupping my breasts in his hands. He leaned down and kissed my throat. I inhaled his familiar scent. Blake's mouth descended to my right nipple while his fingers moved in circles over the left. He spread his warm lips across my puckered skin and sucked, pulling a soft moan from my body.

"That feels amazing. The other one, too," I said, begging him to suck my other exposed nipple.

"I thought you'd never ask." And he moved from one hardened nipple to the other. He ran his tongue slowly from my breasts to my stomach. My deprived body sprang back to life from the attention. He slid his fingertips down my body.

At this point, my bright pink satin panties were the only barrier from his warm hands. I smiled as his skilled hands eased my panties slowly down my legs. He moved the delicate fabric, side to side until he slid the elastic waistband past my matching pink toenails.

I curled my toes in the sand while the cool night air chilled my exposed skin. The wind sent a tremor up my spine. Instantly, my body filled with sensations I had only once imagined or dreamed. My heart started pounding. Heat flushed across my face. All of my senses were ignited; even my sixth sense screamed that this was right—*relax and enjoy him. Live for the moment.*

His warm hands went gliding up the insides of my thighs, caressing me softly. Within seconds, I could hear the excitement in his voice. "Touching you again is like a dream come true."

He traced his thick fingers around the outsides of my pink folds. I did not stop him, but secretly begged him to continue. He began to swirl his fingertip in a circular motion on my most sensitive area. He gently kissed the inside of my thighs. From the glow of the moonlight, I could see his soft kisses and tongue slide across my thigh toward my yearning. His mouth formed a trail of tickles along my flesh. But he deliberately moved slowly. Slow. Steady.

Blake's butterfly kisses were drawn out in an exaggerated reduced pace toward my excited, swollen clit. He teased me, making me beg in excitement.

"What do you want me to do next, Lila?"

I moaned. "Don't stop." He used his tongue skillfully to apply pressure to my most tender, sensitive skin that throbbed for his touch. At the same time, he glided his fingertip along the outermost fold before inserting his thick fingers.

In a slow slide, he thrust his thick fingers inside me. "Relax, Lila." In the next instant, he flicked his tongue expertly, tickling me with an increasing intensity. He began to suck and knew how to put pressure on just the right place. I touched the sides of his head, softly moaning his name. He sucked. He tickled. Faster. Harder. I felt the excitement growing inside me.

I wanted more of him. I needed all of him inside me, but what he was doing felt so good I decided I could wait. He made me come in wave after wave of involuntary contractions until I softly cried out in ecstasy.

But he wasn't done yet. His hands caressed my entire body as if he wanted to remember everything about me. Tonight, he touched me in ways no one ever had before. The enthusiasm he exhibited was the biggest turn-on. With a skilled caress like that, he could make a woman do just about anything.

"I think my kitty is in love," I giggled.

"You mean your pussy . . . cat." He burst out laughing and gazed down at me. "I like everything about you, and I always loved how you taste." And that comment made my blush glow visible, even in the moonlight. "How's it possible that it is even better than I remember?" he asked. *We were like horny teenagers again.*

"And now it's my turn." I unbuttoned his shirt and slid his jeans off. His erection was pushing hard against his boxer briefs. And what a tantalizing sight he was.

"Oh, Lila."

I caught myself staring at the huge bulge and touched his hard, thickening swell. "Is this where you keep your gun? And quite a large one, I must say." And I slowly slid the briefs down his muscular legs.

"Yes," he laughed, "and I keep it fully loaded, so be careful."

I gave him a slight smile. I softly kissed his lips, and then slowly began trailing my tongue along his neck. I brushed my lips across his chest and his rock-solid abdomen muscles. I smiled up at him. "I'm curious if you're as yummy as you look?"

With that comment still lingering in the air, I reached for his hard penis and trailed my tongue across the length of its shaft with my hand cradling the base. "You are tasty." I began licking the head of his penis as if it was an ice cream cone. "Impressive, too." I winked at him.

"He's glad to see you."

"It's so good to see my friend again." I smiled as my hand closed tighter around his shaft and I rubbed up and down. His substantial length continued to grow. Magically, I felt in tune with his desire. I loved the salty taste of his skin—his lips, his chest, all of him.

I stretched my lips across the ultrasensitive rim of his manliness and took him in my mouth. And I continued stroking his hard shaft as I sucked on the tip of his penis. He pushed himself toward me as I stroked him with my tongue. My mouth moved up and down. He pressed himself to the back of my throat. I sucked harder, pulling my cheeks in tight, and instantly feeling him clench his muscles.

Increasing my rhythm, I sucked with more intensity. I squeezed firmly until he began to shudder in response. Before he lost total control, he stopped me. He pulled me close to him, pressed his lips into my cheek. "I need to be inside you. I want to make love to you again," he said, his voice husky with desire. He was excited, like that young man I once knew.

I could feel myself growing wet in anticipation. He had already caressed every inch of me that he could reach, but he wanted more. In that instant, he took me to a new degree of eagerness I had never experienced. Suddenly, I lost all my inhibitions.

He groaned. "I'm hungry for you." And even in the soft, muted light, his eyes glowed in a voracious stare. I could feel his virile energy igniting my skin.

I couldn't wait any longer. "Please make love to me. I want to feel you again," I begged.

He rolled with me until I was on my back. "I need you," he said. He lifted my legs around him and slowly slid inside my welcoming haven.

And when he slipped his throbbing cock deep inside my warm, wet folds, he whispered softly in my ear, "I feel heaven."

He looked into my eyes with a passion I had only dreamed of before now. When I whispered his name, I felt him sigh. For me, it was like the journey of my life ended, and I was finally home. I wondered if he felt the same—bliss.

The waves continued to crash in the distance, and created night music that we moved to as one. While our bodies merged, we danced! And we danced!

From somewhere within me, I found my internal gymnast when he lifted my legs. He placed my ankles on his shoulders so he could pump harder and deeper, just like we had done years ago. *Thank goodness for yoga and Pilates.*

At that angle, he was able to penetrate places deep inside me that I didn't think were possible. No feeling in the world compared to the pleasure his driving force brought to me. Although, for a brief second, I thought he might split me in two. This was like a Thanksgiving feast, and I was the wishbone. But I loved every second of his power and his strength. Secretly, I was giving thanks.

Tears stung my eyes as if the intensity of the emotions seeped out of me. The stars blurred when my eyes filled with joyous tears. After all of these years apart, I did not want these sensations to end.

I could feel his hard shaft pounding inside me as his thrusting rhythm increased. His guttural groans were primal and raw. I moaned underneath him, and felt my muscles clench around him.

At the same instant, I found my eyes fluttering shut as I floated into a dreamlike state. But the expression in his eyes demanded that I stay in the moment that I gaze at him. It had been a long time since a man had looked at me that way with such a hunger. He groaned. I grabbed his buttocks as the incredible sensations built, until finally erupting inside me, bursting through me like an explosion. We cried out almost simultaneously, filling the night air with our passion.

His energy flowed into me, bringing me back to life. I felt completely out of my mind, ecstatic. And within minutes, I was relaxed. We lay locked together, motionless in each other's arms. He sighed. "Our bodies seem made for each other. It's as if they remembered each other from years ago."

I nodded. "Could it really have been more than twenty years since we last touched?"

"It felt so natural, like we had never stopped doing it," he said.

Even snuggling motionless, my face continued to stay flushed in the cool night air. He brushed my temples and looked deep into my eyes. His fingers continued stroking my shoulder, rubbing down my arm. Those soft caresses told me more than his words. I felt appreciated in his touch.

"Do you feel it, too?" I whispered to him. "We're connected. We're linked somehow."

In the next instant, he smiled and pulled the thick blanket on top of us. He wrapped his arms tenderly around me, embracing me in warmth. I wanted to freeze this moment forever.

Could this be what love feels like?

His face softened. "I wanted to make love to you again, Lila, as soon as I saw you. I can't tell you how often I thought about us being together again. I longed to be with you, and here you are snuggled next to me."

"This almost feels like a dream," I said.

"I hope this is the first of many special times for us."

That is music to my ears.

"I'm glad to be back in your arms," I whispered. And then I nestled my head against his chest, basking in the peaceful serenity of our afterglow, and watching the last of the dancing flames. We were silent and took in the wonders of the night as we listened to the crash of the waves, almost hypnotized by the rhythmic pace. The once-crackling fire had burned down to embers, but still emanated warmth.

For the first time in as long as I could remember, everything seemed at peace. I closed my eyes. As he held me tightly, I couldn't help thinking that I never wanted this night to end. I did not want to open my eyes and maybe see it slip away. I enjoyed his body heat pressed against me, shielding me from the nip in the air. I smiled as sleep was taking me at last.

"I missed you," he said.

"I missed you, too," I whispered and then peacefully drifted off into more dreams of passion with Blake.

That was the last thing I remembered.

In the distance, I heard the sound of a dog barking. With a sudden jolt, my eyes popped open. I looked around, disoriented. Light flickered through my rapidly blinking eyelids, although they adjusted quickly to the glare. I could see an elevated yellow fireball in the sky. And there we lay wrapped in blankets, nestled within the dunes, protected from the ocean air. I felt Blake's body wrapped around me.

At the same time, vivid images of our passion, our lust, flashed in bursts, like a strobe light, in my mind. What a night to remember! Simultaneously, the actual world seen through my eyes seemed to change. Recently, I had viewed everything on muted dim, as if in black and white. But now I felt startled by a breathtaking world—filled with vibrant, kaleidoscope colors; and the bright sunlight illuminated this wondrous awakening.

Was there anything better than waking to the warmth of a strong body spooning against my back with his muscular arm draped over my stomach? Still on my side, I curled closer to him and pushed my bottom against his firm erection. His manliness felt long and hard . . . like an exclamation mark pressed into my buttocks.

At the same time, I could feel the steady rise and fall of his chest and his soft breath against my neck. I turned my head slowly to look at him, but carefully, so as not to wake him. Much to my surprise, Blake's entire face smiled down at me.

He stroked my hair while my head nestled in the crook of his arm. The memories of the night before left me with a mixture of emotions. The bottom line was I felt invigorated and younger as if I lost fifteen years in one night. The look we exchanged made it seem as if we shared similar thoughts.

With the sunrise, a new question arrived: Where do we go from here?

This new feeling of vulnerability felt scary and powerful. Should I expose my feelings to him again? And should any of this really be mistaken for love?

Blake interrupted our silence. "A penny for your thoughts."

"You can't afford what's going on in my mind right now," I said. A second later, we both laughed knowingly.

"I feel a little stunned, too. But not as much as I'll feel if one of those beach walkers finds us lying here naked," he said.

"Awkward."

He laughed. "You're right. Since I woke up starving, how about I make us one of my famous omelets?" he asked.

I smiled. "Now that's an offer I can't refuse."

We stood up, dusted the sand from our bodies, and looked around at our clothes scattered in disarray. Quickly gathering our belongings, we dressed in our rumpled clothes. Before we left, we tossed sand on the remaining ash from the fire.

In the distance, we could hear the sound of voices getting louder. But as we stepped over the dunes, we could see only a few people roaming the beach. And none appeared close. When we stepped out from our private enclave and down the side of the mass of sand, we were greeted with a gentle warm ocean breeze.

Blake looked at me, and a wide grin spread across his face. Oh, how I wanted to wake to his smile every day. I held his stare and then glanced toward the ocean.

And there we stood for a while, not speaking, but admiring the view. We took in the beauty of the rising sun glistening across the vast expanse of water. The waves broke white against the sand, crashing noisily in rhythmic repetition, and the incoming tide raced dangerously close to our feet. We ambled, hand-in-hand, along the wet, soft sand, making footprints where we stepped. Blake whistled happily.

While we strolled along enjoying the powerful morning rays, I had numerous thoughts dancing in my head. They all focused on the glorious night I had just had with Blake. One thing was certain: I wanted to have him inside me again.

We disappeared into the house and closed the door. Once inside, I showered while Blake prepared the feast. On the menu were omelets, strawberries, and fresh-squeezed orange juice. While we dined on the deck, we enjoyed the magnificent ocean view without a cloud in the sky.

Nothing seemed the same for me today. Profound joy permeated my being. Food tasted more flavorful than it did yesterday. The splendors of nature astounded me. At this precise instant, all seemed right in the world.

After finishing the last bite of my cheese omelet, my world began to shake apart. That too-familiar stabbing pain gripped my sides. Regardless of my agony, I tried not to wince because I didn't want Blake to see my discomfort. Even though every inch of my body ached, I bit my lip to remain silent. Finally, there was relieving calm after the storm. As I regained my composure, fear set in for me. Was this the beginning of a tsunami of suffering?

Regardless, I didn't want Blake to see this side of me. I didn't want to appear weak or frail because I didn't want to lose him. Overwhelmingly, I felt the need to go home and curl up in my own bed.

And then I decided to make up an excuse that Jenny might be coming to my house, and I needed to return home as soon as possible. Reluctantly, Blake agreed that he had a full work schedule to get back to, as well. By the time we ate, cleaned the dishes, and gathered our belongings, it was almost noon.

As we walked to the front door, Blake looked at me inquisitively. "Do you think we have time for one more go at it? A quickie?" he teased.

I laughed and shoved him in the direction of the door. "No."

He winked. "Can't blame a guy for trying."

"And you can't blame a girl for denying. You turned my legs into Jell-O already," I quipped, but I had to smile at his enthusiasm. And secretly I wished to spend the day in his embrace. *If only . . .*

"Don't blame me if you get back home and realize you should have jumped at the opportunity." He repeated his words with emphasis. "Don't blame me." And he laughed uproariously. He continued grinning as he picked up the bags and walked to the door.

Truth was, I couldn't remember being as happy as I had been in his company. And maybe Blake shared that sentiment. This weekend, he gave me exactly what I needed.

We both grinned and took one last look around at the majestic beach house before closing the door on adventure number one.

During the drive back to Raleigh, we planned our next outing and agreed upon a mountain getaway. "Yes, there it is on my list," I said. Mountain Escape was listed on my pink sheet of paper. I marked an X through it and put the list back in my purse.

When we arrived at my house, Blake kissed me tenderly. "I had an amazing time getting reacquainted this weekend. I have a huge project to complete for work. I will struggle to stay focused, but people are counting on me to finish," he said.

"I know you're a busy guy."

"I'll miss seeing you, but I can't wait until we're together again for our next adventure," he said.

Blake helped me carry my luggage inside the house. Before leaving, he wrapped his powerful arms around me and pulled me close.

We stood together, studying each other, both reluctant to part ways. And when he kissed me good-bye, he held me tenderly. With a sigh, he regretfully tore himself away from our embrace.

In the next instant, he stepped toward the door. With his hand on the doorknob, he turned and stared at my face as if he wanted to freeze that second in time. Like a snapshot, he appeared to want to remember me, what I looked like at that moment.

A sense of loss pulsed through me. Before he could take another step, I ran after him for one last hug. He whispered, "I'll call you. I promise you'll be on my mind."

"It's more than that, though. I've always been a realist. Everything was too perfect this weekend. I know it has to come to an end and that makes me sad," I said.

"We have a lot to be excited about the next time we get together in a few weeks," he reassured me.

I waved as he drove away, and walked back inside and closed the door with a sigh. Yes, we would be together again soon.

CHAPTER 8

In the days following our vacation, I stayed busy with new projects. Sitting behind my art table, my mind began to wander back to the beach with Blake. I longed for his embrace. Before I could dwell on my sadness, the telephone rang. The voice on the other end was Jenny's. "When are you going for that follow-up doctor's appointment?"

"Well." I paused. "I'll make it one of these days." Admittedly, I preferred to skip it altogether. *And that is the reason why I deleted all of those voicemail messages from the doctor.*

I could picture Jenny sitting cross-legged on her dorm room bed with her laptop and books spread across her rumpled sheets. Her long brown hair was probably pulled tightly in a ponytail. And I bet she had on her black workout pants and her favorite UNC sweatshirt.

Today, Jenny sounded a little frustrated. "The doctor's office left their phone number on the last two messages. You know, all those messages I posted on your cork board. I saved their phone number. Should I call them and reschedule for you?" she asked.

"No, it's so sweet of you to remind me, but that won't be necessary. I can take care of it. You stay focused on making those excellent grades."

As we said our good-byes, I caught something in Jenny's voice that made me wonder if she really enjoyed school as much as she claimed. She sounded—worried.

Blake called every night to check on me and discuss the day's events. He cheered me by saying that the memories of us became the highlight of his day. We discussed how neither

Blake nor I could sleep our first nights apart. In our solitude, our thoughts returned to each other, and the fun we shared.

When he called this evening, he told me he dreamed each night of making love to me on the beach. Reluctantly, he began sharing his latest dream, one that he had last night. In a solemn tone, he said, "My dream, or should I say nightmare, started when I held you close. We were stretched out on the sand, and I kissed you lovingly, and then you . . . you disappeared. I cried in my dream and begged, 'I don't want you to leave me again.' And then I woke up gasping for breath. You know, I spent the remainder of the night trying to come to terms with our newly rekindled romance and its effect on me."

"I know. I have been thinking constantly about us," I said.

He sighed and continued. "I must be falling hard for you. This is all happening so fast, and it's bothering me to feel— vulnerable again. Is this just me, or are you feeling stirred? Is this my wishful thinking that you have feelings, too?"

"I want to be with you."

Blake added, "I thought I picked up on a hint of hesitation about something, but I'm not sure if I read your mood correctly. Is there something you feel reluctant about?"

I wasn't sure how to answer. Maybe I wasn't sure what I was holding back. "I'm . . . excited to see you again," I said.

And when we said goodnight, Blake told me he couldn't wait to pick me up this weekend. I only hoped that the waves of pain would not reveal the truth. I kept that secret close to my heart, for me to endure.

Luckily, when the spasms of pain passed, I felt fine again. But I never knew when the next attack would occur. I lived in a state of apprehension. Finally, I relaxed and drifted off to sleep with loving thoughts of him.

I was not awakened by the soft whisper of a handsome gentleman or the calls from my butler telling me the cappuccino and eggs Benedict were ready, but instead from my reality, the whimper of my dog who wanted to go for a walk.

I stood up. "Okay, Elky, let me put on my shoes and grab your leash."

Elky sat down on the floor next to my bed, her tail thumping the ground. Elky watched my every move as I dressed. And she followed close at my heels when I navigated the house to the front door.

I just zipped my jacket when the telephone rang. Looking at my phone, I could tell it was my mother's number. I couldn't imagine why she was calling this early in the morning. And I didn't feel like talking to her until I'd had at least two cups of coffee. What kind of civilized person calls at the crack of dawn?

Without a pang of guilt, I let the call go into voicemail. She seemed unrelenting this morning when she called again. And again. Concerned there could be a problem, I picked up.

"Hello."

"Dixie Elizabeth, this is your mother." As if I needed her introduction. *I knew that voice.* And no one else called me Dixie Elizabeth.

"And how are you, Glenda Louise?" From her huff that followed, I knew my mother was not in the mood for playful banter this morning.

"Jenny told me you still haven't gone to that follow-up doctor's appointment."

You got that right, I wanted to say, but bit my lip instead.

"Mother, I don't want to go. Enough said; case closed," I added in frustration. I tried to remind myself of all the good things she had done over the years. In truth, she had always been there for us. My mother became pregnant with my sister, Susan, while she was still in college. My parents married in a rush wedding weeks after they found out about the baby. Reluctantly, my mother quit school. She gave up her aspiration of becoming a veterinarian to stay home. She was a devoted mother, attending to our every need.

She never acted resentful, but I knew she had bigger dreams. Fortunately, all these years later, my parents were still happily married. My father, Wayne, worked hard as an insurance agent to provide for the family. His magnetic personality drew people to him. He was quick to laugh and made everyone feel welcome. As a result, he built up quite a clientele base until he retired a few years ago.

Through the years, we were a physically active family. The YMCA became our family's favorite destination. When not involved in gymnastics or soccer, my sister and I practically lived at the gym or swimming pool. Susan and I were lucky to have such attentive parents. They stayed busy carting us from one activity to the next. They continued to stay involved and became doting grandparents to Jenny.

My mother had always been a fixture in my life, but sometimes she could be more involved and more rigid than I would like. And now, my mother lived vicariously through my sister. Susan never married but devoted herself full-time to her love of animals. Our entire family shared that love. She opened a veterinary hospital in Florida. My mother, grateful to return to Florida where she grew up, helps her manage the office. And to my mother's delight, she gets to spend her days surrounded by animals and fulfill her childhood dream.

And now that Jenny was grown, the pieces just fell into place for them to follow Susan to Florida. The only sad part of this story was my parents' reluctance to come back to visit. They felt as if it would dredge up too many memories to come back to Raleigh after living most of their adult lives here. And for my father, he lived his entire life in North Carolina. They had made it abundantly clear that if I wanted to see them, then I had to travel. Although the distance between us was probably a good thing, right now. My mother would be in my house daily reminding me to go to the doctor.

"You need to go," she insisted. And in my mind's eye, I could see her pointing her finger when she talked. "And what's this I heard about you seeing Blake again? You know, word gets around fast when you are doing things you shouldn't be doing," she said in a reprimanding voice.

I had become used to her one-sided conversations where she chose not to listen to me and continued with her opinions. *Like a roller coaster taking off . . . here we go . . .*

"That boy is trouble." She said the words matter-of-factly. "He was a bad influence on you then and will be again."

"That was more than twenty years ago." I could hear the petulance in my voice, but I couldn't make it stop.

"Dixie Elizabeth, don't count on his having changed much." She ended her sentence in a shrill tone. I bit harder on my lip; this time I noticed the metallic taste of blood.

Why was it a parent can turn your name into angry expletives and use them almost like curse words? She might as well have been saying, "Silly Shit, he won't change."

But he had become the furthest thing from trouble. Her words almost sounded funny to me, knowing what an admirable person he had proven to be. I mumbled, "Okay," as I wondered who gossiped about my weekend with Blake. It was as if my mother had her eyes over my house and could see my actions.

Being careful with my response, I paused. "I have to go, Mother, but I'll call you tomorrow." As soon as I hung up, I felt relief.

It had taken me half a lifetime to figure out that some people bring a positive energy into one's life, and others just suck the life right out of one's positive energy. I guess I needed to be more understanding and realize that we can all be emotional vampires at one point or another. Not that I was implying anything about my mother; her intentions might be good, even if her delivery could use some—improvement. *Understatement of the day.*

While passing the mailbox after my long stroll with Elky, I realized I hadn't checked it the day before. Sorting through the mail, I spotted a bright pink envelope with scribbled handwriting. I opened it. I pulled out a slip of yellow construction paper covered with glitter. I unfolded the paper that had been cut into the shape of an angel. On it were the words:

Please, be my snow angel. I can't wait to make love to you in the cold mountain air. See you on Friday.
Hugs,
Blake
(Your warm protector from the cold snowflakes . . . I know I got a little carried away with that one. The forecast calls for snow in the mountains!)

I tucked my new treasure under my arm and walked Elky into the house. After hanging the leash in the garage, I tacked the angel onto the cork board over my computer. Just as I was admiring his handiwork, the doorbell rang.

Peering through the glass, I felt relieved to see Jane. I opened the door, greeted her, and motioned her inside.

"Hi. I saw you out walking earlier. Jenny just called me and said to remind you to make a doctor's appointment." She blasted her words with her usual exuberance.

"Oh, no," I screamed out abruptly, startling her.

"What is it, my outfit?" she asked. "You're right. Ruffles never looked good on me. I'll go home, change, and come back," she said flippantly.

"No, your tennis skirt is cute. It's just that you are the third person in the past two days to confront me about that doctor's appointment," I said, feeling my cheerful mood fading. "You know that occasionally I see a therapist to help get me through this divorce. My rule is one doctor is plenty."

"I hear you," she said.

"Why are you looking at me with disappointed eyes?" I asked.

"I'm just concerned about you."

"I'm fine. Seeing my therapist has been more than enough doctor visits for me. And thank goodness for her. A couple times during this past year, I thought I might be losing it." I took a gulping breath. "If overcoming mental anguish makes you stronger, than I should be freaking Wonder Woman by now. And you know, one day I thought I had superpowers, but the therapist lady took them away from me."

Jane wiped her eyes and laughed wholeheartedly. "You're so funny. Lila, you're the strongest person I know. And it's visible to everyone else how tough you really are."

But deep down I was beginning to question my strength.

Finally, she choked out the words, "I know you too well. You were only crazy to stay married to Peter for all of those years. He never did appreciate all that you did for him."

"I agree." I sighed. "And I pay my therapist to agree with me, as well. And you know what, Jane? Joking about the madness of it all makes it easier. My world has been topsy-turvy for a year, but I'm slowly coming to terms with my new reality."

In an unrelenting tone, she asked, "Well, when are you going to make that doctor's appointment?" She blurted out a reprimand before I could reply. "You need to make that appointment."

"Okay. I will," I managed to say before she continued.

"I'm going to take you if you don't take yourself. Don't stay so busy hanging out with your hot ex—Blake—that you forget to take care of yourself." She said her good-byes and left, vowing to check on whether I held true to my words.

It couldn't have been twenty minutes after Jane left that Jenny called. There was a silence on the other end of the line for a second before I heard Jenny speak.

"I made your follow-up appointment for tomorrow morning. Don't tell me you're too busy this time," she warned in a harsh tone. "It doesn't matter if you tear up more of those reminder notes because I'm coming to pick you up regardless. I don't have any classes in the morning, so I'm taking you to the appointment."

"That's nice of you, Jenny, but don't I get a vote? And who is the mother here?" I teased.

"Well, Mom, how would you vote?" she asked.

"You win." I conceded.

"Good. I'll be there at nine a.m. to pick you up," Jenny reaffirmed in a calming tone.

"See you in the morning, sweetheart." I could hardly finish that last word as the chill of fear gripped me by the throat. I struggled to hang up the telephone. *Darn these nervous hands.*

I wished I could distract myself playing in the sand with Blake. Just thinking about us gave me strength. Right now, I needed that because I was crumpling on the inside. I felt like something was taking over my body.

Jenny, always true to her word, pulled her Chevrolet Malibu into my driveway at nine a.m., sharp. She was a darker-haired, perkier version of me and perhaps far more worldly, thanks to church missionary trips. She had spent weeks in Haiti and Kenya helping those in need. Plus, she was quick to volunteer her time within our own community. She devoted hours teaching special needs children how to read, swim, and play soccer. But her true passion was music. For years she had played the flute. Even with all of her outside activities, she maintained nearly perfect grades.

After looking at Jenny seated behind the steering wheel, I pulled down my sun visor and glanced in the tiny mirror. We shared the same light complexion. But her eyes were more blue than green, whereas mine tended to appear more green than blue. And when I looked at her, I often thought we were almost identical. Although, when we looked in the mirror together, or I saw a photo of the two of us, I got a reality slap. Instantly, I realized the effects of age and sunlight on my skin. It was as if each trip to the beach left an indentation in my face. And now, years later, my face was a patchwork quilt of fine lines.

We nervously chatted on the short drive to Dr. Young's office and tried to act nonchalant about the purpose of this appointment. Soon after our arrival, the nurse called me back to the examining room and permitted Jenny to accompany me. Once inside the room, I sat fidgeting in my seat, anxiously attempting to read the latest *People* magazine.

After a lengthy wait in the minuscule, cold room, the doctor greeted us and carefully closed the door behind him. The concerned look on his face shook me. While I shifted on the edge of my seat, my pulse raced so fast I could hardly stand it.

Regardless of my anxiety, I studied him briefly. I thought he was handsome in an intellectual way. He might even be an entertaining guy after he'd had a couple drinks to loosen him up, but his "dateability" level was not the reason for my office visit.

He didn't waste any time getting to the point. He shook his head. "This is very difficult for me," he said, frowning. His medical training did not mask the emotions in his voice.

Tension filled the room. I took a deep breath and held steady for the tornado-force words about to hit me.

Nothing in my life prepared me for what I heard next. Dr. Young looked down at the floor. "There is no easy way to tell you this news." And then he began speaking in technical terms, but only one word registered with me.

Cancer!

The word *cancer* reverberated like shock waves through my body and across the small, sterile office. And then silence.

Before Dr. Young continued speaking in his medical-school-trained, flat, matter-of-fact tone, his steady gaze fixed on me. I could read the concern in his eyes, which sent my stomach into panic knots. I knew there was more. Much more.

The cancer was advanced pancreatic cancer, stage III to be exact. It did not appear to have metastasized or moved to the other major organs of my body. And that was the good news. But there was no hiding the dire reality of my situation.

"There's more," he explained. "I'm sorry to tell you this, but the cancer has become inoperable because it has invaded the major blood vessels immediately surrounding the pancreas. It can't safely be removed by surgery. We should try chemotherapy to help kill the cancer cells, but really we are limited in our ability to treat this aggressive cancer."

I listened with my eyes squeezed tightly and my lips pursed together. I wanted this discussion to end. Then I fell back in my seat feeling faint, letting out a moan.

I fought the urge to throw up. Despite my best efforts to remain strong, I began trembling. A jolt shot through my senses like I had been doused with icy water. I had a primal urge to run away—far away. Run. Run. I wanted and needed to flee the cancer and any other demon that haunted me. I just wanted some peace, even if it were temporary.

Dr. Young handed me a stack of papers. "Here are some pamphlets that should be helpful. Of course, you have the option to refuse treatment. But if you want to try to buy yourself some time, we should start treatment soon. I know this is a lot to process, but unfortunately, you have to make this choice pretty quickly."

Jenny wiped the tears that spilled from her eyes. She shifted uncomfortably in her chair, reached over, and squeezed my hand. She gazed glassy-eyed at the doctor and in a trembling voice asked, "Are you sure about the results?"

"Yes. I will show you how the tumor looks on your imaging scan."

He illuminated the screen and pointed to the outline of the tumor. I had just been introduced to my enemy lurking within, and my eyes were magnetized to the shape that the doctor pointed toward—an unwanted intruder in my body. *And in my life . . .*

It suddenly made sense, all of it. The recurring stabbing pains and my breathlessness had not been products of my imagination. But I didn't find the reality to be a relief. Now I knew the truth, even though I had been hiding from it.

Jenny sniffed. "What about radiation?"

Dr. Young shook his head. "I don't consider radiation an option because of the location of the cancer. There are clinical trials with new types of treatments, but they may produce unexpected side effects. The materials I gave you will discuss those options in greater detail."

All of this technical information seemed almost too daunting for one person to handle alone; I felt grateful for Jenny by my side while I tried to absorb the facts.

"I don't have a solid, viable treatment plan to halt the growing cancer. I wish I did. But we should try chemotherapy. It's not a guarantee, but it's worth trying, in my opinion," he said.

How could all of this be true? My frustration dissipated quickly and turned into utter sorrow. Overall, I had lived a charmed life. I considered myself lucky—until today. Now I felt like I was getting all of that missed bad luck paid to me at once. Times two.

In the forefront of my thoughts was my struggle to fight the cancer growing inside me; in the back of my mind was my concern about how this disease would impact my newly rekindled relationship with Blake.

The doctor looked at me with compassion, although he had probably seen it all before—often. Nonetheless, this must be the most difficult part of his job. Especially in a situation like mine where modern medicine had not yet found the answers to the disease that ravaged my body. I could tell from his concerned expression that this was a frustrating position to be in as a doctor who had devoted his career to treating patients, to give them minimal options for a cure.

"Can we try surgery?" I asked in a weak voice. I could barely get the words out.

"No. If we caught the cancer earlier, that might have been an option."

The sad reality hit me. There was no easy solution. I closed my eyes tightly as if to make the words less painful.

Reluctantly, he continued. "If you decline to be treated, you will need to look into hospice care, as soon as possible. They are an amazing group of people and will be helpful for you in the following months. The literature I gave you should be informative about what to expect."

I sat wide-eyed, listening to my prognosis. *I was under siege, and the enemy within was a sharpshooter.*

Sadly, there weren't many medical options to deliberate over. I did know that, as a result of the uncertainty of success, I opted to forgo the clinical trials. I did not want to suffer in what might be my few remaining months of good health.

Thank goodness for Jenny, but I wished the rest of my family lived closer—at least in my area code would be nice. My parents were older, refused to travel, and lived miles away. Susan couldn't leave the veterinary hospital. I didn't really have any other close relatives to fall back on in tough times. Suddenly, I felt very isolated.

And I wondered what was going to happen next. I didn't want the pain that came on in waves—but fully receded—to settle into my body. I already felt tired. Was this feeling going to consume me in the days to come?

Jenny held my hand as I stumbled to the car, pale and drained. My mind had become numb, and the actions of the world were in slow motion. Finally, I came out of my trance. I glanced out the car window and saw the world as I knew it zoom by. I wondered if my remaining days would have the same feeling as if life whizzed by and I simply watched, frozen. The birds still chirped, and the children still played, but for me everything felt—different.

Then I looked over at Jenny driving without blinking, her hands gripping the steering wheel white-knuckled as she navigated the familiar streets. Sweet Jenny, my pride and joy, who was on the verge of becoming a woman. More than anything, I wanted to see her graduate from college, start a career, and hold her children one day. She had become such a strong person and would be fine without her mother, but I didn't want her to have to live that way. Not yet . . .

Regardless, I did not want to give in to this deadly disease, and I felt determined to fight for my life. *I must fight!*

Ten minutes later, we arrived home. As we walked into the house, I had this overwhelming feeling of living in a bad dream. I pinched myself, trying to wake up from this nightmare. No use. This situation had become powerfully real.

Jenny said the words I had been thinking. "Well, what should we do now?"

"What choice do I have?" I asked in a weak, defeated voice. *I will be strong and face the enemy; I will find strength!*

And then in a louder, stronger voice, I said, "Don't look at me through eyes of grief because I won't look at myself that way. I only have one life, and I'm going to enjoy all of it. I will not waste a moment having a pity party for myself. And I don't want your sympathy, either."

Impetuously, I blinked the tears that tried to fill my eyes, and I gave Jenny a forced smile. My nerves got the best of me, and suddenly I could not stop talking. "I'm not going to let anything get me down," I blurted out, surprising myself with my gumption. "Not the divorce from your father or this cancer. Nothing is going to depress me."

Jenny smiled tight lipped and then hugged me. "I love you, Mommy."

"I love you, too." When I looked at her, I realized I loved her more than I thought was possible. I wanted to protect her from the world. My own mother sometimes seemed overbearing, but really she must feel this protective urge.

"How can I help you?" Jenny asked.

"I know you need to get back to school, dear." Jenny nodded reluctantly. And I added, "I'll be fine."

Jenny looked at me, and with what sounded like forced cheerfulness, said, "Yes, you are the most resilient person I know. But nonetheless, I'll stop by Sunday night. I can pick up a takeout meal for us. Or maybe we can go to a favorite restaurant like the Angus Barn? There's nothing better than a perfect steak."

"That's a great plan, sweetie." I smiled appreciatively. And suddenly I felt a surge of strength.

Jenny glanced at me as if she wondered how I could look so calm and relaxed now. Maybe I had come to peace with how my life was unfolding.

Despite her hesitation to leave, Jenny walked out the door. I followed with Elky at my heels. I stood on the front porch, proudly watching my grown daughter. I loved every day of being a parent; it was the most gratifying experience of my life.

At first, the idea of motherhood had unleashed a series of apprehensive thoughts. But from the first glimpse of my adorable baby girl, I became a devoted mother. Of all the names I had been called in the past, Mommy was my favorite. I tried my best to give my daughter everything. I was always active in the PTA. I embraced every sport, musical, and academic endeavor she pursued over the years.

Just as Jenny was leaving, she stopped and turned in my direction. "Thank you for being a wonderful mother. I know you made sacrifices to put me first. I want you to know that I appreciate you," she said, her voice filled with gratitude. "And if anything ever happened to you, I don't know what I would do. I can't imagine being in this world without you. You've always been my best friend."

Hearing Jenny's sweet words, I was not sure if I felt sorrier for myself or the struggles I would be putting her through. It felt so painful to think about Jenny suffering in any way. But I would insist that she continue her college education, regardless of my health.

Although Jenny looked to be in better spirits than she had been earlier, she still seemed dazed. "Call me if you need anything. I'll be here for you," she said in a scratchy voice. She suddenly looked years older.

In such an ironic twist of events, Jenny wrapped her arms around me as if she were the one comforting a child. She smiled at me, and I found myself smiling back at her.

"Thank you, dear," I said gratefully. "And thank goodness," I sighed, "for your support today."

A moment later, she spun around to leave. And with heart-wrenching sorrow, I watched her walk to her car. Jenny slid into the front seat, closed the door, and waved good-bye. She glanced in the rearview mirror for one last look in my direction. An instant later, she drove out of the driveway, to travel back to Chapel Hill.

I stepped into the silent house. Once safely inside, I jerked forward, sobbing. My body trembling, my throat began to constrict, and I spread my hands across my face, wiping the tears. The long shadow cast by this disease was taking its toll on my emotions.

Although I felt like I was being pulled into a sinkhole, I was determined to fight my way out. I looked at my reflection in the foyer mirror and studied myself with hopeful eyes.

And with lightning speed, I switched my emotions. It was time to ignore the bad scenarios and only focus on good things. *Some circumstances better help one appreciate what one has; that was for sure.* When life gives you a rainy day, play in the puddles. And playing with someone who keeps you laughing will make it that much better. Blake!

A few hours later, the telephone rang. It was my mother again. I let the call go to voicemail. When I retrieved my message, she was on the other end saying, "Dixie Elizabeth, this is your mother." Oh my, I meant to call her as I had promised. Her message continued. "Jenny told me the news, dear. We're sorry to hear about your suffering. I think a few months in Florida with us will help. This was your mother calling." I sighed. *I love my parents and feel grateful they are in my life, but I think I'll stay here.*

Before I had time to reconsider, the doorbell rang. Standing on my front porch was Jane, looking unusually serious. I opened the door. She grabbed me, threw her arms around my shoulders, and squeezed so hard I had to pry myself free.

Jane wiped her eyes and gave a sympathetic smile. "Jenny just called and shared your news. I hope you're not mad. She knew you wouldn't tell me."

"She was probably right," I said. *And how could I be mad at people who cared enough to worry about me?*

"Would you like to talk about your doctor's appointment?" she asked.

"To be honest, I'm tired of crying. Let's go have fun and play some tennis instead."

"Are you sure you're feeling up to it?"

"I think so; anyway, I have some nervous energy that I need to work out of my system."

Without hesitation, Jane said, "Okay, I'll meet you on the court in fifteen minutes."

Our club consisted of a large, pillared brick building. The two-story structure overlooked the tennis courts. Along the back of the property was an Olympic-sized swimming pool. And next to it was a bathhouse.

When I arrived at the club, I saw Jane's minivan parked in front. Her car was easy to spot with all the magnets that hugged her bumper. She was clearly proud of her honor students and her dog.

I stopped and greeted a few ladies from my supper club and headed toward the tennis gate. As I approached the first court, I saw Jane stretching.

"You're going to need a bigger car soon. Those magnets are multiplying and taking over," I said.

Laughter flickered in her eyes. "My kids keep getting me those. At first a few magnets were cute. But now it looks like I'm driving a big refrigerator."

For the first time all day, I laughed. "I especially like the one that reads: *It doesn't get any better than this*."

Jane giggled. "Did you notice that I put that magnet on top of the dent in my car? If you peel it off, you will see silver duct tape."

"I didn't even see the dent. I'm going to make you one in the shape of a tennis racket that reads: *Game, set, match . . . don't mess with my hatch*."

"No, I don't think I have anything to worry about," she said. "No one's going to bother that mom mobile. One glance inside the car and a thief would run away in disgust."

"I remember those days. For such small people, kids sure have a lot of stuff," I said, touching my toes.

"You got that right." She lunged forward with her left leg and straightened her right.

"That would be fun to make humorous magnets."

"You're the artist. Can you make me one in the shape of a swimming pool that reads: *Game, set, match . . . if you look like Chase, come play with my snatch?*" She tossed her head back and laughed. "You know I'm joking, right?"

"I saw the way you were leering at him. I'm not so sure," I teased.

"We better get on the court before I start daydreaming about having a pool of my own," she said. She stopped stretching. "I'll take the side with glare, if you serve first."

"Sure, I'll take the shaded side. Thanks."

"Did I see you talking to Darla and Lacey from our supper club?" she asked, unzipping her tennis bag.

"Yes. It's been a bit awkward to go to the dinners alone, but I haven't been kicked out yet," I said, walking onto the court.

"Nor will you. It's not a requirement to bring a husband."

"Maybe not, but I'm the only single person there."

"Just because you're divorced doesn't mean you have to make new friends." She slid on her visor. "Are you ready to play?"

"Let's just hit back and forth first. I haven't been out here in months."

"You got it."

Twenty minutes later, I wiped the sweat off my brow. "That's it for me. You wore me out," I said in a breathless voice.

As we stepped off the court, Jane said, "You did great. Let's play again soon."

"You were nice letting me win one game." Just last year, she couldn't get a game on me. I could play for hours. And now I was struggling to keep up with her.

"Don't look up," Jane said, glancing toward the balcony dining area full of people.

My smiled faded. "What are you talking about?"

She turned her attention back to me. "Trust me. Let's just go."

I quickly gathered my belongings and walked off the court. Out of the corner of my eye, I caught a glimpse of what upset Jane. Standing by the rail overlooking the courts, I saw her. It was a younger version of me, holding a baby.

I gasped. "When did Sabrina start coming to the club?" I lowered my voice. "She's staring at us." *Why is she staring? She has my husband.*

"Let's just keep walking," Jane warned. "I didn't want you to have to deal with that sight. I saw her here last week and hoped you'd never cross paths. I'm especially sorry you saw her today."

I sighed. "Now I can't even relax on the tennis court."

"It's not surprising that your no-good ex-husband couldn't find a different club to join."

"I'm going home to finish my art project," I said, approaching our cars. "Thanks for kicking my bottom on the courts."

"Let's play again soon. And next time, it's all you," she said. "Please call me or stop by if you need anything."

"Thank you," I said, closing the car door and fighting the urge to look in Sabrina's direction. Really, what's the point of dwelling on the past? But still, the image of her baby stayed with me. I wondered if Sabrina knew just how much her baby looked like Jenny at that age.

The next morning, I woke up with a feeling of inexplicable hope and a plan of action. Numerous times I had heard of holistic medicine but had never taken an interest in it—until now. I planned to see a nutrition specialist for a vitamin therapy regimen. Maybe acupuncture would be part of the plan and an occasional massage. And sleep—lots of rest to help my body rejuvenate.

This plan of action probably wasn't going to shrink the growing tumor, but why not try?

Before I could think of other options, the telephone rang, startling me. As I fumbled to answer, I saw that it was Blake.

"Hello," I said excitedly. I could hear the faint sound of Usher's song "OMG" in the background.

"I'm missing you," he said. I could picture him dancing in his boxer briefs. I wanted to rub my hands down his ripped abs.

I sighed. "I know we talk on the phone every day. But I want to snuggle up to you."

"For now, I'm counting the days and nights until I see you again. Four days to be exact. I'll check in with you later," he said.

"It can't get here soon enough for me. In fact, I am having my imaginary way with you right now."

"Take it easy on me in your fantasy." Blake laughed. "Better yet, be rough with me. Bye, babe."

"Good-bye."

Finally, the day arrived, for Blake, to set foot in my door. And when he did, I gasped because that first sight of him always took my breath away. Call it love; call it infatuation or simply raw desire. Nonetheless, his presence made my heart flutter.

Blake rushed over. He gave me a bear hug as if we had been apart for months and boomed, "I missed you, baby." He smiled brightly, filling me with cheer. I felt the excitement in the air.

He scanned the room and saw a framed photograph of us back in college, just before a formal party. He walked over, picked up the photograph, and stared at it without blinking. "Is that really us?" he asked.

"I was wondering if you would notice that picture. I found it the other day. I thought you would get a kick out of seeing it. Does it take you down memory lane?" I asked, all ears.

Blake turned to face me. "You bet, like I'm racing full speed in my old Camaro with sexy you sitting next to me. We're relaxed and happy like we don't have a care in the world. You remember how it used to be?"

"I sure do."

"Well, I would like a copy of it when you get a chance," he said, putting the picture back on the table. "You know I tore up all of our old photos and sent them to you after we broke up, along with your shocking letter."

I had to look away after that comment. "Yes, I remember that day clearly." I refrained from giving him an earful about how angry those shredded pictures made me. Instead, I said cheerfully, focusing on today, "I packed my camera to take some new pictures this weekend. To better days . . . I'm ready, if you are."

Blake gave me a bright grin. "Let's start this new adventure."

CHAPTER 9

Blake grabbed my bag and put his other arm around me, and we walked to his light blue Corvette parked on the driveway. We were leaving for our next destination, the Appalachian Mountains. As Blake slid into the driver's seat, I gushed, "I love your new car. But please don't drive faster than our guardian angels can keep up."

He nodded. "This car has an incredible amount of power, but I promise I won't use it all today. And if I do get pulled over, apparently saying, 'I thought you wanted to race,' is not, I repeat, *not* a good way to get out of a speeding ticket."

I laughed. "Now you're making me a little apprehensive about this trip," I said, closing my door.

Driving out of Raleigh, we lowered our windows so we could enjoy the crisp October air. The mountain forecast predicted unseasonably low temperatures and snow. I leaned my head back on the beige leather seat and thought about how wonderful it was to begin another adventure. As soon as that thought crossed my mind, Blake leaned over and caressed my leg.

Fortunately, we never ran out of conversation. A couple of hours into our trip, the Appalachian Mountains appeared to erupt from the landscape as we ascended the mountain highway. While journeying into the elevations, Blake reached for the control panel and turned on our heated seats.

Seeing the peaks hovering above us, from the crest of the first incline, reminded me how majestic nature can be in its varying forms. On this fall day, it was a true symphony of colors with vivid shades of red, yellow, orange, and green blending in harmony. The vantage point from this high elevation offered a sweeping spectacular panoramic view, and the rolling hills seemed to go on forever.

After talking effortlessly, like best friends, Blake cleared his throat nervously.

I glanced over. "Is everything all right?" I asked.

His jaw tensed. "You left me with so many words unspoken. I'm not sure if this is the right time to bring up the subject. But this question has tormented me for years," he said.

My smile vanished. I shifted my weight in the seat, trying to feel more comfortable, but nothing worked.

I pressed the glass and felt the cold air seeping inside. Even with the cool air spilling into the car, I almost choked on the tension. We both knew this talk was inevitable, whether we liked it or not. A lot of questions had crossed our minds over the years. We needed to discuss the past because it was like a dark cloud looming over us.

I paused. "I guess we have some unfinished business to take care of, don't we?" I asked. The trip was beginning to feel bittersweet.

Finally, Blake began to speak. "We were so much in love back then." He looked at me with years of pent-up frustration visible on his strained face. "This question has always puzzled me. Why did you break up with me? I thought we were happy together. Were you angry about the scholarship?"

Suddenly, it was like being trapped in a heat wave. The tension was so thick that it altered my breathing rate.

I hesitated while trying to find the right words. "After I transferred, we were going to different colleges and had separate lives."

"That's true, Lila, but why the complete break from me?" He glanced over, and I could see the question in his eyes. "We could have stayed in each other's lives. It would have taken more effort, but we could have done it." Blake grimaced as if he tried not to let his words sound harsh or mean.

I looked at him curiously. "Maybe."

He fumbled with the radio. It seemed like he was searching for a distraction. Finally, he shut it off. "You know, I was devastated. I missed you so much. You broke my heart. In fact, you were the only one . . . ever . . . to hurt me."

"Looking at you now, Blake, I feel like I missed a lifetime of joy with you. In my mind, you're the one who left me," I said defensively. "You just didn't realize it at the time. But I felt like you slipped away from me. It was too painful for me even to think about what you were doing with other girls when we weren't together. And I heard stories of your shenanigans, plenty of them."

"Really?" he asked. Blake pressed the tips of his lips together until they turned white as if holding in secrets. He looked at me quizzically, opened his mouth as if to say something else, and then closed it.

"It was difficult going to different schools." He listened to me intently with a dismayed look. "The first couple years we were together were amazing. We had so much love and passion. But when I switched schools, everything changed between us."

Blake sighed. "How?"

I paused briefly. "You know, for weeks, I felt like you were still my boyfriend, but I kept hearing stories of you and other girls. In the end, I thought it was easier *not* to have you in my life at all than to deal with that pain." I watched his face and tried to read what lay underneath but couldn't. He bit his lower lip and stayed silent while I voiced my point of view. "And now you want to twist things around and make me feel like I'm the one to blame. Well, keep twisting back toward yourself, too. We were both players as our relationship—deteriorated."

He snapped his face in my direction and looked almost too stunned to respond. A moment later, he turned forward and stared at the road. "What do you mean?"

I nervously continued, "At the end of our relationship, after I transferred, I felt like I didn't even know you. You were rarely available to talk or see me. And all those stories I heard about you with other girls. I wasn't sure what was true, but I'd had enough."

Blake threw his hands up in frustration and then clutched the steering wheel. "Are you saying it was my fault? You know I always felt terrible about the accident. I replayed that scene a thousand times, each time wishing I caught your fingers when you slipped. I grind my teeth at night thinking about how stupid it was to have sex on that ledge. I'm sorry. I never wanted you to transfer."

"We were reckless, but it was more than that."

Blake rolled his eyes in frustration. "No matter what you thought at the time, I never betrayed your trust. I would never do anything to hurt you."

Those words flowed off his lips, but that didn't make them true.

"Well, I'm here with you now. And I want to try again," I said.

"The same goes for me. And I can't do anything about what happened years ago, but I can show you the person I am now," he said.

My voice softened to a whisper. "Believe it or not, I always loved you." I surprised myself with my admission. I hadn't expected to say those words.

And that silenced him completely. He looked at me with a twisted mixture of emotions. As if, at one time he would have given anything to hear those words, but now it made him feel angry and confused.

"How can you say that you loved me, when you didn't give us a chance?" he asked.

"You became so distant that I stopped trying."

He frowned. "Well, you had it all wrong."

I stared at him. "It didn't feel that way at the time."

"You were the only girl for me." His voice elevated. "I have only *really* loved one woman in my life. That woman, of course, is you."

I looked at him in disbelief as I sat in stunned silence. None of this news occurred to me. Ever. Now, I didn't know what to believe.

"Why? Why me?"

He glanced at me out of the corner of his eye but did not turn his head. "I'm not exactly sure how to express my feelings. There's just something about you that warms me up inside. You always could."

At that exact moment, freezing rain began crashing onto the windshield. Blake clicked on the wipers, and clumps of wetness smeared across the glass. Our momentary silence was interrupted by the repetitive swish from the blades.

"I was devastated when you broke up with me," Blake said and cleared his throat. "I felt sad and guilty because you lost your scholarship. It felt like my chest squeezed until a chunk of my heart broke off. Almost like an iceberg snapping off a glacier and jarring into the sea."

I sat, startled by his admission. He must write some powerful short stories. The eloquence with which the words flowed out of him stunned me. I questioned the truth as I stared out the side window at the wet flurries surrounding us. The grass now had a dusting of flakes.

He didn't stop. "And those shattered, broken fragments of my heart that remained were as cold as ice. My fractured heart sent nothing but chilly blood coursing through my body." He turned and looked deep into my eyes. "I missed you beyond words." As he spoke, I tried to size up his sincerity.

"Why didn't you tell me years ago?" I asked, looking away and choking on my words.

Blake shrugged his broad shoulders, stared at the road, and sighed mournfully. "Well, I didn't try to win you back because of my young, foolish ego. You broke up with me. I had too much pride to let you know how I really felt about you."

I soaked in his words and searched for the real story. My heart ached at the thought of his pain from our breakup. But was it true? I swallowed hard. I really had no idea that I had even hurt him. I didn't think he cared; after all, he shut me out after I switched schools. From my perspective, he cut me out of his life and became distant.

Blake glanced over and met my stare head-on. He looked back at the road. "I'm trying my best to let go of the frustration and the pain from the past. But my question is, can you? Can you meet me halfway?" he asked.

"I'm not sure what you're asking."

"Can we both put away the things that other people did to hurt us in the past? Including the hurt and pain we caused each other?" he asked.

"Everything revolves around trust," I said.

"I think we can have something special together." He went on, the words pouring out. "I feel like we have a second chance to see if this works for us."

"Each sunrise brings another opportunity." I laughed. "I must sound like an inspirational poster."

"Maybe just a little bit. But today is a new day to get love right. I don't want to put pressure on us. But I want you to know that I always felt like you were the one who got away. I always looked for *you* in the women I dated." He glanced over and smiled. "Maybe this is our time in the universe!"

"You think our paths crossed again for a reason?"

He hesitated and when he did speak his voice cracked. "You hurt me in the past, but I want to look forward. Years ago, I tried to pretend you never existed so I could get on with my life. But I couldn't simply remove your images from my mind. Young love is some powerful stuff."

"I don't think many people forget their first love or the way it hurt when it ended," I said.

"We were just kids then," Blake said. "We didn't know any better, about any of it. We don't have that excuse anymore. I know what I like at this point. I've seen a lot. And I know you are the best sight I've seen."

Bewilderment must have flashed across my face, and it was replaced almost immediately with a look of remorse. I didn't know what to believe.

For what began to feel like hours, he didn't speak. His eyes didn't blink, as if he were caught up in his memories. Finally, he said, "I did eventually move on. I married a woman I met in the service. We weren't really compatible, but it felt right at the time. The marriage fell apart quickly. I have dated plenty over the years. But it was more about fun than love. I just stopped becoming emotionally involved because no one else captured my heart."

He clicked the windshield wipers on medium, smearing the wet, sticky snow. Even though it was daytime, our car lights were beaming. We drove slowly, cautiously along the winding road. Trucks going in the opposite direction, however, did not slow down, spraying chunks of the wet slosh against the glass.

Taking in every word, I stared at Blake with my emotions in turmoil. My stomach twisted in knots. Hearing Blake talk about the other women in his life was very difficult for me; it might be tough for any woman. I hadn't asked earlier because I didn't want to know. I cringed and looked away.

There was no point in denying the stab of jealousy I felt at the thought of Blake touching other women. I knew there had been plenty in my absence. *He was mine at one point. Was I foolish for letting him go?*

Now he had a lifetime of memories with other women. Could it have just been me all of this time?

I was not sure what to say to him. Finally, I repeated the words that swirled in my head whenever I looked at him. "I'm sorry. I wish I could get that time back. Maybe if we had talked more—other than me listening to my friends—it would've worked out between us. I was angry. Mostly, I was afraid of being hurt, so I hurt you instead."

"And you have no idea how much it did."

I studied Blake. "My words may seem hollow, but it's the truth," I said, trying my best not to display frustration now. I felt my cheeks heat. "It was immature to shut you out completely, without even a discussion about our relationship. I was a coward and broke up in a letter. That was the wrong behavior. I know that now. We should have at least talked about things. I didn't give you a chance to defend yourself or have any closure."

We drove for miles in silence. The freezing rain mixture from earlier had become large flakes. He flipped the wipers from medium to high. Finally, I broke in and said, "Maybe we both learned not to shut the other one out, if we want to make this work? I think we each have enough life lessons behind us that we can get through problems better than when we were younger."

He nodded. "Communication is best. Let's try to talk through problems if we encounter any."

I thought the discussion was over, until Blake released a sarcastic laugh. "Ironically, I stood courageously in battle, but now I feel fear. I have decided it's worth the possibility of hurt and disappointment to try to create a new relationship with you." There was warmth in his voice as he continued. "It's scary to open myself up to so much vulnerability, but you're worth the risk. Even if, in the end, you hurt me twice, it will be better to have loved you twice than to have never loved you at all."

I put my hand on Blake's arm. "I feel thankful to have another chance," I said.

A moment later, we pulled up to the resort. I breathed a sigh of relief. The hotel was nestled in a valley next to an enchanting lake—quite an idyllic setting. All around us, snow covered the landscape like a soft blanket. And beyond the lake, we saw soaring white-peaked mountains that provided the backdrop for this picture-perfect scene.

Blake pulled the car under the portico. "Let's unload here and check in. Then I'll park the car," he said.

"Thanks, handsome."

While unpacking, I began to feel that too-familiar stabbing pain in my side. I bent over, gasping for air. After a few seconds, I staggered around the car in an attempt to hide my sickness.

And just as quickly as it struck, the wave of suffering passed. My frustration was on maximum. I made a point of resting during our time apart. I wanted to have plenty of energy for this weekend. And I hoped to ward off any further episodes. The pain followed me anyway.

I glanced around the car at Blake and wondered if it was time to share my secret. Maintaining a facade of normalcy was becoming too much, since I had a secret growing inside me. But when should I tell him?

When Blake walked over to me, I sighed softly. If only we could share a future together. But I could feel the painful waves growing more intense every time. I knew the cancer was spreading in my body, like weeds taking over a garden. This weekend, I would pretend to be healthy. A mountain getaway was exactly what I needed.

And as if by magic, upon entering the hotel, I felt a sudden surge of energy—rejuvenation. Carrying my bag, Blake ushered me into the hotel.

After looking around the lodge, I said, "It's lovely in here. What would you call this décor, rustic opulence?"

"You're the artist. I'm going with your interpretation," he said, smiling down at me.

I lifted up on my tiptoes to brush a kiss across his lips. "I'm so excited to be here with you."

"Me, too. I can't wait to get checked in and then check you out." He winked and then glanced around the lobby.

While Blake went to the reservation desk, I looked around our homey surroundings. Next to the lobby was a sitting area that had oversized leather chairs and a matching leather sofa. Mixed in the seating area was an assortment of bulky wooden furniture and a pile of magazines. I plopped down in a chair that almost sucked me into the pillowy cushions, picked up the latest issue of *Cosmopolitan* magazine, and began flipping through the pages.

A few minutes later, Blake walked up and said, "Take your time and finish reading your magazine. I'll deliver our bags to the room. Here's your keycard for our room, 226. See you there." I nodded, extended my hand, and reached for the key. I only glanced his way out of the corner of my eye, watched him grab my bag and my purse, and then continued reading my article on fall fashions.

About five minutes later, I snapped my magazine shut, tossed it on the coffee table, and began my search for the room.

Stepping out of the elevator, I saw a sign, rooms 200-225 to the left and rooms 227-250 to the right. *Well, that is odd.* What about room 226? Where was it? An uncomfortable sting pulsated through my nervous system. Maybe room 226 was a separate suite, perhaps around the corner? No. Only an alcove with an ice machine.

I strolled up and down the halls, floundering in disbelief, and continued looking for room 226. I searched the maze of rooms. And searched. In the silence of the corridor, I only heard the faint drumming sound from my beating heart. I could hear my pulse thumping in my ears. Two more laps around the second floor. Now the drums were beating furiously, whooshing through my head.

After wandering up and down breathlessly for several minutes, a woman with flowing red hair from housekeeping, pushed her cart into the hall. I almost grabbed hold of her cart as I exhaled. "Excuse me, miss, where's room 226?"

The plump-faced housekeeper looked at me curiously. She hesitated and then said in what sounded like a French accent, "There's no room 226 in this hotel. Is that the room you were told? Well, it doesn't exist."

My smile vanished. A visible shiver traveled through me. "Are you okay?" she asked. I must have looked like I was having a seizure. I nodded and walked away without even realizing what I was doing. *I know Blake said room 226.*

In haste, I took my phone from my pocket. I punched in Blake's cell phone number and listened while it rang straight to voicemail, but I refused to leave a message. Maybe I could text him to verify the room number. I sent him a text while clutching my phone, and waited.

A few agonizing minutes passed. Nothing. No reply. As I walked the corridor, the walls began to feel as if they were closing in on me, constricting me, like a vise—closer, tighter.

I needed fresh air.

And then the unthinkable, the possibility of *revenge* occurred to me. How well did I really know him?

Had he become the kind of person who could scheme and lure me out on false pretenses? Could he really be angry enough to pretend he desired me and wanted to spend time together when in reality he set me up?

A shiver buzzed through me as if I stepped outside, in this frosty air. Did he lead me to believe we would be vacationing together and then leave? Would he do something so awful?

I sent another text and waited. Once again, no reply. I called Blake again. When his voicemail answered, I became alarmed. Adrenaline shot through my body. *Would he abandon me like an unwanted animal? Am I chasing after Blake like I'm a lost puppy?*

What should I do next? Well, I couldn't go to the car to look for him because he dropped me off. I had no idea where he parked. He took my purse. He had everything. I stood lost in thought.

Maybe he had an elaborate plan of cruel vengeance all along. He did tell me he had been angry with me. Did he really do this? Did he just drop me off and go somewhere else or back home?

Foolishly, I let him take my purse. I trusted him. I thought we had so much fun on our last outing, or was that just a setup to reel me in further? Could he be so spiteful and cruel? Maybe our renewed happiness was all a smoke-screen, a well-laid out plan of revenge. *It worked, Blake. This hurts.*

At last, I gave up on the idea of finding Blake or the missing room. I began searching for the front desk to get my answers. I shuffled across the corridor, my head down, becoming dizzy staring at the geometric patterns on the endless stretch of carpet. Around and around I went; I felt lost in a labyrinth.

With my mind in a fog, I was not sure if I could navigate my way to the front lobby, but somehow I stumbled upon it. I knew I looked pale when I finally reached my destination, leaned across the reservation desk, and with a fretful smile asked, "Where's room 226?"

The young man at the front desk combed his nails through his stringy blond hair that hung almost to his shoulders and gave me a blank stare. His booming voice conveyed confidence well beyond his years and didn't match his skateboarder appearance as he repeated what I had already been told. "Sorry, but there's no room 226." I cringed. Chills raced down my back.

I inspected the lobby as if searching for answers. He just watched me in silence. I avoided eye contact by rotating my head to look at his name tag. "Eddie, why do you have a resort with a missing room number?"

He shrugged.

I looked down at my tightly woven hands while I squeezed so hard it turned my fingers beet red. "If it were room 13, I might understand, but 226? This makes no sense," I said.

"I agree. Not much our eccentric owner does makes sense, but this is his hotel, and he has an issue with the number 226." He leaned forward. "Most people don't notice it's skipped, which is good because we don't know the full story behind the missing number. But I do have to explain this scenario often enough that I feel frustrated," he said in a ponderous tone.

"Whatever pleases the owner?" I sighed from this setback. "Will you look up my friend's name and see if I have the correct room number?"

I gave him the name Blake Benton and Lila Baxter. He searched the computer screen and shook his head. "I'm sorry to tell you this, but those names are not in my computer or checked in to this resort."

My stomach dropped like an elevator with the cable cut, careening out of control.

I rolled my eyes toward my eyebrows as if searching my brain for answers. I leaned in closer. "Are you sure that's correct? Will you look again?"

Eddie would not meet my gaze when he answered, as if not wanting to witness my embarrassment and pain. "Sorry, ma'am; there's no one checked in under those names."

I automatically nodded at his response, because my mind had already left the conversation. It took a minute for my brain to put the mental puzzle pieces together and register what he had told me. Blake never checked in to the hotel! I stood frozen, baffled. This was mystifyingly unreal.

Absorbed in thought, I stepped away from the reservation desk. What was going on here? I believed we had a connection, but I thought wrong.

I walked outside and scanned the parking lot, looking for any sign of him. I did not see Blake's Corvette anywhere. I began to pace nervously up and down the endless rows of cars. I searched and searched. Ten minutes passed, and still, I didn't see Blake's car anywhere.

My head began to throb as I fought off mental images of Blake laughing while he spun away—with my purse and my suitcase, too. Our getaway weekend had become a living nightmare.

I sat down on the curb, dropping my face into my hands, and cried. If our relationship hadn't worked the first time, what made me think it was a good idea reuniting with him now? Was sexual attraction stronger than good judgment? And I thought that night on the beach meant something to him. *Stupid me. Sex is sex and never means commitment or anything else to a man. Women are so easily confused by a man's touch.*

Just because I easily could fall head over heels in love with him again, doesn't mean he had fallen in love with me. I guess that weekend at the beach was just a fling for him. And this weekend was a joke. Well, I guess he got the last laugh. I must be a dreamer for believing it would work between us a second time around.

After hesitating, I wrote a text that read: *How long did you plan this one?* And hit send. Convinced that Blake had left, I started to send a hostile second text that read: *You just had to be the one to leave me this time. Well, we are even. Did you plan this revenge all along?* With my finger hovering above the send button, my blood boiled.

I placed my finger on the button and hesitated. Should I press it? Shouldn't I?

At that instant, a familiar voice called out my name. "Lila! What in the world are you doing outside?" I jumped, startled by Blake's voice. I dropped my phone. My entire body lurched, and I spun around. I twisted around so quickly that I flipped backward and toppled over the curb.

After that awkward gymnastics routine, I tried to act nonchalant. I stood slowly, wiping the gravel from my clothes, and picked up my phone. I checked him out—up and down—to make sure it was actually Blake. I regained my footing and composure, but I was hurting.

So now I just stared at him, confused. I could see the questions in his eyes, and to my amazement, he gave me a concerned gaze. "Finally." He tossed his hands in the air and elevated his voice. "Why didn't you come to the room? I waited and waited and then started looking for you."

My lower jaw dropped sharply, and my mouth looked like a giant *O. What the heck?* My stare questioned him, but I found no words for a response.

He continued speaking, with his voice sounding serious. "I was having trouble getting phone reception here in the mountains, so I walked the halls for an hour looking for you." He paused, catching his breath. "Why were you just sitting outside on the curb? Is everything okay?"

I released a huge sigh of relief. Simultaneously, his words sank into my brain, and my heart filled with joy.

And when I finally regained my speech, the merriment in my voice was back. My words gushed out in a squeaky high-pitched tone. "I started to think you changed your mind about our weekend together, but I didn't understand since we had a fabulous time on our last trip." I laughed shakily and added, "Or so I thought."

He looked at me perplexed. "Of course, I loved our last trip together."

"I looked all over for room 226, but there's no room 226 in this hotel." Just saying those words out loud sounded amusing to me, now that Blake was here, standing in front of me.

"Lila, baby," he laughed, "I said 206."

"I thought you said 226. And can you believe it, there's no 226 in this hotel?"

It appeared to take a second for him to understand what I was saying. "So you have been walking around this enormous hotel trying to find a room that doesn't exist? What kind of hotel is missing one room number anyway?"

I shrugged. "A hotel with an eccentric owner, I was told. And to make matters worse, when I checked the front desk for our names, they weren't registered. So you can understand my confusion."

"That's probably because I made the reservation using a friend's name. He had a special discount pass for this resort. My name should have been on everything, too. They probably made a mistake and keyed it in wrong. I never put your name down since I wanted to pay for everything."

I smiled both inwardly and outwardly. I could not remember the last time I had been so relieved. "I don't want you to pay for everything, but we can work that out when we check out."

"And if you were looking for my car, this lot is full. I had to park on the hill over there," he said, pointing into the distance.

I nodded, not knowing what to say next. And then I thought of my last text message I *almost* sent. Glad I didn't react too hastily. Lesson learned; don't jump to conclusions next time. *But please, no next time.*

The fact that I was concerned he would and could play a cruel trick on me made me start to wonder if this was really a good idea, getting reattached to my ex-boyfriend. Was it a good idea to have feelings again for someone when it did not work out the first time? *Something to think about when my nerves finally calm down.*

He grinned. "Enough of this nonsense. Let's have a good time." He rubbed my arm. "You must be starving. I know I am. I made reservations for dinner at the main dining room for six o'clock. If we hurry, we can make it in time," he said.

"I'm starting to get hungry."

He took my hand, and we walked to the room to freshen up for dinner. *Room 206!* I was not yet aware of the scrumptious feast that awaited me. Feeling my stomach growl, I quickly dressed for dinner in my black wool skirt, knee-high boots, and cashmere sweater.

Before we left the room, Blake said, "Grab your jacket because we might want to step out on the veranda later."

"I got it and my gloves."

"We're all set then." He laughed. "This time I'm not letting you out of my sight." As we walked down the hall, he squeezed my hand and held it tightly.

Blake pushed open the heavy mahogany doors, and the hostess greeted us. She ushered us to a reserved table by the wide picture window. I felt eyes on us as we walked to our table. I noticed ladies staring at Blake. One woman froze with her fork suspended in mid-bite. I wanted to walk over, maneuver her jaws, and help her continue eating. But instead, I smiled at Blake.

We took our seats and looked out across the expansive lake. The sun was setting over the mountains, casting a luminous yellow light.

While enjoying the scenery, Blake rubbed the back of my neck, releasing the day's tension. Overall, I was as relaxed as I could remember. The conversation became lively as we discussed current events and shared humorous stories.

Our discussion slowed only after the waiter brought our first course and we relished every bite of our creamy Caesar salads. We were equally enthralled with our main course. Blake selected the filet mignon wrapped in bacon drizzled in béarnaise sauce with a side of mashed potatoes. I opted for the sea bass glazed in a chive butter sauce on top of spinach sautéed in garlic.

We ate slowly, savoring every delectable morsel, although I eyed Blake's filet mignon enviously. "Do you mind if I try a piece?" I asked.

"Help yourself," he said. "What's mine is yours." And when I took a bite of food off his plate, there was an implied familiarity to it that reminded me of dinners from years ago.

I glanced around, trying to stay in the moment. All the while, I could feel Blake's eyes on me. When I turned in his direction, he was grinning. It was impossible not to smile back at such a handsome face.

Beyond the windows, I could see the sky darkening. Pinks and yellows gave way to crimsons and purples as the sun slid behind the mountains. As the natural light in the restaurant dwindled, the flickering candle in the center of our table appeared to be waving. A few minutes later, the room was nearly dark except for the lights positioned in the far corners.

The soft murmur of voices could be heard. Suddenly, the room became more intimate as the man sitting behind the baby grand piano began his rendition of Frank Sinatra's "Luck Be a Lady," drowning out the hushed, whispered background sounds.

With Blake's insistence, I reluctantly ordered the triple chocolate layer cake. Without a hint of hesitation, Blake eagerly selected the crème brûlée. A few minutes later, the waiter returned with the desserts on a silver tray. We asked him to take our picture. When the waiter leaned in with the camera, we tilted our heads together and smiled. New memories to treasure.

I looked down at the triple layer dessert centered on a small plate. The moist chocolate cake and thick frosting were drizzled with a red raspberry sauce that swirled in loops. As I bit into the sinfully rich treat, an explosion of flavors burst in my mouth.

Blake licked his lips. "You must taste this one."

I nodded my head eagerly. He leaned forward and put a heaping spoonful of crème brûlée into my mouth. Instantly, I tasted the sweetness.

I toyed with him as I closed my lips around the spoon, easing the creamy mixture off in a sweeping sensual motion, at the same time, purring, "Mmmm. That's so delicious."

"I bet you're even more delectable," he said, repeating my gesture. He performed a slow motion lick of the creamy dessert from his spoon, at the same time shooting me a smoldering gaze. I felt my anticipation build. And I had to avert my eyes as he tried subtly to adjust himself under the table.

"This chocolate cake is sinfully rich. Try it," I said, reaching over, placing the fork inside his parted mouth and nudging his lips with the cake.

He wrapped his hand around mine. "I feel lucky to be here with you tonight. And that frosting stuck to your top lip is making me think dirty thoughts." He laughed. "Let's order a piece of chocolate cake from room service later, and I'll finger-paint your body with the frosting," he said, smiling mischievously.

"Now, Blake," I replied in a disapproving tone, finding it hard not to laugh.

"What, Lila? You want me to begin with your nipples or your toes?" I squirmed in my seat, thinking about his rugged thick fingers tracing frosting streaks across my chest.

I made a silly face and then poked out my tongue. "Should we start in the middle?"

"I have a place where you can put that tongue," he said. He leaned forward, kissing me softly and flicking his tongue seductively across my lips, lapping up the remaining frosting.

At the same instant, the waiter arrived with our coffee, clearing his throat to announce his arrival. "Looks to me like things are already heating up in here," he said. The waiter grinned while placing the steaming coffee cups beside us. I glanced away to hide my embarrassment.

The waiter, realizing his mistake, quickly cleared the table and returned to the kitchen. After he was out of sight, I elbowed Blake teasingly and mouthed the words, *"Later, I'm yours."*

"Yummy, but I want you now," he whispered in my ear in a warm, breathy voice only I could hear. Taking my earlobe in his lips, he sucked softly and continued down the nape of my neck, sending goose bumps up my spine.

"I want more of that," I purred.

"Oh, I promise you will, baby, until you scream for me to stop," he said, keeping his voice low so only I could hear. "And, by the way, I have an idea the daring side of you will love," he said, looking beyond the window. We watched the last speck of light from the day fade into darkness.

"Hmmm."

"It already snowed about an inch. I bet we will get another five inches," he said.

"Or more," I added with a tilted smile.

Blake turned toward me, his bright eyes twinkling with mischief. His face lit up with a playful grin. "Come play with me in the snow?" he pleaded. "I'll make it a night you'll never forget." Those golden eyes implored me, and I reluctantly obliged. Yes, I would go. *What does he have in mind?*

I tried to register exactly what he was asking here. I felt titillated by the thought of frolicking in the snow with this handsome man. But do I dare step into the darkness with him?

So many "what ifs" invaded my mind. I tried to gather my courage, and I searched deep inside to awaken my latent adventurous spirit that was somewhere in there. I knew it. *I just need to locate it and then channel it. Do it!*

I looked at him sheepishly, nodding while taking his outstretched hand. He wrapped his large fingers around my hand, and then we exchanged a scandalous look meant only for each other. Our eyes gleamed with excitement.

CHAPTER 10

After charging the dinner to the room and swallowing the last sip of his coffee, Blake excitedly said, "Ready to go, dear."

"There's no stopping us now," I said. And with both of us grinning, he escorted me toward the exit.

Before stepping into the night, I saw him searching inside his jacket. He pulled out a small blanket and flashlight he had discreetly tucked away. Evidently, he had been secretly planning this adventure. No wonder he sighed in relief when I agreed to go.

Blake and I stepped outside. Fortunately, the moon was full and lit up a huge mass of shimmering snow clouds. Looking into the sky, I saw the snow illuminate the night with dancing lights. We were greeted by the biting cold air and the winter wind that carried a slight smell of chimney smoke. It was invigorating.

The frozen wetness smacked my face. I wiped the soft snowflakes away, turned up the faux fur collar on my coat, and pulled my wool hat over my ears. I stood captivated by the crystals that fluttered furiously around us. "The snow is like diamonds falling from the sky," I shouted.

"It's a lovely sight," he said, watching me waving my arms in the air, spinning in circles.

White dusted the ground everywhere around us, like creamy frosting on a wedding cake. Looking out past the resort, the snow cast a luminous glow onto the rolling hills. But in the distant sky an ominous bank of thick, churning clouds warned of pounding snow yet to come. We agreed not to stray too far from the resort, and then we forged ahead.

Blake leaned over, picked up a handful of powdery flakes, and pretended to fling it at me. "Wow, it's seriously cold out here. You better zip your jacket," he said.

"Good advice."

He tossed the fistful of snow to the ground in a shower of crystal sparkles and wiggled his fingers in the air, showing off his thick leather gloves. "The military provides these top-rate gloves. Would you like to wear mine?"

I shook my head. "Thanks for watching out for me. My gloves should be fine. If not, maybe you can help keep me warm." I smiled up at Blake and brushed the snowflakes off his broad shoulders.

"My pleasure."

"I think this crisp air is exhilarating. And is there really anything more beautiful than falling snow?" I asked, watching the tiny crystals fly through the air.

"You are and seem to get more so each day. You really found the fountain of youth." He smiled, squeezing my hand. I smiled back at him, loving every sweet word that flowed from his lips.

We strolled along the path that bordered the lake, letting the silvery light from the moon become our guide. In the distance, we could hear the faint whistle of a train.

As we continued walking, Blake encouraged me to step slightly ahead of him while he lagged behind. The entire time I could feel his eyes staring intensely at me.

"Ouch!" he cried out. "Stay focused on the ground," I heard him whisper under his breath.

"Is everything okay?" I stopped, turned, and was bewildered to see Blake rubbing his leg.

"Yes, babe. I stared so intently at the sway of your hips that I forgot to watch the ground in front of me. My ankle twisted slightly on that upturned branch, but I'll be fine."

"Should we go back?" I asked, turning to see the trail of footprints we created. With each crunching step in the compacted snow, my boots left imprints.

"No, I became hypnotized by your magnificent bottom. It must be the static electricity because your skirt is grabbing your rear end like plastic wrap and clinging to your curves."

"Ah, so that's what you're doing behind me," I said, smacking him lightly on the arm. "You're making me laugh so hard, I'm warming me up inside. I'm thrilled to share this glorious night with you."

"You haven't seen anything yet," he said.

"Well, Mother Nature is giving us a spectacular show."

"I've been enjoying one, all right. Watching your curvaceous booty is giving me quite a show. Maybe too good because I just fell over ogling you," he said, looking a little embarrassed. "Does that bother you that I just shared my inner male thoughts? Should I keep them to myself next time?"

"Are you kidding? Share anything you want with me." After walking a few feet, I shouted, "I bet it snowed two inches since we first stepped out here. Careful, there are some slick spots." Our voices became less audible; drowned out by the crackling ice beneath our feet.

Blake let out a command. "Just lift those feet. Pretend you're on the balance beam, and you'll be fine."

"I forgot what that was like."

"I know what you mean. I haven't played football in years. And really, after my last slip on the ice, maybe we should both move a little slower."

I lumbered along the path and reached for his hand for reassurance. He surprised me by saying, "Come with me. Let me show you the way."

Not sure what to think of his comment, I looked at him and lifted an eyebrow. Did he mean for me to follow him along this particular path or in life? Either way, I was along for the journey.

He pointed. "I bet the view is stunning from that hill over there. It's not too far away. Are you up for it?"

"I wouldn't miss it for the world." We took slow and measured steps. I let Blake take the lead as we brazenly forged ahead with our ascent and climbed the snowy embankment. The hillside we traversed was steep, but we didn't have far to travel to reach the top. The climb quickened our breath and we stopped talking. Midway up the slope, I trudged along at a reduced pace. "I'm just glad I fueled up on that strong coffee before we left," I joked.

Blake turned to see me struggling to navigate the icy surface. "You can do it. Give me your hand," Blake ordered protectively. I reached upward and grabbed his outstretched hand, and he took my fingers. He helped guide me along the slippery path to the peak.

Standing on the crest of the knoll, we strained our eyes to see the lights from the distant hotel through the swirling snow. Looking out toward the lake, even in the downpour, we were mesmerized by the glistening reflection of the moonlight across the water. Every direction we looked, snow had become a shadowy veil of glowing white cascading across the darkened rocky peaks.

Blake squeezed my hand and led me to what I thought was a secluded area among the dense mass of trees. He opened his jacket and pulled out the blanket.

"Thanks for thinking ahead," I said.

He shrugged, slightly embarrassed. "I try to be prepared."

"Nice job."

"Although, life does throw some curveballs just when you think you have the game mastered, especially with love," he said.

"I haven't been very good in the past," I said.

"It's not any easy game to win." He looked at me and smiled. "I can't remember the last time I was this energized. Want to play in the snow with me?"

And to my surprise, he opened the blanket in one quick jerk and spread the wool cloth across the snow. Laughing at the silliness of it all, we lay down on the blanket, sinking into the powdery snow.

"I'll keep you warm tonight." He leaned on one shoulder and looked deep into my eyes. And he said in an undertone, "I'll keep you warm for as long as you'd like." Although, I was certain he wanted those words private.

And I was about to discover he was right. It would be a night to remember for a lifetime.

Suddenly, it was as if the night sky shattered into a million glittering pieces and poured on top of us. While on my back, I looked up into the sky and watched the snow fall on top of me.

I tried to look Blake in the eyes, but the fluffy flakes stuck to my long lashes.

I blinked rapidly to release their grip before finally wiping my eyes. Blake realized I was almost drowning in snowflakes, and he leaned over me, shielding me from the downpour of snow. He was so close to me that his steamy breath warmed my chilly cheeks.

Looking up toward his face, I smiled, fascinated by his unusual aura created by the shadowy light. His lips curved upward in a teasing smile, and even his eyes were smiling as he looked longingly into mine. Blake could see me inviting him with my eyes. I watched him lean toward me, and with the skill of an expert, he kissed me seductively, using his warm mouth to melt the snow from my lips.

Excitedly, I pulled him closer, causing the heat from our kiss to ride through me. I could smell the warm scent of his heated flesh, and I could taste his desire. My senses were on red alert, and even in the cold night air I could feel myself starting to flush.

Blake removed his gloves as quickly as possible and slipped his hands beneath my skirt, revealing my black thong panties. "These panties are so small, my dear, why bother at all? But I'm not complaining. You rock these dental floss undies." He pulled the tiny sliver of black lace off in one swift motion and tossed the fabric hastily into the snow.

I caught his hand and held it tightly as he started to unzip my knee-length boots. "Look at the snow piling up around us. These boots stay on."

"You're so unbelievably sexy. Those boots and your naked bottom are driving me wild."

I thought I heard a loud cracking sound from somewhere in the distance and looked at him wide-eyed in surprise. "What if someone sees us?" I cried out in fear.

"Don't worry, Lila. With this wind whipping, there are lots of unusual sounds."

Nonetheless, I sat up, alarmed, and gripped Blake's arm for reassurance, quickly glancing around, keeping a watchful eye for movement in the shadows. I thought I saw something coming toward us. I stared. Blake started to say something, but

I grabbed his hand and squeezed it as a warning. My ears strained for any sound to indicate a presence. I put a finger to my lips, glanced around, and listened for the sound of footsteps or voices but heard nothing.

"My chattering teeth are probably what you heard." He looked around and added, "Anyway, in this blizzard a person would have to be standing next to us to see us clearly. Secretly, you like to be watched, don't you, Lila?"

I shrugged. Maybe he pegged me correctly. I started to feel hot just thinking about someone hidden among the trees, watching us. And he was right; we could barely see past our hands in the swirling flakes. Plus, the wind speed had intensified, causing the nearby branches to creak and sway. Looking around, I saw nothing except the wind stirring the falling snow.

The only sound I heard other than the swaying trees were Blake's breaths while he kissed my throat. At that moment, excitement eclipsed my fears.

"Lie back down and relax. We can keep each other warm," he said. He blew out frosty air. In the next instant, he pulled me down on my back next to him. I shivered from excitement as well as from the cold, but I could feel the heat coming from his body. I felt his excitement even through his layers of clothing.

"Even with the chilly wind, you're starting to heat me up," I said.

We stared into each other's eyes briefly. He rubbed his hand across my cheek to warm me and keep my teeth from chattering. Barely able to see his own hands, he fumbled through the layers of winter clothes until he was finally able to unzip and pull down his pants. I placed my trembling hand on his briefs. I watched his growing erection begin to push its way toward the top of his tight waistband. "How about I rub you on the outside of your clothes?" I giggled while circling my hands around his hardening shaft, stroking up and down.

"Do it hard," he said. His warm pant rushed toward my ear.

While stretched out on the blanket, an arctic blast of air blew my skirt up, catching me by surprise. The icy air surged toward my naked bottom; the cold air licked at my wet pleasure center, causing my damp skin to explode with sensations. I trembled as my exposed moist flesh burst in a delicious wave of tingles. At the same time, Blake began stroking my thigh, causing me to catch my breath in anticipation.

"Would you like me to touch you?" he asked. "And warm my fingers inside you?"

I looked into his eyes and nodded eagerly. He slowly slipped his two cold fingers inside my warm folds. The sensation set off little shivers of pleasure. Those tremors were the start of my avalanche of desire that rumbled through every part of my body.

Blake twirled his tongue against mine as he slowly thrust his fingers inside my hungry body. He moved his fingers inside me in rhythm with his probing kiss. I spread my thighs wide. The flesh between my legs ached and throbbed for more; my entire body begged for his touch. I moaned softly and pressed my body closer to his.

"You like that?" he asked.

"Yes."

"You want more?"

I moaned. "I do."

Instantly, his breathing rate increased. With his fingers swiveling inside me, he used the palm of his hand to rub gently on my throbbing clit. As he steadily applied circular pulsing pressure, I could feel my orgasm beginning to build.

Meanwhile, the whipping wind picked up its momentum, whirling the snowflakes; the blustery gusts made us feel like we were being swirled inside a vacuum. The billowy forces of nature surrounding us heightened every level of stimulation. Every nerve ending on my skin became invigorated.

Blake could not wait another minute to be sheathed by my warmth. He whispered in my ear, eagerly telling me, "I want you to come when I'm inside you—feel my heat—my burning desire for you." His words ignited a slight tremor of anticipation within me. I wanted him.

In one swift motion, Blake rolled on top of me, blanketing me with his hot body. His towering presence protected me from the cold flakes. The scent that emanated from his fiery flesh was an intoxicating blend of cologne and pure desire. I took a deep breath to inhale his manly essence in the invigorating, frigid air.

As I trembled beneath him with my legs spread wide, I reached between his legs and continued stroking his growing erection. Blake breathed faster from the excitement, and I could feel his heart pounding even through his sweater. His hot puffs of air warmed my face. And his fervent touch lit up my entire body.

My breathing accelerated. I shivered in anticipation as he slid his underpants down to expose his rock-hard cock. *Must act quickly, before the cold ruins our fun.* I used my hands to help slide him inside my welcoming haven.

I thrust my hips against him, pushing his manliness inside me. Instantly, he groaned as my hot, moist walls tightened around him. Blazing heat blasted through me. I let out a moan of pleasure. Excitedly, I raised my hips to pull him closer, his path eased by the rush of my warm fluids.

"You feel so hot," he said.

"I like you inside me."

Growing even larger, I could feel the length of his cock nearly pressing against my spine, sending pleasure pulsing through me. The frozen snowflakes showered on top of his prone body and all around us. For an instant, I lost perception of my surroundings except for his closeness. The only sounds were his rapid breaths and the wind that whistled.

In spite of the crisp air, my body was on fire with desire. Blake's tongue danced with mine. The icy flakes poured in a steady flow and became a welcome relief from the heat coming from my boiling skin. Each snowflake seemed to sizzle on my face as if they were dropping on a hot skillet. I almost could hear the hissing sound and feel the zing as the flakes touched down on my flushed cheeks.

I moved my pelvis against him. He radiated warmth inside me as he thrust hard, creating burning heat from the friction. My loins felt tingly and hot under my skin, but the surface layer felt icy cold.

He drove his hard cock deeper inside me. The rhythm of his pulsating movements made me throb in ecstasy. The warmth of his touch reminded me that I was alive, and that was exactly what I needed. I closed my eyes and exhaled. "Blake, Blake . . . don't stop," I moaned eagerly, my voice barely a whisper.

My buildup of excitement caused me to clench my muscles, making my passage even tighter. I could feel the heat building with each of his thrusts. The cold snow pressed against my bare bottom, and his hot flesh pounded inside me. The cold air stung the outside of my body, but I was sizzling on the inside from Blake's erupting passion. His tickling kisses brought every sensation in my body alive.

A moan erupted from the back of my throat, making him burn wilder with desire. His eyes flickered with excitement. He looked into my eyes. He breathed heavily in my ear. He groaned. "Oh, Lila."

Electric heat shot through my body. I moaned his name, the sound of my pleasure driving him closer to the edge. My cry mingled with the pattering drops of snow, and both resonated through the night air.

I managed to gasp a single word in my excitement. "Yes."

All at once, my body began to take over; my contractions of bliss came in a tidal wave of shuddering euphoric pulsations. My release was explosive; my paroxysm of excitement shattered the night air as I moaned in the darkness.

At that instant, he, too, began to burst in delight. I arched my head back as my body pulled tight in a spasm that clenched his manliness. I squeezed. And squeezed so hard he, too, came in an exhilarating explosion of energy.

My body took over—it just happened—I cried his name. "Blake," my voice shouted. And my frenzied sounds drifted through the wind.

He groaned something in my ear as I came, but I could not distinguish his words over my moans of pleasure. Did he just tell me he loved me? Maybe my imagination was playing tricks on me.

And for a little while, we lay breathless in each other's arms, covered in snow. I smiled, and neither of us said anything. With the soft pattering around us, we seemed alone in the universe.

He gently brushed the snow from my face and ran his fingers through my tangled hair. I wondered if anything could be better than what just happened, our passion more intense than anything I had ever felt.

I finally felt the nerve to ask him. "Did you just say something to me?"

He looked at me and smiled. "You make me very happy," he finally answered.

Although we had just become reacquainted weeks before, I had a feeling like we had been together for years. We just fit together—perfectly.

Blake said with a conviction I had not heard from him before, "That was incredible. I feel like my world changed before my eyes." His warm lips kissed my cheeks. "I have a renewed feeling of excitement for life, and definitely an insatiable hunger to make love to you. Thank you for inspiring me and helping me remember what it's like to feel true passion."

I was feeling the same exuberance. Our lovemaking was hotter than my fantasies—even on this, one of the coldest nights. My elation carried over in my words. "That orgasm was the most amazing feeling in the world. I didn't want it to stop. And I never want our time together to end," I said.

"Bliss," he whispered. "Being with you is like finding a slice of paradise."

"I agree."

"And how many more orgasms can I give you before this glorious night ends?" Blake started to shiver. "We should get in from the cold. Come on, let's get a drink to warm us up and see what other fun we can find this evening."

I laughed. "I'm game."

He slowly stood up. "You look like an angel spread out there . . . my snow angel."

"I love that comparison, but this snow angel is getting cold snow on her bottom." I giggled, trying to get up gracefully, only to slip in the attempt.

"Can I help you?"

"I got it." I stood and dusted the snow off my skirt. "Have you seen my panties?"

I spun around, searching the ground, but only saw indentations in the snow.

He shrugged. "No, I think I just tossed them in the air in the excitement of it all. There's no telling where that tiny sliver you call underpants went in this powdery stuff."

I knelt down and patted across the snow, as far as I could reach. "The snow probably buried them an inch or two by now." I shoved my hand in the snow. After a few futile minutes, I gave up looking. "I guess I'll just leave them here."

"Sorry I flung your undies. I wasn't thinking."

I mused over the thought of someone finding my panties once the snow melted. "Well, at least they don't have my name printed on them," I said in resignation.

Blake let out a gleeful laugh. "No, but they should read *hot, sexy lady*."

"But only the first two letters of 'hot' would fit, and don't even go there," I warned jokingly while narrowing my eyes to give my message added emphasis.

A loud delighted laugh burst out of him, followed by a roaring, "*HO, HO, HO!* I like you naughtier than nice!" He continued chuckling, rubbing his belly, giving me his best Santa Claus impression. Although his rippling stomach muscles didn't quite have the same jiggling effect, he was nevertheless a cute sight.

He didn't stop there with his jokes. "This is like a winter wonderland. And I feel like I just—unwrapped—some Christmas magic."

"Very funny, Santa," I said.

"And I'll take some more sugar cookies, please. You are making me hungry for more tasty treats." He let out a pretend growl like he was a hungry bear.

I let out a delighted giggle. "We need to get you back to the resort before someone gets injured."

As we laughed together, I realized I would have to walk through the hotel without my panties. "Blake, you better behave when we walk through the hotel. I don't have any panties on under this skirt."

Trying to disguise a snicker, he said in a slightly more serious tone, "I won't lift your skirt and embarrass you. But I might shout 'commando' when you walk by me."

I looked at his smirking face while I twisted my skirt that was off-center. "You know I will be cracking up about all of this tomorrow, but right now I'm a little worried."

"Yes, I remember you're the kind of gal who will randomly start laughing about something that happened yesterday. I always liked that about you. You remember to laugh, and you know how to play."

I smiled. "Being with you has reminded me how to have fun, because I think I'd forgotten how to let go and enjoy myself."

"Well, you didn't seem to have trouble finding your wild side in the snow," he said.

With a sigh of regret about leaving our play spot behind, we trekked back in the direction of the resort. We emerged from the tangle of arched branches and walked toward the ridge that overlooked the lake.

Looking down, we could see the edge of the resort through the falling snow. It was picture perfect.

"Enchanting, isn't it?" I sighed. "If I could capture this view and keep it with me somehow."

"Maybe you can make a snow globe depicting the two of us playing in the glittery snow, encapsulated and captured in time, for all of eternity," he said.

"What a great idea. Just think—our own personalized snow globe to help us remember this night."

We turned toward each other and smiled, this instant frozen in time, forever, if only in our minds.

Blake reached for my shoulders. He looked deep into my eyes. "From now on, every time you look into a snow globe, I want you to think about this evening of hot and frosty passion. And when you shake the snow globe and the snow swirls, always compare that image to how we shook up the chilly night."

"I might not put that snow globe down."

Blake smiled. "I promise to remember this night forever. For me, these are memories to treasure for a lifetime."

A sudden jolt of fear shot through me as I remembered my doctor's words. Yes, these were memories to enjoy for a lifetime. *Tick, tick, tick . . . I can feel an imaginary clock ticking faster and faster inside me.* I shook that alarming thought from my head and smiled up at Blake.

We continued our journey back to the hotel, wearing satisfied expressions. As we began descending the steep hill, neither of us felt the need to speak. We just enjoyed the peaceful elements of nature. Blake pointed out things I hadn't even noticed, like the beauty in the snow clustered in the treetops.

At last the downward incline began to level, and we reached the outer fringes of the resort. We plodded into the parking lot along the perimeter of the resort. Upon entering the lot, Blake saw something that really caught his eye. He motioned to a nearby sign, and we fixed our eyes on the large yellow cautionary diamond.

Laughter made his golden eyes sparkle while he pointed at the sign. Maybe we should have seen this warning before we ventured in the wild; he laughed out loud as he pointed. I looked up at the sign and read the words: SLIPPERY WHEN WET.

For a minute, I was not sure how to respond and finally found my words. "Yes, that warning sign has taken on a new meaning for me." I shook my head and laughed.

Blake shot back, "I think it has a lot of meaning for us, all fun."

"There's no slowing you down." I giggled.

"Let's take it as a suggestion. How about we have some more slippery fun? How about a bubble bath in the Jacuzzi tub tomorrow morning? I'll lather you. But first I have some other ideas for us. Are you up for another adventure?"

I hesitated and nodded. "Forget a sign as a warning. I need some of that yellow caution tape with you."

"Hmmm," said Blake. "Now you're onto something."

"Come on, comedian, let's go warm up before this cold air permeates my bones and coagulates my blood," I said, picking up my pace. Blake had me thoroughly heated earlier, but now I was freezing, despite all my layers of clothing.

I looked into the distant sky and saw the menacing, dense cluster of snow clouds approaching. The wind that had blown steadily now snarled like a roaring beast; a nasty storm was brewing. I shivered, thinking of the blizzard yet to come.

Fortunately, we quickly approached the entrance to the resort. Two women in ski jackets came out the main doors. One lady nudged the other as we crossed paths, as if the blanket he clutched and our flushed faces gave away our naughty tale. Or were they staring at Blake?

After a few steps, the glass doors slid open, and we swiftly stepped inside the warm hotel, shaking the last of the snow from our hair. I sighed. At that moment, I had no idea of the adventure ahead. Blake had promised a night I would never forget, and he intended to hold true to his word.

CHAPTER 11

Once inside the building, Blake took my arm. We walked across the lobby, admiring the décor. I gravitated toward the seating area beside the giant fireplace. We paused, gazing into the amber swaying flames, and thawing our nearly frostbitten, rosy cheeks.

A couple of minutes later, we left the warmth. I thought we were headed to our room, but Blake had other ideas. We made a quick detour into the dimly lit hotel bar.

The focal point of the room was a stone wall that was dominated by another mammoth fireplace. This time, I sat down on the stone hearth in front of the blazing flames and waited for Blake to get our drinks.

While Blake was away, two men sat on either side of me. The men between whom I was sandwiched began talking to me and eyeing me approvingly. As Blake approached, he turned his attention to the men seated beside me.

In an act of territorial assertion, Blake swaggered up to me with a broad smile. He placed his hand on my shoulders while kissing the top of my head. He handed me the glass of wine. Blake announced in a booming voice with a hint of humor, "Let the games begin." I blushed slightly and had to avert my eyes from the other men's view.

I looked up at Blake inquisitively. "What?"

"Have a good time, gentlemen. I know I will," he said, smiling at the other men as he took my hand, somewhat possessively. He helped me to my feet. I watched Blake in amusement and blushed. I had to laugh inwardly and felt flattered that he had jealous feelings, even if they were unwarranted.

"What adventure are you taking me on now?" I asked.

"Let's go entertain ourselves." He whispered, "You know, I was just messing around with those guys back there. I wasn't really jealous. You know how I like to joke."

"Okay, lover boy. Are you a lover or a fighter? You just keep me guessing, which has me thoroughly entertained."

Before Blake could reply, a blond man in top physical form, about our age, approached. "Hey there, buddy," the new arrival said. He extended his hand to shake Blake's and used his free hand to grab Blake's arm.

"Ted, good buddy," said Blake, reaching out to give the man a hug. "Imagine running into you here." Blake smiled while greeting him, and turned to introduce me to his friend from Camp Lejeune. Blake made the formal introductions while I studied the two distinguished men. I liked the way they both carried themselves in a dignified manner with confidence, but not too much that they seemed arrogant. I was fascinated by them. Sleek. *Forget eye candy. These two are like eye caffeine. I feel energized just looking at them.*

"You're with a terrific guy here, one of the best," said Ted. "We have served together in the same unit. I would trust him with my life."

"Wow, that sounds like the highest compliment," I responded. To hear such praise, my heart swelled with pride.

"I assure you, it is," confirmed Ted, and we engaged in friendly conversation for a few minutes before he excused himself.

A moment later, we walked toward the dance floor. With a jazz trio playing in the background, Blake talked above the music. "Would you care to dance with me, my lady?" He bowed in a supplicating motion.

I chuckled, amused by his teasing gesture. "I left my dancing shoes back in Raleigh, but I'll try. Don't toss me around too much. Remember, I'm naked beneath this skirt." In the next instant, he pulled my reluctant body toward him. Before I could make more excuses, he twirled me in a playful motion, and we glided across the floor. Thankfully, my skirt stayed in place, sparing me any embarrassment.

The music slowed. He draped his arms across my back. At the same time, I wrapped my arms lovingly around him and held him tightly. He pressed his cheek next to mine. We swayed and moved together, almost floating across the dance floor.

Blake smiled down at me, and his face sent a clear message that holding me close like this made him want to explore my body further.

We walked hand-in-hand, strolling out of the bar and across the lobby to find our room. After we rounded the corner, the fitness room sign came into sight. In the distance, we could hear the faint music drifting through the air. Blake pointed to the sign. "I have an idea I think the gymnast in you will like."

Even though he nudged my arm with his elbow, I ignored his remark. Finally, I slowed my pace. "Isn't it a little late for a workout?"

He stopped me, turned in my direction, and flashed that mischievous smile. "Let's check and see if maybe the door is unlocked. And go in," he said, with imploring eyes.

Much to our surprise, the door was slightly ajar. But I wasn't sure if I wanted to enter. "Come with me." He motioned me forward without any compunction. And with that gesture, my pendulum of indecision vacillated.

Before I could say no, he tugged the door open, and the musky smell of stale sweat greeted us, stinging my scrunched-up nose. "Whew, sorry I got a whiff of that powerful stuff," I exclaimed, watching him peek his head in the door. "Wait, don't go in," I said, gripping my fingers around his toned bicep as the pungent smell spilled out of the room. "Are you sure you want to go in there?"

"I didn't know you were such a squeamish girly-girl. Don't worry about anything. Trust me," assured Blake emphatically, without a qualm.

Peering cautiously into the darkened room, we found it to be empty. As we began to sneak inside, I hesitated. Before I knew what happened, Blake grabbed my hand, yanked it forward, and scuttled me inside the chamber. He smiled down at me reassuringly.

Thankfully, most of the stale scent had drifted into the hallway. The room was still; we were alone in the darkness. There was something in the eerie silence of the room that bothered me. Although I heard nothing, strangely enough, for some inexplicable reason, I sensed a presence in the room.

Did I hear whispering? Surely, I must be mistaken. I tried to fine tune and sharpen my senses to figure out what was stirring me. I listened. There was nothing except for the slight ticking from the clock and my pulse pounding in my ears.

Nonetheless, I shivered despite the stagnant, warm temperatures and tried to glance into the murky recesses. I felt an uneasiness that Blake quickly picked up on; he sensed my hesitation and cajoled me forward.

"Relax," he urged. But even with his coaxing, I could not assuage my internal trepidation. My inner alarms were blaring, but maybe that added to the intrigue and excitement.

It took us an instant for our eyes to adjust. When they did, we could barely make out our surroundings. We searched the dim room, and we caught sight of the mirrored walls and padded floors.

We were surrounded by fitness equipment, barbells, and medicine balls. These were all basic fitness room items, but there was something more, some kind of enigmatic energy in the room; it was a mystery indeed.

Without turning the lights on, Blake guided me to the mirrored back corner. There were slivers of light shining through the broken blinds. Looking at the yoga balls, Blake asked with a shadowed wink, "Ever try one of these?"

"Sure, I have one at home."

Then Blake stunned me by saying, "No, I mean have you ever played on one of these?" He gazed at me, filled with eagerness. I could not conceal my surprise. My wide-eyed stare said more than words ever could.

"I have always admired your zest for living and I'm definitely open to trying new things, but this one has me second-guessing my feelings," I said. His amused expression made me question his intentions.

With my voice barely above a whisper, I asked, "What do you want me to do?" My surprised reactions did not go unnoticed, causing further delight to dance in his eyes.

"I'll show you," he said, giving me a naughty smile. He stroked my cheek, threaded his large fingers through my hair, and pressed his warm lips on mine.

Although the room was quiet, Blake and I began to create our own music as our mouths danced to our song of passion. I longed for more. And I suddenly had this overwhelming desire to please him.

And before I knew what happened, Blake twisted my hands behind my back and gently pushed me over the yoga ball with a fluid transition move. After falling forward and landing in a splayed position across the ball, the air emptied out of me. I released a quiet sort of cry.

Taking a deep breath, I regained my composure. I wiggled on the ball. "Don't get up," he insisted with surprising firmness. As he maneuvered me slightly forward, his powerful body descended upon me and melded into my back. I was helpless. His stomach molded against me, and his body began to sink onto mine. He positioned himself so that he was resting slightly on top of me, but not with his full weight.

As he pressed against my bottom, I could feel his arousal; his excitement was obvious. His erection was making a statement, and I was listening. *I'm listening . . . hard.*

Before I could get too excited, I just wanted to get my balance. I wobbled back and forth. I tried not to squirm. Most of all, I wanted to keep my arms from flailing and flapping. *Looking like a bird is not sexy.*

Lying across the ball, I stretched out and straightened my arms in front of me. Even though I wore boots, I tried to point my toes daintily, as if I had become a graceful Superwoman flying through the sky.

I tried to keep my balance, but to no avail; I couldn't keep myself from teetering and propelling forward. I pitched headfirst and began to slide over the ball toward my face, getting my long hair tangled under the ball. I cried out, "My hair is stuck. Help me."

When Blake realized what I was talking about, he lifted me enough to release my trapped hair, all the while nearly falling over in laughter. My giggles, however, were muffled against the plastic ball.

"Well, aren't you dirty and fun, wrapped up in one?" I teased. Next, I stumbled and pushed myself back into position. But this time, I used my hands to grip the ball, and I clung to it.

Blake repositioned himself on top of me and slid his erect penis between my bottom cheeks. "I have wicked thoughts about how to bring you pleasure. I want you more than anything," he whispered, his hot breath against my neck.

"Fair enough, but don't even think about going in the back door now. I don't have any lube with me. Another time, please. No ifs, ands, or buttttttts about it." I chuckled, hoping Blake got my silly joke.

I was relieved to hear him laugh, but to my surprise he added, "I do intend to have my twisted way with you." He lifted strands of my hair and began sucking on the nape of my neck, stopping only to say, "I can be very persuasive. Better yet, I'm going to make you beg for it," he said with complete resolve.

He tapped a hidden desire I didn't even know existed. I had always liked his commanding personality, and I was completely turned on by the power he emanated. And now, his demands were getting me hot.

Tonight, I realized that being dominated happened to be one of my secret fantasies. He wanted to take me to the edge and back.

My thoughts were interrupted by that sudden feeling of being watched. My gaze stretched to see beyond our physical bodies, seeking and looking into the darkness, only to see more shades of black.

Maybe my senses were in overdrive and spooked by the shadows of the room, but I still had this lingering suspicion that if I looked around a second earlier, I would have seen a figure moving in the shadows. *Enough of this silliness. I need to chill and enjoy Blake.*

While trying to relax and get back in the moment, I whispered in my most seductive voice, "Do what you want with me. Tonight, I'm yours to enjoy." And I meant those words because I was his, for the taking, his for the discovery.

It wasn't every day that I got tossed around like a "sex kitten ragdoll." I loved every second of it. In my mind, I was a gymnast again, preparing to do a front flip or at least a somersault.

But that gymnastics routine was in my mind, and with my actual body, I didn't flinch. I waited for my next instruction. Instead, he lifted my skirt, exposing my bare bottom. In one swift yank, he tugged off my sweater and tossed it to the floor.

Exposed and vulnerable, I felt a jolt of excitement shoot through me. My entire body shook and trembled in anticipation of what was next. Blake wove his fingers through the back of my hair. He twisted the long tendrils of brown waves around his wrist and pulled it gently, revealing my bare flesh. He leaned in to kiss and nibble the soft dent of delicate skin at my nape. In the next instant, he released my hair, and it fell softly over my shoulders.

As he lightly caressed the skin along my back, I felt a slight tickle radiate down my spine. Blake followed that path with his mouth. He gently sucked, kissed, and licked his way down. I shivered with each delicate butterfly kiss. Along the way, he inhaled my perfume now mixed with my natural scent; they blended together to create an intoxicating combination of fragrant spices mixed with the faint scent of sex. He inhaled deeply, drinking me in as if hungry for more.

When he reached the base of my spine, he gently began to massage my flesh in tight circles at the small of my back and hips with his strong hands. Blake dropped to his knees, knelt next to me, and began kissing the slight indentation where the curvature of my bottom merged with my back. I lay almost naked, spread eagle across the ball, defenseless against his desires.

His large hands curved around my soft flesh, and he began to squeeze my round bottom. I released a slight moan of desire. And just as I gave in and lost myself in pleasure, he slapped my left buttocks cheek—hard.

I cried out, "Ouch! What was—" and before I could get out my next words, he slapped my right bare buttocks cheek. For an instant, I was taken off guard, but the gasp of surprise quickly turned into a moan of pleasure. My vocal exclamations further aroused him. I tried hard to maintain control but struggled.

And before I could recover from the shock of it all, he did it again. Much to my surprise, he slapped both bare cheeks hard, twice, in quick succession. I wanted to cry out, but then he stopped to knead the stinging flesh. I was sure my bottom cheeks were covered with splotches that were as red as my flushed face.

"You like that?" he asked.

"Yes."

"I knew you would."

At first I resisted these sensations, but then I quickly discovered the pain brought every nerve to the surface and made me feel alive. His controlling presence felt so powerful, so carnal, and so real.

I turned to look at him. "Is this your alter-ego playing with me now?" I asked.

"Yes, you like him?" His smile was accompanied with a smoldering gaze.

"Hmm, I'm not sure if I'm ready and can handle him. How about I send in my stunt double?" I teased.

"Does that mean I get to play with you both?" He laughed wickedly. "I'm kidding. You don't need a stunt double, and besides, you don't want to miss the fun," he responded jovially while he pulled my legs apart. In the next instant, he slipped his pants and briefs down his legs and off his ankles. I glanced in the mirror at his reflection, admiring his thick, hard cock.

He whispered, "Just relax. I won't hurt you, unless you want me to?" And he rubbed his hands along my thighs in an upward sweep.

"Is the landing going to be as rough as the takeoff on this ride?" I asked.

"I'll try to go as easy on you as I can, for now." He raised a brow and added, "I intend to show you the time of your life. Hang on, baby."

And with that comment, I turned at a sharp angle. I looked over my shoulder at him inquisitively to see what he had planned for me. He proudly flashed that naughty smile that I took such delight in seeing. *I could get used to that mischievous look—it is the face of fun.*

Not slowing down his momentum for a second, he bent over and kissed my lips hard, pressing my cheek into the plastic yoga ball. I kissed him back with increased intensity and urgency. I wanted him, needed him. His mouth slipped from my lips to my shoulders. He began sucking the muscle between my shoulder and my neck. And to my astonishment, in a quick rushing move, he clamped his teeth down on my flesh.

I cried out, "Another party scar, Blake!"

He released his bite. "No, I'll stop, this time," he said in a low groan. He leaned on top of me again, and caught me off guard as he surged forward with his movements. His hand slid upward, continuing along my leg to where my thighs converged. All the while, I shivered in anticipation.

He reached his hand between my legs, tickling me as he caressed my smooth lower lips. He made me moan softly in delight. As if my pleasure sounds called him to action, he used his middle finger to slide along the parting of my folds. He dipped his finger inside me, penetrating me. Teasing me, he slowly slipped his finger in and out.

I raised my hips as if begging for more and also so he had easier access to satisfy my throbbing desire. He pushed a second finger inside me, pumping faster and deeper. I felt his warm breath against my hair. "You like it when I'm inside you, don't you?" he asked.

Both his hands and his words toyed with me. I nodded, hungry for more, although he had already touched hidden erogenous zones, places and parts I didn't even know existed. He continued stroking my body. "What do you want me to do next?" he asked in a voice husky with lust. Meanwhile, I squirmed under his weight, eager for more.

"I want you inside me. I want your hard cock inside me." I groaned but wanted to shout.

Blake rolled me slightly forward on the ball, thrusting gently, gliding only the head of his penis inside me, enough to stroke the sensitive skin near my clitoris. The entire area was throbbing for his touch. As if manhandling me, he brusquely lifted my hips and further entered from behind—but only slightly. I moaned.

Honestly, I wanted him to slam his entire shaft deep inside me and bring me over the edge of ecstasy, but he had his own ideas. I tried to push myself back onto him. He held me steady with his powerful grip. He continued to rock me back and forth across the ball, keeping his cock near the outside of my wet throbbing flesh. The swollen head of his penis stroked my sensitive skin just within my folds. But that sensation was just a tease. I wanted more inside me; I wanted all of him.

I clenched my muscles, trying to pull him deeper within me. I felt the beginning of a spasm as the excitement of my orgasm began to build. I was hungry for him—all of him. We pulsated. I tightened around him.

"I want to feel that sensation from deep inside," he whispered as he pushed in one swift thrust his hard cock into my hot, wet desire. "When I make you scream I want you to press your face into the plastic to muffle your cries."

"Presumptuous of you," I giggled. But before I knew it, he was true to his word. He had me on the edge. My body begged for more. He thrust deep and pulled back. "You tease," I moaned. *Wicked man with your wicked games*. My entire body quivered in excitement.

"What do you want me to do, Lila?" A low guttural growl rumbled in his throat.

"Give it to me hard," I begged.

And with those words, he finally slammed all of his huge manliness inside me, making me shudder with mind-numbing pleasure. I managed to gasp a single word in my excitement. "More," I said. He banged me harder . . . again . . . and again . . . and again.

I moved easily in rhythm with his motions; each movement drove him wilder. He felt me squeeze and tighten around him. My inner muscles clenched, pulling him closer, until I trembled and moaned against him. I pressed my face up against the bouncy ball, but even my muffled sounds seemed loud in the quiet room.

"I like when you moan," Blake said.

At that same time, he reached around me and eased his thumb between my thighs, stroking my damp flesh in time with his thrusts. He lightly pinched my clit. The extra sensation added just what I needed to send me over the edge, making my orgasm ignite like a rocket launching. We both exploded in unison.

Our cries broke the stillness of the room. And for a minute we didn't move; we lay motionless except for our panting breaths.

Sweat glimmered on his skin. I continued to be amazed that he still had his youthful energy. He had enough vigor and vitality for the both of us.

He beamed. "They're going to kick us out of this hotel if we keep doing this," he said.

"You're sexing me senseless," I said breathlessly. "Don't stop. I love every minute of it, and I'm having the time of my life."

Blake jumped in and added, "You haven't seen the end of this escapade."

Our eyes met in the mirror as he pushed himself against me. In my peripheral vision from the corner of the room, a slight movement caught my attention. Blake zoomed in on the disturbance, as well. Was there something lurking in the darkness a few feet away? My eyes darted wildly, trying to cut through the obscurity of the never-ending blackness.

In that instant, a loud rustling noise captured our attention, taking the complete focus away from our pleasure. The sound propelled us back to reality.

I all but jumped, even with Blake on top of me. My head quickly spun toward the noise. At the same time, I arched my back, as much as possible, to get a better view. I caught sight of the faint, outlined silhouette of what might have been a human figure gliding into my sight line. Was that a person lurking in the shadows? Was someone else in the room?

I heard what I thought was muffled breathing. Blake glanced at me, looking uneasy. A shiver of awareness swept through me when I realized we were being watched. The hairs along my spine spiked to upright attention like soldiers jumping to action.

It was Blake's eyes that saw an image first. I watched his eyes widen as he gazed into the dark recesses of the room. What did he see? He drew in a deep breath, and I froze, wondering what caused his alarm. Only my eyes moved as they strained and jerked from side to side trying to pierce the black. I glanced up at Blake, into our reflection in the mirror, and back at the shadowy figure.

Because of the muted light, it took a few seconds for me to discern what was happening. Simultaneously, we saw it: glowing blue eyes peered through the shadows as if materializing through wafting smoke. Slowly, the profile of a soft face appeared. My eyes followed the movement, but still, I could see only the outline of her body.

I wanted to cry out in distress, but instead, I squeezed my eyes shut, wishing the image in front of me would disappear. When I reopened them, her entire body emerged from the shadows. She stepped into the streak of bright light that shone through a broken window blind and reflected off the mirrored walls. I stared riveted on the image in front of us while the form took shape and moved closer. And now I could see a woman with flowing red hair. Her face was rosy and plump like a cherub.

Up until now, she had been all but invisible in the ebony corners. There was no telling how long she had been concealed or what she had seen. Stunned, I threw Blake a glance to see his reaction. He stared curiously at the mysterious woman. I saw the intrigue in his eyes, the strangest expression on his face, but he was no longer alarmed.

The voice that followed was in broken English, maybe a French accent. "Your dance of desire was certainly impressive. I must say, I was watching with considerable interest," she said. She appeared to be holding a rag and spray, perhaps with the intention of cleaning the mirror.

Hearing her words made the heat from my flushed cheeks drain away, leaving my face cool. We were so preoccupied with each other we didn't see her lurking in the shadows.

She sighed. "Your moans reverberated through the room, masking my heavy breathing, allowing me to watch you undetected from the shadows. And you had me practically panting," she said.

"Who are you?" I asked.

"I work here," the stranger said. "So, where do I get a personal trainer like him?"

We looked at each other and then at her. We laughed at the comment. Blake lifted himself off me and the release of his weight catapulted me to my feet, blocking his naked body. And from the sharp angle that she strained her neck, I could tell she wanted to see more of him. We reached for our clothes and quickly dressed.

"Didn't I see you earlier today looking for a missing room?" she asked. "It sure looks like you found your man. Or at least, you found a fast replacement." My eyes flicked from hers to Blake, and I could see amusement in both.

"I found my man. He was in room 206, not 226." I laughed. All that angst from earlier now seemed funny. I mustered the courage to ask, "Do you always clean in the dark and this late at night?"

"No," she answered, "but I'm glad I did tonight. Actually, I left something in here earlier today and came back in to retrieve it. And then you two walked in. I was going to slip out, but I became fascinated by your," she cleared her throat, "performance."

The tension of the moment was released by the laughter that followed. And Blake and I continued to be amused while we gathered our few belongings and prepared to slip out the door.

"Good night," we said to her.

"See you at the same time tomorrow night?" the housekeeper joked. Blake winked at me while brushing his fingers through his disheveled hair.

"Let's meet at the hot tub instead," I contributed, trying not to sound serious. There was more laughter while we all walked out together.

I slipped my hand into the crook of his arm, and he gripped it with his large fingers. We exchanged glances, trying not to smirk, and could feel the employee's eyes on us as we dashed toward the elevator. We continued racing along without even a backward glance toward our observer. Blake whispered to me,

"Well, it seemed like a good idea at the time." *It felt like a good idea and what a workout!*

We walked arm-in-arm down the hall. Suddenly I found myself wishing this night could go on forever.

As if reading my thoughts, Blake chimed in, "I'm so hot for you. I've had a fantasy night."

"What a night it has been. I think it's almost morning though," I said.

"It feels like it just keeps getting better and more exciting, if that is possible. We have been taking our discovery of each other to new heights."

I was thinking similar thoughts. I didn't dare share that we had more sex in the past few hours than I'd had in years.

Blake looked down at me and smiled his seductive smile. "Let's go back to the room, where I intend to have my way with you," he said.

"And you haven't already, my dear?" Meanwhile, I secretly wondered if I could handle any more excitement tonight. I couldn't tell Blake that I enjoyed holding on to his arm for closeness, but I also held on to it for support. My legs were feeling shaky as if I might drop to the ground. My muscles had turned soft like butter. *I was melting.*

We watched the elevator doors open, and we stepped inside, ready to go back to the room. But first he placed his hand on my bottom. "I'm going to impound you with my passion, right here, right now." He laughed, filling the small elevator with his vivacious presence. "I'm just kidding, Lila. I felt you tense up. Scared you, right?"

While finger combing his hair, he said, "Let's just go back to the room."

I sighed in relief. Unlike so many I had heard about, I was not excited by confined spaces like elevators or airplane bathrooms. But if he insisted, I might try to find the fun in it. Gratefully, he didn't.

When the elevator stopped on our floor, we stepped out into the empty hall. As we scurried down the corridor, I was giddy like a schoolgirl, and I couldn't remember the last time I'd had this much fun. I begged my body to keep up.

In the privacy of our room, Blake quickly undressed down to his green camouflage boxer briefs while I watched, smiling in admiration. "Do they teach you to undress that quickly in the military?" I teased.

"You're a funny lady. I've learned many skills over the years. Would you like me to show you a few examples?" His eyes twinkled.

"Not so fast there, soldier." My eyes looked at his bare legs while I spoke. "Look how muscular your thighs are."

"We're often required to carry heavy gear. My thighs used to be so big they would rub together."

"Now that's a fascinating image." My gaze gravitated toward the outline of his burgeoning cock that pressed against his briefs. "I love those boxer briefs, but I like you better without them. May I slide those down your legs and salute you?" I giggled.

But Blake didn't give me the chance; instead, he motioned me with his finger to step closer. The next thing I knew, he encircled his muscular arms around me, pressing his partially nude body against mine. "I can't get enough of you," he whispered, kissing the curve of my shoulder. His eyes were eager, hungry. I felt turned on again from his touch, but my body was fading quickly.

"Blake, you're insatiable."

"Only for you, my dear. You just keep me fired up and ready to go."

I sighed. How did I get so lucky this time, to have a man who was so enthusiastic for me? My mind longed for Blake, similar to the manner in which he lusted after me, but my energy level was critically low. *That man does need caution tape around him. I could get hurt trying to keep up with him.* Was I beginning to feel my knees buckle? I let out a loud sigh of pleasure or maybe just fatigue. I did not want him to become aware of my reluctance. Nor did I want to disappoint him or diminish his enthusiasm. My spirit felt engaged and eager to continue, but my flesh grew weary. *Better stop now before I collapse.* Although I felt drained, I loved every second of his touch.

Blake must have sensed my hesitation. He surprised me by saying, "I have an idea. How about I just give you a back rub and we snuggle. Would you like that? And tomorrow morning we can enjoy that bubble bath together."

I wanted to shout out with joy. Instead, I only nodded my head. I assumed he said all of this for my sake because he didn't look tired. But I was exhausted. Was this a ploy to get me into bed? I was really uncertain when he took my hand. "Come with me and let me teach you about staying in bed on a cold snowy night," he said.

"You mean rather than lie in the freezing snow?" I asked. We burst with laughter. I did not have a second to hesitate and ponder his offer. Before I could say another word, he pulled me on the soft bed. We lay down, side by side, while he caressed my smooth skin. However, Blake held true to his word—he only massaged and held me.

In the silence, we could hear the freezing rain, and escalating wind tapping against the windows. We wrapped the blankets around us and cuddled. Stroking my arm and gazing into my eyes, Blake said, "I want to wake up with you every day and see your beautiful smile first thing. It warms my heart and my soul. Each day that you're in my life is happier than the one before."

I exhaled. "I feel young again in your arms." I saw happiness dance in his eyes, and I continued. "You could hurt your lovers with your voracity."

There was a pause, and then he burst out laughing. But as soon as I made the joke, I thought about how I only wanted him for myself. And I felt a pang of jealousy at the thought of him with another woman. That conversation used the last of my energy. I snuggled on his chest, and began to fall asleep. He kissed my bare shoulders, and his fingers continued to stroke my arm in downward sweeps. I nestled against his neck, and he held me tightly.

As if feeling his affectionate gaze, I opened my eyes to meet his as he stared down at me. I almost could see a warm wave of tenderness sweep over him. For a brief second, he held his hand over his heart. Could he be surprised by a strange feeling? Maybe his heart was beginning to heal.

Looking deep into his eyes, I knew it was almost time to share my secret. *I don't think you want to know my secret.* I wanted to tell Blake, but not yet. I did not want him to be with me only because he felt pity for me. I had to know if it was real.

We lay there memorizing each other's faces as if we never wanted this special time to end. I knew I would cherish the memory of this magical night. At that exact instant, I felt a throbbing pain in my side. I tried to take slow, deep breaths to keep from writhing in agony. I did not want him to see my fear.

His strong arms were enclosed around me, holding me against his chest. Using his free hand, he rubbed tenderly up and down on my exposed arm. He wrapped his leg around mine, creating a protective barrier. For that instant, I felt safe from the world. As I nestled in his arms, I wished the pain would go away. *Breathe deep. Relax.* And with that thought, the pain eased. I drifted peacefully to sleep.

CHAPTER 12

The next morning, I woke with an overall feeling that something was wrong. I lay frozen in fear. I grimaced from stinging abdominal pain that made my ribcage throb. Opening my eyes in a flash, I discovered the room spinning, so I quickly shut them.

When I finally did pry my eyes open, the room was filled with sunlight. I felt disoriented and confused. After a few seconds, I tried to focus and looked around the bedroom. I edged myself onto my elbow and looked for Blake. Where was he? And where was I? I shook my head, trying to release that muddled feeling.

The last time I woke up feeling this way, I'd been drinking tequila. But that experience was years ago—one tequila, two tequila, three tequila . . . floor. "To-kill-you." My friends would joke about their tequila-filled nights. And I was feeling like the punch line to their jokes.

But oddly, I'd had only a couple glasses of wine last night, and it had never affected me this way before. Was this a hangover? No, it couldn't be. I swallowed hard. My mouth was dry, and my stomach ached. I felt as if I'd been eating sandpaper. And I'd never been this thirsty.

I tried to recall the events of the prior day. Vague visions flashed through my mind—of the snow and the fitness room. But beyond those bursts of thought, my mind was hazy. Slowly, I began to visualize yesterday's fun. Last night was exciting, but I didn't do anything to cause this kind of physical response.

Finally, I collected myself and jerked my head sharply toward the clock. I blinked frantically. What time was it? I still couldn't read those blurry numbers. I rolled my entire body over and studied the clock. Did it flash one o'clock p.m.? Could that really be possible?

I tried to untangle myself from the sheets, swung my legs over the edge of the bed, and stood. My legs turned to jelly. I teetered back and forth. I stumbled and fell limp into the bed. It was a futile effort. Maybe sex for a day straight could wear out anyone. I sighed; evidently not Blake.

A moment later I tried to rise again, but this time more slowly. I felt my knees shaking and stood a minute to gather my composure. For some reason, I was finding it hard to breathe. I felt nauseous and dragged myself to the bathroom and risked a glance in the mirror. Bad idea; I was a mess.

I turned the faucet on full blast, and it gushed with a whooshing sound. Next, I splashed cold water on my face. No help. I still felt trapped in someone else's body. I closed my eyes and wished to be healthy again. At the same time, I heard Blake enter the hotel room. "Lila," he shouted. My heart beat faster from the sound of his voice.

I whimpered, "I'll be out briefly." And I remembered my doctor's cautionary words: *"Take it easy."*

Blake shouted and rapped on the closed bathroom door. "Are you in there?" A minute later, he charged into the bathroom, looking alarmed.

The sight he saw could not have been pretty. I was sitting on the vanity chair with my head pressed against the mirror, eyes swollen and half-closed. Even delirious, I could read the sudden surprised look on his face and his shudder of shock—unmistakable. There was no hiding my plight. My health had declined so rapidly overnight, the sight of me now made his breath gasp. I must have looked up with an empty stare and pained appearance. Blake viewed me with his mouth open in horror.

Blake declared, "No. No. What happened?"

I know I must look haggard, but this was not the response I wanted to hear. In a toneless voice I heard myself say, "I think I need help getting back into bed." My words sounded distorted, almost swirling in my head, and I wondered if someone else was speaking them. *Am I just mumbling nebulous phrases, or can he understand me? And am I saying my words out loud?*

From my fumbling words, and glassy-eyed gaze, we both knew the situation had turned abysmal. My entire appearance must have altered from the vivacious woman he had held the night before. The fun ideas we had planned for the day all but disappeared.

But once I finally regained some of my composure, I took careful note of the vision in front of me. In my fleeting seconds of lucidity, I saw that Blake looked exceptional in his tight running pants and form-fitting shirt stretched tight across his chest. *He is fireman-level gorgeous.*

And there was no mistaking the contrast between us. This afternoon, I knew my face looked sick, pale, and pasty, and he looked so healthy, energetic, and vibrant.

He gently stroked my hair. "How are you feeling, sweetness?"

After a long silence, I gave an enervated response that was more of a mumble. "Better now that I see your gorgeous, sweaty body."

He laughed. "Well, at least you still have your sense of humor. I'm a little drenched. I just finished an eight-mile run." But I was barely listening, because I was only thinking about how exhausted I felt and hoped I wouldn't collapse. Blake interrupted my daze. "Maybe your caffeine level is getting critically low. How about I get you some and fuel you back up?"

"Are you teasing me again?" I asked. I stood, but I staggered and faltered when I took my first step.

He grabbed my arm and led me back to the bed; his touch instantly soothed me. "Rest may help you. You looked so peaceful earlier. I didn't want to wake you. So I had breakfast, read the paper, and worked out." I only could marvel at his stamina. Blake was something else with his high energy level and perpetually pleasant demeanor.

Sitting on the edge of the bed, swinging my legs, I said, "Maybe my equilibrium is just a little off?"

He shook his head. "What were you—sneaking shots of vodka throughout the day?"

I tilted my head and made a pouty face. "Funny guy. I'm just having a rough day, and maybe I'm fighting off a cold." Even I could hear how exhausted I sounded. And my words were not fooling anyone.

"Are you sure there isn't something else we need to discuss?" he asked.

After shaking my head, he helped me climb under the covers. He tucked the blankets around me and kissed my forehead. Even feeling sick, he brought out my smile. I flashed grateful eyes at him. "You're the light in my darkness," I said.

"You're my light," he whispered. He jumped to his feet and bolted toward the door. I listened to his footsteps fading. And then with a sigh I clutched the sheets around myself. I closed my eyes; I wished I had the energy to keep up with him today. I heard the door close.

"Wait," I called after him. "I didn't mean to send you running for your life." I shouted.

The door opened, and Blake peeked in. "Lila, didn't you hear me? I said I'm getting you a soda."

I pulled the sheet over my mouth. "Oh." A moment later, I sat upright. I tried to give him my best welcoming smile when he returned.

He handed me the cold soda, but I was too exhausted to drink more than a couple sips. I lay back on the pillows, and the need for sleep began to overpower me.

Blake sat by my side while I started to drift peacefully to sleep. My breathing rate slowed and became shallow. I muttered incoherent words. I could see Blake leaning in to hear my babble, trying to make out what I said.

In my delirium, I panicked about my sickness. I wanted to tell Blake, but I was afraid. *Did I just mumble something? Did I just say out loud, "I'm leaving you . . . I'm going to have to leave you?"* No, I must have thought those words. In my confused state, I wasn't sure what was real. But I thought I saw Blake stare at me in wide-eyed silence while he grabbed for his stomach. A moment later, he rushed out of the room and slammed the door. My head felt fuzzy, confused, and I quickly drifted to sleep.

When I woke up an hour later, I was myself again, almost euphoric to feel good again. However, that elated feeling quickly passed when I saw Blake's bags packed by the door. He stood by the window, his spine stiff and his arms crossed. My smile faded fast.

He was silent, almost brooding, and had a grim look as if he had swallowed cough medicine. Blake turned toward me, his eyes narrowed. An unusual expression crossed his eyes, and then it vanished.

Instantly, I could see from Blake's pursed mouth that he was holding back something. *But what?*

I shrugged. "Is something wrong?" I asked guardedly. "Did I say or do something to upset you?"

Reluctantly, I eyed Blake, waiting for an answer. Silence. He refused to look directly at me. And his eyes skipped away when I tried to catch them. *Why are you being so evasive?*

I tried to distract myself by looking at my fingernails. Still no response. *I can hold my breath while I wait.* I began counting. *One, two, three, four, and five. Okay . . . breathe.*

"Why do we need to rush home? I thought we had another full day at the resort?" I asked, pressing for an answer.

He shrugged with a downcast face.

I pouted. "Were you upset because I slept all day? I'm sorry that I didn't feel well and ruined our fun. I'm feeling much better now."

He shook his head. "Of course not. I'm glad you recovered." But I didn't feel right about the way his eyes shifted when he answered, and that dour expression on his face left me mystified.

"Thanks."

Blake looked at me and said impatiently, "I need to go." His lips curved up slightly; however, that smile seemed fake, more like a sneer.

"Sure," I said.

And he added through his false smile, "I have some business to take care of and need to get back." *What did I do?* Blake asked me indignantly, "Would you like me to help you pack?"

Shaking my head, I quickly gathered my things, my happiness all but forgotten.

I persisted with the questions. "Are you mad at me?"

"No." His curt response didn't help me find answers.

"What is going on?" I asked. Blake jerked his hand in the air as if to stop me mid-sentence. And my eyes popped wide open. It was interesting how such a small gesture could tell so much, without saying a word.

I rushed my packing; meanwhile, Blake stood watching me, clearly impatient. What was going on behind those angry eyes? I wanted to shout at him, but instead I stood next to my packed bags with a limp smile.

The ride home was tense and uncomfortable. The two of us barely exchanged a word except for a brief discussion about the quickest route back to Raleigh. I was relieved that the snow had stopped, and the roads were cleared. Regardless, it was dreary both outside and in; there was no escaping the lingering gray clouds.

To ease the tension, I removed a magazine from my travel bag and scanned it. I acted like I took incredible pleasure in reading my article, but occasionally I slid a glance his direction and saw his eyes fixed on the road in front of us.

And rather than comprehend the written words, my mind was running a mental marathon—going over every detail from the weekend. *What changed his mind?*

I didn't even try to carry on cheerful conversation because Blake immersed himself in what felt like interminable silence. Out of the corner of my eye, I saw him glance over toward me with something like a scowl on his face as I continued pretending to read.

Why the cold treatment after such a hot weekend? I wanted to tell him, "I am through trying to understand you." *I don't get you at all!* But really I just wanted our fun back.

CHAPTER 13

We arrived at my house almost four agonizing hours later. Blake carried my bags inside and set them down in the living room. When I stepped toward him, he backed away and bumped into the couch. *What is he hiding from me? His eyes haven't met my gaze all afternoon.*

As if reading my thoughts, he looked me straight in the eye with his inscrutable gaze. He cleared his throat. "Look, I have been doing a lot of thinking," he said. He raked his fingers through his tousled hair and rubbed his head.

I couldn't help but focus on his magnificence. And, oh my, was he perfect, even distraught or angry, whatever it was. *But this lead-up did not sound good. Just tell me what you need to tell me.* "Okay," I said.

There was an uncomfortable pause. "I'm not sure how to . . . say this."

My body responded instinctively. The muscles on the back of my neck tightened; the contractions continued down my legs and left my feet numb. I reached for a solid surface—a table— to brace myself. And, of course, just my luck, I grabbed my grandmother's fragile antique table. I knocked it forward, sending the table tumbling to the ground. "Darn it," I muttered, watching it crash to the floor. I was a calamity waiting to happen.

Blake shook his head. He looked at me with pity.

"As I was saying, Lila, before you started tossing furniture around. I have been giving this a lot of thought." His voice sounded colder than his usual warm intonation. "I have come to a conclusion: things are going too quickly for me."

"Really?"

He continued in that unfamiliar harsh voice. "Maybe we should slow this down and not see each other." I spun on my heels and looked at him with my eyes bulging. Blake saw the utter surprise on my face, but his expression was indecipherable. He paused a few seconds to let me absorb the depths of what he was saying. "I've been thinking a lot about us, and I just don't think this is working for us." Blake watched my stricken expression as he said the words.

Instantly, I wanted to shout at him . . . what? I felt like the relationship was progressing and then, smack, this bombshell. I needed to press him for answers, but instead I crossed my arms. I squeezed myself in an effort to quell my hurt. And I said nothing.

I looked at him, dumbfounded, and asked him when I finally caught my breath, "I thought we were having an amazing time. What changed your mind?"

He shrugged. "Nothing."

And there I stood, cast in the shadow of his doubt, with him avoiding my eyes.

I felt a surge of fiery anger rip through me. I was raging inside, and it pushed out of me with driving power. My rushing hostility made me speak before thinking clearly, and I blurted out, "You just needed to be the one to break up with me this time."

Blake snapped back with equal force. "You're just too upset to be rational about anything. This just doesn't work." But his eyes appeared to say something else.

My confusion escalated. And so did my temper. "I thought the sweet things you said to me the past few weeks were true. Silly me, for believing you. For believing in you."

"I never promised you anything. Why are you so upset?"

My temper continued to light up quickly. I was letting him see one more side of me I tried to hide—my fire. Finally, I took a deep breath, trying to regain control. "I guess I'm like a firecracker—once you light my fuse, there's no turning back," I said.

Blake huffed. "Are you telling me I should run for cover?"

I stood with my hands pressed into my hip bones. "I said firecracker, not bomb, for crying out loud," I snapped.

Blake looked at me and laughed. "Good one."

He stretched his fingers across his cheek and scratched. I could hear the faint sound of his fingertips rubbing against his dark stubble. For a moment, I thought about the coarse feel of his whiskers between my thighs. But then the reality of his words struck me again.

My jaw tensed. "Was this what you strived for all along, to make me want you and then cast me aside? You know, you made me think you cared about me." *Why did I ever think this was a good idea, us reuniting?*

Blake did not hesitate before he spoke. "I guess you got it all wrong."

My mind was racing full force. *I want you in my life. I do.* "Are you tossing me aside the way you think I did to you years ago?" I paused, waiting for him to say something. He just gaped at me in silence.

Blake looked as if he felt anger surge within him, but was forcing himself to remain calm. He turned away, possibly trying to contain his boiling rage. At last, he found his words and grumbled in an annoyed tone, "You're a piece of work, you know that?"

I glanced out the window and saw a small brown bird standing on the windowsill. It looked toward the glass as if wanting to come inside. At that instant, there was a slight break between the dense clouds. A shaft of sunlight cut across the sky. And then I watched the bird fly away. *I want to take off, too.*

A lump swelled in my throat, and in a voice that quavered, I continued. "Blake, I'm sorry for speaking out of anger. I know we have years of frustration built up within us. Just yesterday you told me kind and special words. And then today, this . . . revelation. I'm angry and confused."

His voice wavered. "I want out. I have nothing left to say."

Finally, I managed to get another question out, trying to stay composed. "But I have to ask you again. What happened today that made you feel this way?"

I watched for the faintest change of expression on his face, but there was none. *He made his decision. Let it go. Let him go . . . again.* Yet, he was still in my house discussing our situation. He wouldn't still be here if he didn't care.

"Really, there's nothing to discuss," he said in an explosive voice that overrode my faltering, soft words. The booming sound of his voice must have startled him, for he lowered it. He softened his tone as he continued. "It's over."

I sulked and asked him with my eyes if it had to be this way. No response; he looked away. I had to face the truth: in his mind, this was over. *But he is still here, so there is a chance.* His mind might not be entirely made up . . . yet.

In my confusion I started to wonder, was that what happened when you shared such a powerful attraction—you repelled each other with equal power? Certainly that couldn't be right. Could it?

He stared at me, nostrils flaring and broke the silence. "Well, do you think you can just weave in and out of my life as you please?"

"Blake, what are you talking about? We discussed in great detail what happened years ago. I thought we were past all of that."

I caught a pained looked that flashed across his face. "Believe it or not, I cared about you, about us. Once. . . ." As Blake continued to speak, the telephone rang. "Get that," he said through gritted teeth. "I need to sort out my thoughts anyway."

I, too, was grateful to have a momentary change of focus.

When I returned, he surprised me by slamming his fist on the back of the chair. "You broke my heart. I was upset for a long time. I got over it, of course, but I was really hurt. Youthful love carries some powerful feelings. Your first love stays in your heart . . . always."

"Yes."

He stared at me with an intensity I had not seen before now. I flinched as he spoke, looking away to avoid his searing gaze. "Be careful who you choose, right? Aren't those your words? You were my heart's desire. Now my heart is scarred deep. It grew cold around those scars."

"Mine, too."

Are the people who have become cold-hearted the ones who once cared too much?

He rolled his head downward, staring from under lowered brows, and continued lecturing me. "Now just because you feel ready to love again, you just think I can forgive and forget. No way. Don't get me wrong. The sex is still amazing, but sex is just sex."

He did not just say that.

"Is that how you feel?"

"As far as love, I just can't love you back."

I must have looked like a small child staring bewildered at an angry grown-up as I asked in a voice higher than my own, "What about those times recently when you said I was all you ever needed? What about all of that?" My voice grew tighter. "Why did you tell me those things?"

He looked down and could not meet my gaze. "I guess I'm creative. I enjoy writing a good story—but my stories are pure fiction."

I gasped and stared at him, my eyes full of pain. "Ouch. That stung."

"That's why we need to stop seeing each other." Blake just stood in rigid silence, staring at the wall. "I don't want to lead you on or for you to think this is more than it is. And besides, I have to be honest, our breakup years ago taints my view of a future with you. Can you blame me?"

I flinched. "I did end it abruptly years ago. Maybe we shouldn't have tried it again." I shook my head. "I thought we could try it as adults, but I guess our lives don't mix at close range." In the end, I guess none of our discussions really mattered if he was going to stay angry with me. But I felt the unrelenting urge to ask if we could keep trying. "Can't we just have fun and enjoy each other? It's not as if I'm proposing marriage here. Does it really have to be all or nothing?"

In the silence that followed, I could hear Blake release a sigh.

He smiled a twisted grin. "You're completely unafraid because you have never been hurt by me before. Well, I have . . . so I walked very slowly into this one. And now it is time for me to leave."

"How can you say that when you haven't even given us a second chance," I said. I studied him with such intensity. "You have me craving an eggroll with sweet and sour sauce."

He looked at me curiously. "What in the world are you talking about now?"

"You can be so sweet, but you can also be so damn sour." Simultaneously, with the last word I spoke, I felt a slight throbbing discomfort in my side—fortunately, not quite as severe as the stabbing pain I usually felt.

He glared. "Why do you think I'm sour, just because I have doubts and I'm not sure about any of this?"

I shook my head. "Could we even take this relationship back to the level we had in college? Honestly, I don't think either of us can feel that kind of love anymore."

"I know."

I pushed my fingers through my hair. "We have too many scars and walls that we have put up over the years. We have learned to be more guarded with our feelings, so we can't be hurt as easily."

He said nothing for a moment. "Maybe it is better we not try again."

I gasped. "We know better than to jump in feet first. That naive innocence we once had is gone. I think we can still have something special. It'll just be different."

We could never move forward if he kept looking back. Did I need to get on my knees and beg? Honestly, maybe Blake and I had nothing but a fling. Just because, I fell in love with him again, didn't mean he had fallen in love with me. Now I had no choice but to face the truth; it was over.

Suddenly the pain in my abdomen surged again; this time it surfaced as a sharp sensation that pressed inward. For the first time, I barely noticed, as if I could not even feel it through the ache in my heart.

At that same moment, Blake must have registered the pained look that flashed across my face. He shot me a thoughtful glance. "I'm sorry if I upset you. I just didn't think I could handle being hurt again. The first time tore me up. I can't imagine what a second time would feel like," he said, as gently as he could manage.

He stepped toward me. Only a couple feet separated us.

"Until this afternoon, I thought everything was going great," I said. It might have been the sight of me so emotional, or in physical pain, that made Blake realize how much his words upset me. Something changed in his attitude.

He smiled. "I didn't fully realize how much I cared about you until I saw the way you reacted to my harsh words. But you don't need to look so hurt anymore. I just saw it in your sad stare and heard it in your voice. You do want this relationship to work. And, honestly, so do I, more than anything," he said, in a soothing voice.

"I thought it was working." *I am confused now.* My brain was buzzing.

Blake hesitated. "I get it now—we both have feelings. But if you're serious about having a relationship with me, then why did you tell me you were leaving me?"

"What are you talking about?"

"Lila, let me ask you something. Earlier today you told me in your mumbling state –when you were falling asleep—you said that you're leaving me. Do you remember that one? Care to elaborate?"

I shot him a puzzled glance. "Is that what you were upset about? I remember lying down on the bed, but after that it gets hazy. Was that what you heard me say? And was that what this sudden departure is all about?" The realization finally hit me. *He thought I wanted out again!*

"Well . . ."

I sighed. "I'm so sorry if that's what you have been thinking, but that is the furthest from the truth. I want you in my life, more than anything."

He shocked me with his next question. Blake looked me square in the eyes. "Are you sure you want to be with me? Maybe you just need a man; any man will do."

"That's not true! I have been living by myself and doing just fine, thank you. I don't *need* a man in my life. You have enhanced my life, but I don't require a man to feel complete. I want to share adventures with *you*." I put extra emphasis on the word "you" so he could understand that this discussion was about him and only him.

That hard glint in Blake's eye softened. Suddenly an understanding look replaced the anger in my eyes. He had been afraid of getting hurt again. *I get it now.*

And with this new comprehension of the situation, I wondered if maybe it was time to share my secret. He deserved to know the full truth. *Maybe I could pretend none of this sickness was happening—and just live in denial.*

I almost blurted out my secret, but decided it was not the right time to reveal my news. *When is the right time to divulge that you are dying?* I contemplated. I don't want him staying with me out of guilt or obligation. If only I could tell him. . . .

What would he say if he found out my news? Was he going to dart for the door? And if he did, I would have to accept it, regardless.

Not wanting to lose another opportunity with him, I decided to share my feelings. I announced with conviction, "I'm falling in love with you again, Blake. Don't feel like you have to say anything in return."

With a relieved sigh, he reached out and pulled me close, burying his face in my neck. "I don't want this to end. I was afraid you were leaving me again. I thought I needed to be the one to break away, but the reality is that I want this to work." I smiled, hearing the joy in his voice again. "You know I have always wanted to be with you," he said.

Blake sighed as he locked his arms around me. The greatest pleasure was enjoying his strong hands lovingly rubbing on my skin. I knew that I never wanted a lover so bad in my entire life. I never experienced anything so gratifying. The feeling of him inside me had become a drug. And I was addicted.

CHAPTER 14

Blake smoothed my long hair and pushed it away from my face. He placed his fingers on my temples to rotate my face toward him and gazed into my eyes. He stroked my face, tilted my chin upwards, and brought his mouth down on mine. He kissed me tenderly. At the same time, his arousal pressed against me. While he continued kissing my lips, I could feel him growing larger in excitement. I had become insatiable for him, and from Blake's eagerness toward me, the feeling was mutual.

Just as I wondered how far he would take his caresses, he released our embrace and began to untie my dress. I felt my passion erupt as the dress slid down my body, pooling at my feet. He unhooked my bra and pulled down my panties. I stood before him naked except for my long hair draped across my bare chest.

"I'm entranced by your beauty," he said. He stood still and drank me in, my bare body enticing him.

I looked down. "I was afraid it was over."

"Look at me, Lila." He stared into my eyes. "I don't want to lose you again."

Everything felt perfect. I knew I did not have a flawless figure, but he made me feel irresistible and sexy. For that brief instant, I did not have a care in the world. It was just the two of us. And we could not get enough of each other.

Blake kissed my shoulders tenderly. "You fill me with desire, my dear," he said. His lips pressed against my throat. He turned me so that he could kiss the nape of my neck. Standing behind me, Blake reached his arms around and cupped my tender breasts, fondling my hard nipples.

"That feels good," I whispered in a voice that was breathy and excited.

He brushed his fingertips across my nipples, giving each one a gentle tug. I gasped in surprise, but that quickly turned into a sigh of enjoyment, causing me to moan in time with his caressing touch. His kisses slid from the top of my neck and traveled slowly down my spine. When he reached my shoulder blades, I turned back around to embrace him.

"I'm so turned on by you," Blake whispered, gazing into my eyes. The enthusiastic expression in his eyes demanded that I stay focused on him.

Looking deep into his eyes, I thought I could see everything he was feeling. At the moment, his pleading eyes begged me to be one with him. He pressed my hand against his zipper.

He leaned in to kiss me softly, and he deepened the kiss, his tongue dancing with mine. I lifted his shirt and tossed it onto the couch. I slid my fingers down his toned chest and across the firm ridges of his stomach. Groaning in delight, he slowly began to kiss between my breasts and down my stomach. Lower and lower, until I, too, moaned in anticipation.

Much to both of our surprise, at that instant, I pulled away, doubled over, clutching my arms around my sides. Pure agony ripped through my midsection like someone stabbing me with a sharp knife. I almost fell forward but instead stumbled to the couch. I curled my body into the fetal position in the corner, hoping for the sharp sensations to pass. About a minute later, I felt normal again.

When I straightened up, trying to regain my composure, I glanced over at Blake. The horrified expression on his face said more than words ever could. His eyes were as round as saucers, and his lips contorted in a frightened grimace. Perhaps he thought I was horrified by his touch. Either way, I had some explaining to do.

Blake sat down beside me and spread a cotton blanket across my body. I felt his hands touch my shoulders, gently pulling me close to him. I did not resist. I tilted my head toward him with my eyes half-closed, enjoying the closeness. I felt his warmth, his arm draped over me protectively while I snuggled against him. I felt like I was exactly where I belonged, in his arms.

He sighed and lowered his head slightly. He gazed into my eyes as if searching for answers. Could he see into me? Could he see through me like glass—like the broken fragments I had become?

His eyes were kind, but questioning. Nonetheless, he sat in silence. He kneaded the strained muscles across my back. As the tight muscles relaxed, the tension I held fell away. When he finally spoke, his voice was filled with regret, and it trembled with emotion as if he were apologizing for being so hard on me earlier. "What's going on here, Lila?"

I guess I was not transparent after all if he still searched for answers. Eventually, I was going to have to tell him the truth. *Just do it.* I had been planning how to share my news for days. I had rehearsed it in my mind, over and over.

I sat up and wrapped the blanket around me. Really, I had no choice but to plunge right in and begin. "I think you know I have something to tell you." My voice sounded different, forced and distant. "I have something very important I need to tell you, but I'm not sure how."

And with these words, my eyes filled with tears that poured down my cheeks. I could barely see. A sudden feeling of self-consciousness washed over me, and I covered my face with my hands, trying to hide the streaks.

Blake looked concerned. "Are you saying good-bye again with those tears? I thought we reached a good place. What is it?"

"I never want to lose you again, Blake." I blinked my eyes to fight back more tears. "But I need to share something with you." I could feel my heart pounding while he stared.

"You can tell me anything."

My voice dropped in volume to barely above a whisper. "I have stage three pancreatic cancer. It's inoperable because it has spread to my major blood vessels." My words echoed in the air.

His head jerked back in disbelief. When he finally did turn to look at me, his face was frozen and his eyes wide. He swallowed hard as if he had a lump stuck in his throat.

Although Blake looked alarmed, he also had an expression as if my behavior now made sense to him. Quite possibly he had noticed my more pronounced dark circles and tired eyes. Maybe he saw me wince in pain a few times but had brushed those thoughts aside.

There was a painful silence, but he recovered quickly. "Why didn't you tell me earlier? I want to be here for you."

I looked at him. I could see the care and concern in his eyes. After hesitating, I said, "I'll be all right." But my pained face was not fooling him.

In the next instant, he encircled his arms around me and held me. I glanced at him gratefully.

"I'll do anything for you, if you just let me," he said.

I replied with a limp smile. "I don't expect anyone to solve all of my problems. That's not fair to you."

He looked at me as if he were losing everything. Quickly, Blake turned his now-pale face away from me and looked toward the window. He seemed to gaze out at the lustrous sky while he collected his thoughts; maybe he did not want me to see his fear.

The cloudless blue sky seemed so vast, like it could go on forever. Why couldn't life be like that—endless—an infinite journey? Why did mine have to stop when I just turned a corner and started in a new direction? To lose each other just when we found pleasure again seemed so cruel. *I am afraid the cancer will rob us of our second chance to get it right. With my secret finally exposed, will this shatter my dream of our happily ever after?*

After taking a deep breath, he looked at me. There was something less definable in Blake's expression. Perhaps there was something about my eyes that seemed to trouble him. Defeat? Did I give him a dull stare, as if I had given up on life? And maybe at that moment my desire to fight was fading.

Blake stared at me as if reading my thoughts. He looked determined to revive me. He glanced down and brushed his fingers along his eyes, wiping his welling tears. I heard him try to disguise a sniffle by clearing his throat. Was he trying to be strong for me? He knew I was scared.

I sighed. "You know, this type of cancer usually wins, especially in the late stages. But I still think I have a chance, somehow," I said.

Blake choked through his words. "This is your fight, but I want to help you." He cleared his throat until his normal voice returned. "I'm a trained fighter in the military. I'm just the right person to help. We will defeat this enemy invasion."

"This is not a military drill, my dear."

He shook his head. "I just want to be here for you, but I'm not sure how," he said in an unwavering voice. "It will be a tough battle, but we can do this; we will get through this—together."

"I'm trying to be strong," I said.

Blake's voice raised several levels to accentuate his words. "Do not give up! I'll never stop fighting for you and with you."

"Thank you."

His emphatic voice commanded, "We will win. We will put up a unified front. You invited me on this journey, and I'm not about to end it now. We only just started marking off the items on your list. And I have a list of my own to merge with yours—for us to enjoy."

The tears trickled down my cheeks. I could tell by his furrowed brow and steady gaze that he was not going to change his stance. I had seen that expression before and knew that when he had made up his mind, there was no changing it. He was determined to be with me during this challenge. And I was grateful.

Although I loved his support, I knew it was not that easy. Was I supposed to believe we could wish the sickness away, and it would be gone? And how do you fight the enemy within?

He turned to me and reached out with his big, strong hands and swept me into his arms. I flung my body readily into his welcoming embrace. I clung to him for dear life—or so it felt. His warm lips pressed against my tear-streaked cheek, and he gently stroked my hair as if I were a fragile porcelain doll.

He began patting my back like my mother did when I was a child seeking comfort. "Look at me. We can win this battle," he said in a forceful tone. And following those words, I clung to him for security as if we were attached by Velcro. He squeezed me tighter, and for that brief instant, all of my fears dissolved.

After several deep breaths, I pulled back and looked at him, gazing through my swollen eyelids, nodding my head silently, and trying to smile valiantly through my tears. "I'm being realistic about this situation. Just help me forget about the pain for a while." I sniffed.

But I knew that even with his comforting support, I could not overlook the struggle that lay ahead—it was more than a speed bump; it was a brick wall in front of me. But maybe with a boost, with him to hoist me, I could climb the wall and escape. *That is, indeed, wishful thinking.*

The reality was different. Deep down, I felt sad that our exciting journey together was about to come to an end when it had only just started. I wished for more time . . . more time with him. I begged the sickness to leave my body. But the truth was I knew that some wishes couldn't come true, no matter how much you wanted them to reign free.

A part of me felt exhausted and defeated. But at the same time, I was grateful for Blake, and I couldn't remember when anyone was as good to me as he had been these past few months. I needed to draw from his strength, even more than I realized. He leaned over and wrapped his warm arms around me again as if creating a force field, empowering me with its shielding energy.

He held me for a couple of minutes until my tears stopped flowing. "Lila, you can be fiercely independent. I like that about you, but this time, allow me to add to your strength. I want to help you. Whatever the future brings, I'll be there for you, if you let me."

I wiped my eyes and looked up at him. "I don't want you to feel like you have to rescue me. I'm not helpless."

"I know. Even tough people need a friend," he said.

We had miraculously found each other just before my downward spiral, and his added strength was empowering me.

"Thank you for reminding me how resilient I am. I'm not going to wither, shrivel, or cower from this battle. I haven't always been the most competitive person, but that is about to change."

"I saw you win a lot of gymnastics trophies. You are a winner."

"Well, win or lose, I'll fight to enjoy the time I have left. I'm not going to curl up in a corner and give up. I want to live life to the fullest and try my best to keep my mind, body, and soul healthy."

"I'm on your team."

"Thank you for reminding me that I have a substantial inner strength. Sometimes we all get lost and need a little boost to get on the right path." My voice was hoarse from sobbing.

He shrugged and sniffled. "I thought I was going to comfort you, and look at my tears welling. Maybe it is the ice from my heart melting and dripping out of me."

"You're making me feel better. But, Blake, you deserve more than I have to give you."

His loud voice softened. "I was just a rogue player until you came back into my life. Now I'm all in . . . with you. You have become my friend again. And I have always loved you."

I smiled through my tears. "I'm so lucky to have you in my life twice. I love you."

I looked deep into his eyes and could see his energy, determination, and love. I was grateful to have Blake by my side and on my team. But I also knew that I had to find the inner strength to deal with this disease and its effects. Whatever the outcome of this looming battle, I would appreciate each moment with friends, every glorious event from nature, and celebrate each new day!

Sadly, even dealing with the life-altering effects of a sickness, the details of life continued. Blake had a busy work schedule to return to for the next few weeks and could not guarantee a date for our next adventure. He returned to Jacksonville and back to work. We made several visits to see each other and enjoyed our time together.

A few weeks later, he disclosed the shocker. The timing was unfortunate, but Blake was being sent overseas on temporary assignment. He said he could possibly find a way out of going, if I thought that was necessary. I assured him I would be fine.

Before he left, he made me promise I would take care of myself. And I vowed to rest and not exert myself while he was away. He called me as soon as he arrived. "I can't bear to be away from you. I should be there holding your hand during your chemo. I feel like I'm letting my best friend down during her time of need."

I held the telephone next to my ear, wishing it was Blake rubbing against me, not this cold metal. "Don't worry about me. The chemo isn't too bad. I'll be fine. We can call each other and text. And Jenny is only miles away if there's a problem." But deep inside I felt like I was starting to sink— slowly being pulled into quicksand—with no rope to grab. My pain intensified. The stabbing sensation, which had been progressively getting worse, stepped up another notch. Secretly, I knew the enemy within was taking over my body.

I woke up at seven a.m. one Saturday morning, anxious to start my day. Once again, I was relieved to have another lonely night behind me. I had a full day of projects scheduled, which included a trip to my favorite craft store, where I could spend hours searching for just the right shade of colored glass. My imagination would whirl with ideas when I selected the large, fragile sheets.

After walking Elky, showering, and cooking breakfast, I was ready to go shopping. Just as I picked up my purse, the telephone rang. Jenny wanted to come home and spend the weekend relaxing and hanging out. Of course, I was thrilled. I had just enough time to shop and pick up lunch.

I had converted my sunroom into the art studio. In the center of the room, I had a work table and glass grinder. In the far corner, I had a large television and shelves filled with glass waiting to be transformed and brought to life.

I just sat down at my art table when Jenny walked in the sun-filled room. She rushed over, gave me a huge hug, and sat down next to me.

"Will you help me with a glass project this weekend?" she asked, looking down at the blue sheet of glass on the edge of the table.

I smiled. "I would love that, Jenny. Would you like to sell it in my art gallery?"

She looked at me curiously. "Are you really going to do it? You've been dreaming of opening that gallery as long as I can remember."

I looked up at the window in front of me. My eyes locked on the oval stained glass featuring a black horse standing beside a red barn. Instead of walls, the sunroom had floor-to-ceiling windows. Each window had a different glass creation suspended at the top. Each piece of art was unique. Most were my creations, but Jenny made a few. And my favorites were the ones we made together.

I turned to my left to stare at the hanging rectangle comprised of mostly purple glass. Jenny and I made this spectacular creation years ago which featured a tree in bloom on a hill above a field of lavender. We worked on it for months. We had always dreamed of going to France to visit the lavender fields. But time had passed, and we never went. Now that it was almost springtime, I wished we had finally planned a trip. And with Jenny in college, could she even get away? Maybe next year . . .

"Yes. I am going to open an art gallery," I said softly. "I'm going to use the money from the settlement with your dad and from the sale of the house."

Jenny hesitated and looked down at her hands. She spun the ruby ring I gave her for graduation. "I'm so excited for you . . . to have that opportunity."

I turned and looked at her. "I'm not exactly ignoring my sickness. I spent hours getting my financial information and other important documents organized for you. They're in the filing cabinet."

She took a gulping breath. "You know I don't want to talk about any of those details."

I cleared my dry throat. "Yes, I understand; however, it's important for you to know where my documents are located. Maybe you can glance at the paperwork today and see if you have any questions?"

"Perhaps later." She sighed, releasing a deep breath.

"I bought you a pattern book this morning. You want to look at it?" I lifted a shopping bag and pulled out a book.

Flipping through the pages, her breathing rate returned to normal. "These are mostly flower designs. I like them all," she said.

"As far as the gallery is concerned, I'm going to sell the stained glass, paintings, and jewelry I created over the years. But my main goal is to showcase a variety of artists."

"What a great idea. You have accumulated quite a collection."

"Ideally, the gallery will be profitable, but I hope my art will bring joy and maybe inspiration to others. And I look forward to working with local artists," I said, focusing on the sheet of cobalt blue glass between my fingers.

"You're very skilled at your craft," Jenny said, looking down at my hand moving the cutter along the glass.

I snapped the piece in half. "Thank you. Glass is an unforgiving material to work with, but the end result can be stunning. Just like the pieces you've created, Jenny."

"Well, I still have a lot to learn," she said, marking a page in the pattern book. "Where are you thinking of locating the gallery?"

"I don't know yet. Downtown would be nice, and I could get a small condo close to it." I placed my pattern piece on the glass and traced the edges with my marker. "Right now, I just want to create beautiful art while I wait for this house to sell."

"It'll be good for you to have less upkeep," she said.

"I haven't actually made any final decisions. I probably shouldn't take on too much right now," I said cautiously. "Although . . . I have my mind set that I'm going to beat this disease. I know it's not very realistic, but I'm still making plans for the future."

"I love your attitude. And the art pieces you've created the past few months are the best I've seen you do."

"I have some artist friends who make it fun. We get together for coffee, gossip, and work on our craft." I paused and looked directly at her. "I'm so proud of you, Jenny. With your grades, you'll be able to do whatever you want."

"This might surprise you, but I've been thinking about going to medical school," she said.

"You will make the best doctor. What a wonderful idea," I said, putting the glass aside. "Why don't you tell me all about school while we eat? I know you must be starving. How do barbeque ribs, spinach salad, baked beans, and pecan pie sound to you?"

She giggled. "I'm hungry, and you know my favorites."

"Great. I'll have the table set in a few minutes. See you in the kitchen."

After lunch, we flipped through the pattern book and selected a flower design for Jenny to create. We worked diligently throughout the weekend. As our fingers transformed the glass, we laughed and talked for hours. By Monday morning, our projects were complete. I hung Jenny's hummingbird and pink flower design in the window. Next to it, I suspended my sunrise and pier creation. We stood, admiring our efforts. A few minutes later, we hugged good-bye and agreed to have a similar weekend again soon.

CHAPTER 15

Jenny spent weekends with me when it worked with her schedule. The sunroom windows were lined with our artistic creations. She spent the holidays with me except for a few detour trips to visit her dad. She never discussed her time with him and his new family. And I never asked.

Winter was mild this year. Jane and I continued to play tennis; even if I lasted only a few pitiful minutes on the court, we still tried. As the weeks passed, I felt too weak to play tennis, even for a few minutes. Although, Jane encouraged me to get out of the house, I usually stayed home.

We began playing card games in the sunroom instead of tennis, but even that grew too difficult for me. I could not concentrate. I started making excuses every time Jane insisted she come over. I was not sure why I had this sudden urge to be alone.

Blake called every day, twice a day if he could do it. We sent funny text messages and e-mails, but the miles between us seemed greater each day.

I was sitting at my art table in the middle of the sunroom when the telephone rang. I placed the glass cutter on the table and answered the phone. Blake's voice, on the other end, sounded exactly as it had in college. "I miss you so much— you're in my night, and my daydreams," he said.

"Miss you . . . more."

"I promise that I'll be back soon."

I looked down at my chipped fingernails. "I'm excited to be with you again," I said. Secretly, I was nervous for Blake to see me in my frail condition.

"Why do I have this strong feeling there's something you're not telling me?"

I slid to the edge of my seat. "I don't know."

"Your voice sounds weak. Are you getting enough rest? Is the chemotherapy making you feel worse?"

His question startled me. I wanted to hide my weakening state. I didn't let him know just how brutal the chemotherapy had been on my body. I refused to share my suffering with anyone, even those closest to me. To the world, I put on my happy face or no face at all because I rarely ventured outside.

I had a full range of negative side effects, but fortunately, my hair had not fallen out, only thinned significantly. My skin was a different issue altogether; the healthy color faded and looked sallow. I didn't feel like eating. And when I finally did eat, it didn't stay with me. My list of issues started there. Just today, for example, wearily, I tried to eat a cheese omelet. And after two bites, I raced to the bathroom. I didn't try again. The doctor offered medication to help with the nausea, but I resisted.

Even though I had hardly eaten in days, I tried to stay tough. I forced myself to stay mentally strong. *I can do this. I will do this. I will make each day count.*

I tried not to sound surprised that Blake detected my distress. "Don't be concerned. The medicine is not as bad as you might think. I'm just sad because I miss your superb bedside manner," I joked. Fate may be taking everything, but for now, I still had my sense of humor and hoped it would be one of the last things to go. I needed to keep a positive outlook.

He sighed. "I can't wait to crawl in bed with you again. In fact, I'm admiring your picture right now. It's my screensaver. You know, the one we took at the restaurant."

I took a deep, agonizing breath. "I want you here, right now."

"It won't be much longer. Are you sure you're okay?"

"Sometimes I do too much. I've been bustling about with all of my art and home projects, trying to keep distracted. I've had several people tour my house, but no serious buyer. By the end of the day, I'm drained." I lowered my voice to a whisper, secretly struggling for air and trying to hide my raspy breath.

Thank goodness we went old school and stuck with the telephone, not video communication. If he could have seen me, he would have known I was gasping for air between words. I tried my best to hide my ordeal by covering the phone when I took a deep breath. I closed my eyes. I visualized his handsome face when he spoke. His image brought me pleasure and relaxed me.

"Get some rest. Before we know it, we will be enjoying our next adventure," he said.

"Hurry back so we can get started."

Part of me wanted to include him in my struggles, but at the same time, Blake had his own issues. This was my fight. I was determined not to feel overwhelmed and have a pity party. I tried to be stronger than that. But at the same time, my weakened condition had me living a sequestered life.

I was counseled to avoid being out in public with my immune system severely compromised from the chemo, especially close-quarter events like movies, restaurants, or sports. Plus, I didn't have the energy for my usual activities and had begun to isolate myself. I probably needed more help, but my pride kept me from reaching out—to anyone.

I managed to make my doctor's appointments; however, that took my remaining energy. At this point, I rarely answered my door or my telephone, unless it was Blake. When I did talk to Jenny, Jane, my mother, or anyone else, I put on a happy front and pretended I was fine, but I wasn't. And, of course, I always put on my game face for Blake.

Jenny was busy with school. She stopped by when she could manage it. Sometimes friends brought meals or groceries that I didn't even open. I found myself napping more than awake. In fact, the only place I could find relief was curled up in bed.

The days grew warmer as spring approached. Weeks stretched into months that Blake was away. I started to feel like I would never see him again. And this time when Blake called, I couldn't answer. I was physically depleted. Honestly, I had been lucky to have as many good days as I'd had up until now, but the tables had turned. I was on a slippery slope, careening out of control. There was no traction—only a downward plunge. I could barely get out of bed and just wanted to sleep. And sleep.

Tucked under the covers with the curtains pulled, I faintly heard my name. The male voice grew louder and louder along with the sound of footsteps and my door opening. Using my remaining energy, I lifted my eyes to see a man. His focus was fixed on me from across the room. Was that Blake? The man looking at me wrapped his hand across his mouth and let out a muffled cry.

Without a doubt, I was just a shell of the person he had known. The last time I glanced in the mirror, I looked pale with charcoal circles that skimmed along underneath my lower lashes. My eyes looked like bulging marbles as the thin skin beneath them sank deeper into my face. I had hollowed cheeks. The hair I had left hadn't been washed or combed in days.

I had struggled to fight the disease. *And lost my drive.* The enemy within was getting the upper hand. I used my remaining energy to turn my head to look at him. I signaled with my face for him to come closer to me. My vision had become blurry through my swollen eyelids. I squinted at him in the dark room and tried to slow my breath because I was practically hyperventilating. I felt like I was getting air through a straw.

Unable to steady my respiration rate, I cried out with panic in my voice. "Blake, is that you?" I could hardly speak the words from my dry, scratchy throat.

Even in the dim light, I knew he could see how frail I had become. "Yes, my love," he said in a voice tinged with guilt, as he opened the curtain, letting the sunlight flow into the room.

He stared at me for a long, agonizing moment. As the bright rays poured into the room, I could see him standing over me. I was certain the light shining on me accentuated my paleness. The air was still except for the sound of our breathing—his rapid and mine shallow. No outside noise, not even a peep.

He fumbled in his pocket for his telephone and called for paramedics. In the next instant, he took my frail body into his powerful arms and held me next to his broad chest. He stroked my hair like I was a child. At that moment, maybe I was childlike in my vulnerability. I wanted to bawl like a little girl, but I didn't. I needed to stay strong because I knew if I let loose, I would be inconsolable.

I murmured, "You came back." My face pressed into his neck, distorting my weary, weak voice. The sounds I made, I hardly recognized.

"I kept my word. I'm sorry I was away for so long. I won't leave again," he said.

Seconds turned into minutes that he held me. He sighed as if months of anguish surged out of him. "My heart melted the instant I touched you. I'm here for you," he said.

He held my head up like a baby. Blake stared into my eyes, but I could barely keep them open long enough to return his gaze. My body was failing quickly. I felt so weak and floppy, like a wet noodle. And when I looked at him, I hoped my eyes had a hint of brightness.

He sighed. "What can I do for you, my love?" He fell silent, waiting for my reply.

I whispered in Blake's ear. "Thank you for loving me." I knew my once-rosy cheeks were gone. My face looked gaunt— my beauty, but a memory. However, I was still me, even in the body of a stranger.

I forced myself to look at him through my swollen eyelids and winced from the stabbing pain. But for some strange reason, the pain reminded me I was still alive; even if in agony, I was alive. With the last bit of my strength, I squeezed enough air from my lungs to mumble, "I love you."

Blake stroked my cheek. "I love you . . . always."

My brain was not working any better than my body. My mind felt creaky and confused. When we made eye contact one last time, I mouthed the word, "Blake."

I turned slightly and gave him a confused look, before closing my eyes. Had I actually enjoyed his touch again? Were these thoughts, figments of my imagination, perhaps, nighttime dreams leaking into daytime reality? Were they illusions formed in my altered physical and mental state? I felt like I was underwater and couldn't tell which way was up, but I felt peaceful, floating perhaps. In my delirium, I suddenly found myself wishing to be an unborn baby waiting to see the world.

But most of all, I just wanted to sleep, to close my eyes and slip into a state of oblivion so I could escape the pain. I felt so tired. My breathing became shallow, paltry puffs of air. Slower. Slow.

Blake sat with an intense stare at the window. He cradled me in his arms. "Where's that ambulance?" he whispered.

I was trying my best to stay conscious and aware, but the pain was shutting down my body and jumbling my thoughts. To deal with the excruciating pain, I became numb to everything. Every sensation slipped away. I felt invisible. Peaceful.

I exhaled and fell limp in his arms. At the same time, he laid his head down on my chest and cried out loud. "Don't give up." My breathing rate remained weak, almost nonexistent. "No, don't leave again, Lila," he shouted. Without releasing his grip from my body, he reached beside my pillow for an envelope with his name on it. He pulled out the slip of paper and began reading out loud:

Dearest Blake,
The time we have spent together has been the time of my life! I loved you when you were a boy, and I can't even express with words how much I love the man you have become. And the word love does not even seem powerful enough to express how I truly feel. Maybe infinite love better exemplifies the true spirit of our bond.

Your inspirational words brought me strength in these final months. Your love has filled me with warmth. And your intimate touch gave me the greatest pleasure. I have been the luckiest woman to enjoy you in my life, twice. Oh, if only we could bind together the missing pieces of time when we were apart. I will not cry over our lost days. They just helped me realize how precious and special every instant is that we do share.

I will always be grateful. You are a part of me. I am so sad to say a final good-bye, and for our journey to end. Your love was the best feeling I ever had.
Lila

He whispered in my ear, "Love the ones you treasure with everything you have because really, they are *happiness*. Nothing else really matters in this world but friendship and love."

I felt his lips touch my forehead. "Lila." While he held and rocked me, I felt wetness drip on my cheek.

Simultaneously, the wail of sirens cut through the still air, and everything seemed to happen in a blur. The medics rushed into the room with armfuls of supplies. They went to work quickly, pumping air into my body, covering my mouth with some kind of mask and tubes. I gasped for air. I heard a man's voice shouting. "Breathe deep. Focus on inhaling and exhaling." *Were they trying to keep me conscious? Was this all a dream? Am I the center of this drama?*

Lifting the outside corner of my right eye, there was Blake pacing in what looked like a frenzied panic, watching the medics in action. This experience felt almost surreal, like I was floating above watching the scene play out, wondering if my body would spring back to life.

Meanwhile, Blake stood with his hand on his throat while the paramedics hoisted me onto the stretcher. I saw his eyes gravitate to a framed photo on the nightstand of the two of us, young, smiling in the bright sunlight. He reached for the frame, pulled it to his chest, and hugged it tightly. Blake appeared lost in thought as his gaze fixed on the photo, and then he looked at me. Clenching the photo in one hand, he flicked the lights off and followed the stretcher out of the bedroom.

The ambulance rushed me to the hospital, where they pumped fluids into my dehydrated body. My skin had become saggy and thin, like I had been crawling through a hot desert for days. I was placed in intensive care, where I continued to fight for my life. A feeding tube pumped in extra vital nutrients. The rehydration proved successful.

Day after day, Blake sat by my side, holding my hand while I clung to life. When Jenny could break free from her busy class schedule, she, too, comforted me. At the same time, she got acquainted with Blake. Other friends passed in and out. Of course, my mother called daily.

Jane, too, stopped by frequently with looks of sorrow and guilt because she did not realize my rapid decline. No one had—toward the end I had successfully sequestered myself from everyday life.

In my dreamy state, I could see Blake next to me, holding me, wrapping me in loving warmth. I knew he was there, not just in body, but in spirit. He stayed by my side, like a German shepherd—always protective. Day after day, my fight continued, and miraculously, I grew stronger. And the medication helped manage my pain.

In hindsight, I felt like my body and my mind were trying to alert me about my sickness for months. Warning bells had been ringing, but I kept ignoring all of the unusual signals my body sent. And I avoided my doctor for weeks, out of fear of hearing bad news. By the time the cancer was detected, it had already spread. As a result, the disease had become fully entrenched in my body.

Perhaps my own behavior contributed to this near shutdown. I did not eat right or get enough rest. I even stopped drinking liquids when I was thirsty. I felt that tired. And I almost lost this battle completely—prematurely.

My biggest mistake could have been avoided. I hid my struggles from the people closest to me because I didn't want to burden anyone. *Actually, we all need help sometimes, I guess.* I am grateful that Blake intervened during my time of need.

My road to full strength would be a challenging one. The chemotherapy had taken a toll on my body and my mind. Thankfully, the amazing team of doctors and nurses helped get my downward spiral under control.

Here at the hospital, the doctors told me, I was very lucky. Much to their surprise, the chemotherapy reduced the cancer impinging on my major blood vessels. The smaller tumor that remained in my pancreas could be removed with surgery. The doctors did not really have the words from science to describe what was happening to me—they were baffled. They referred to it as an amazing phenomenon.

The morning after my surgery, Dr. Young poked his head into my room. "How is my miracle patient?" he asked.

I managed a limp smile. "I'm feeling better by the minute, which is good because I don't want to be on the sidelines anymore. I want to be right back in the game," I said in a soft, weak voice.

"I'm elated to hear you're feeling better. I will be back to see you in an hour for a complete checkup. We can discuss how long I want you to stay here and work out a plan to get you back home."

Just as the doctor stepped away, Blake walked into my room, carrying a red rose. "You're a wondrous sight," he said. I could hear the joy in his voice. He sat on the edge of the bed and hugged me until I pulled away. I could feel his positive, healing energy flowing into my body. *I was starting to feel like me again.*

I motioned for him to sit back and share my pillows. After he propped up his feet on my bed, he turned and looked at me. I tried not to be concerned about my disheveled hair and tear-streaked cheeks. "These are tears of happiness," I said, wiping my eyes and the wetness that streamed down my face.

For a few minutes, we engaged in light conversation before I changed the mood with my apology. "I'm sorry I didn't warn you about how dire my condition had become. Maybe I didn't realize it myself until it was careening out of control. I didn't want you to worry; plus, you had an important job to focus on."

"You fooled me and everyone else. Don't do something like that again," he said.

"Thank you for getting me medical care when I needed it so desperately. I'm forever grateful."

"I'm just sorry I couldn't be there for you earlier."

"I never wanted to bother you with my illness. You have enough going on with your father's Alzheimer's disease and your career."

"Let that be my choice. I want to help as much as I can. Maybe I couldn't get to you in time to help, but I could have called someone. And I would have, if you had told me."

"I'll remember that in the future."

"You successfully tricked everyone close to you into believing that you were okay. We now know that you weren't.

Being strong is one thing, but sometimes we all need a friend," he said.

"I made a mistake. I should have asked for help. I just didn't want sadness or to carve out time for tearful good-byes. I had this urge to live life to the fullest. And I still do, until, well, I lose my battle."

"I'm ready to take us on our next adventure."

I smiled. "Wonderful. I hope my fight is over. Maybe I'm as good as new. Time will tell. But for now I'll rejoice in this milestone victory. Did you hear? The surgery was a success," I said in triumph. "They were able to remove the tumor without causing irreparable damage to my body and believe I should be strong again pretty soon. Hopefully, I'm cancer-free. The doctors think I'll be healthy enough to go home in a week or two."

And when it was time to go home, Blake was there to make my homecoming a joyous event. I looked up at him in the bright sunlight when he carried me tenderly in his arms into the house, like he was carrying his new bride across the threshold. The yellow rays from the light gave him a sun-kissed glow—almost as if he had on a halo—and made him look like an angel.

He kissed my cheek. At the same time, we could hear the sound of the birds chirping in unison as if welcoming my arrival. Spring was here. And like the flowers growing in my garden, I felt my body coming back to life. I didn't know if I ever would be quite the same person I was before, but I felt grateful to have a second chance. I would not waste a moment of this gift dwelling on the negative. Indeed, I had been skeptical of the power of positive energy, but now I was a believer.

He whispered softly, "You have my heart, my whole heart."

"What, no more, Mr. Iceman?" I giggled.

"No, Frosty has melted again, thank you."

"Thank you for helping me," I said.

"It was not me; it was you. And we need to give modern medicine credit, as well," he said.

I sighed. "I feel like I was dragged to the edge and looked down into the abyss but was lucky enough to escape the fall.

Blake, you are the one who pulled me back to safety." My voice cracked. "I'm so lucky to get a second chance to be with you. I'm grateful for you, for cheering me on and saying you believed in me, even when I stopped believing in myself."

"I thought I lost you this time," he whispered. "You mean everything to me." We shared grins that promised a future of happiness together.

"We found each other again."

A smile lit his face. "I'll always find a way back to you."

Without another word, we exchanged a look that said, *love you . . . always*. He hugged me tenderly and gently helped me to the leather couch. I had a sudden burst of energy. "Come here, handsome," I said in a silken voice and winked. Blake smiled at me with his entire face.

"But first, I have something to share with you," I said. I took the pink list from my pocket and read out loud, "Number three on my list, Tropical Escape." He was bringing my fantasies to life, whether he realized it or not.

PLEASE VISIT MY WEB SITE AT
www.BOOKSBYDEBRAKAY.com